Lost

A HARP SECURITY NOVEL

Laura K. Curtis

BY LAURA K. CURTIS

THE HARP SECURITY SERIES
Twisted
Lost
Echoes
Mind Games

THE GOODY'S GOODIES SERIES
Toying with His Affections
Gaming the System

This is a work of fiction. Names, characters, places, and incidents either are the product of the author's imagination or are used fictitiously, and any resemblance to persons living or dead, business establishments, or events is entirely coincidental.

This book was originally published by InterMix in May, 2014

For all the everyday heroes who go out of their way to
help others without hope of remuneration.

CHAPTER ONE

THE DINNER HORN blew while Tara was literally mending fences. After five weeks with the Chosen, she was allowed to work alone, though always in sight of others. The various areas of the twenty-nine-hundred-acre compound were divided by a multitude of different types of fencing, all of which needed regular maintenance. Plain white pickets created a welcoming atmosphere at the front, despite the guards on duty. Eight-foot chain-link surrounded the buildings where group activities took place. Critter fencing protected the gardens, nets covered the fruit trees, and a hefty, wrought-iron barrier kept the unwelcome out of the Leader's private domain.

At the sound of the air horn, Tara put down the wood-handled saw she'd been using to cut away the oak tree limb that had pushed its way through the chain-link on the northeast side of the complex and wiped the sweat from her forehead. She rolled her shoulders to relieve the ache that had settled in about half an hour before. What she wouldn't give for a long, hot shower. But she had only twenty minutes to put her tools away, splash some water on her hands and face, and get to the mess hall before dinner was served. She'd learned the hard way that if you missed pre-dinner prayers, you missed dinner.

She slid inside the cavernous dining hall just before the sentries shut the door and took her place at one of the long trestle tables next to a woman named Joy, who had been assigned to show her around her first day at the compound. Dark-haired and dark-eyed, Joy's broad face gave her a vaguely Mexican look, but she spoke with a typical Texas drawl.

"Thanks for saving me a spot," Tara said as she settled in beside the older woman. "I was out on the northern edge and I wasn't sure I'd make it!"

"Is the fence repaired?"

"Not yet. I'm still getting the tree cut away. Then I can patch it."

"One of the men should help you."

Tara thought so, too, but she wasn't about to complain. A chance to be alone among the Chosen was too valuable to squander. "They have their work. I can manage, even if I can't go as quickly."

Joy might have replied, but the sound of chimes indicated that the Leader was about to take the stage for the blessing of the meal. And this was no "Good bread, good meat, good God, let's eat" prayer, like the ones Tara had grown up with. No, the Leader usually droned on for a good fifteen minutes about the Powers and their importance and their great beneficence before shutting up and letting his followers eat. This was also the time he introduced any newcomers to the group.

Tara glanced at the small table at the front where those who were taking their first meal with the Chosen sat. She remembered her own dinner at that table. Having spent the day with Joy, she had been distressed to find herself left alone. The analytical part of her mind had understood: separating her from the woman who had been her guide left her vulnerable, more likely to look for security in the group dynamic. But men like the Leader used those techniques because they worked and, despite her recognition of the manipulation, they'd worked on her. She *had* appreciated it when the Leader sat with her, when he introduced her and everyone made her feel welcome.

At the table tonight were a man and three women, the most people Tara had ever seen at one time coming into the group. But then, the holidays were approaching, and the lost and lonely became needier when the leaves started to fall.

After the Leader finished his mumbo jumbo about not polluting the bodies that housed the eternal souls granted us by the Powers, he asked the newcomers to join him on the stage, leaning down to offer a hand to each of the three women as they climbed the stairs. The man followed behind them, shoulders stooped, with a slight hitch in his gait.

It wasn't until all four faced the audience that Tara recognized him. All the blood rushed out of her head, and a wave of dizziness assailed her.

"Are you all right?" Joy whispered in her ear, a hand on Tara's arm.

"I just . . . low blood sugar or something," Tara choked out.

Good God, what was Jacob Nolan doing there? Did the FBI have something on the Chosen? But last she'd heard, Nolan had left the Bureau and was working full-time at computer programming. Of course, it had been months since she'd been in touch with anyone from her past. Perhaps he'd gone back to work.

If the FBI had sent Jake, what did that mean for Andrea, the girl whose disappearance had prompted Tara's involvement with the Chosen? She blinked back the dizziness and concentrated on the Leader's words.

"As you know, we welcome all who come to us seeking refuge from the troubles of the world outside. Here you will find the peace that comes with the acceptance of the Powers' rule, and when you accept them into your heart, you will be accepted in turn."

He put a hand on the first woman's head. "This was Eloise.

She has visited us off and on for almost three months, so many of you may recognize her. Today, she joins us and becomes Rachel."

"Hello, Rachel, and welcome," said the crowd.

"You may also recognize Janet, who has helped us with the harvest for several days. Today she joins our community as Mary."

"Hello, Mary, and welcome." Tara wondered how many of the members of the Chosen had been to Alcoholics Anonymous meetings and whether the greetings sounded familiar to them.

"This was Suzanne. She heard about us and came from Louisiana to join us. Today, as a member of the Chosen, she becomes Charity." Suzanne was petite, blonde, and curvy, and the Leader's hand lingered on her head.

Then he turned to Jake. "Jason has also sought us out. Today, he is Chosen and becomes Jacob." *Neat trick.* How had Jake convinced the Leader that he should be given the name Jacob? The Chosen were given names in a peculiar range from Old Testament reference to New Age sentiment, but it was too coincidental that Jake should be given his own back.

Dinner was served, and Tara mechanically put the food into her mouth, chewed, and swallowed. The vegetable stew and homemade bread filled her belly, but she could barely taste them, so engrossed was she in her thoughts. How could she get close to Jake? As a new member, he would be assigned first-level chores and he would always have another man with him as a "guide." She had at least another day on the fencing, and then she'd be given some other job to do, either alone or with another woman — rarely did the sexes mingle. With the exception of Sunday afternoons, when they were allowed a few hours of freedom, the acolytes' days were scheduled from dawn to dusk, and most of them liked it that way. If she raised a fuss, or tried to buck the system, she'd never find Andrea.

Was it possible Jake knew Tara was in the group? Surely not. Which meant he was here on some kind of official business, since she didn't believe for a minute he'd decided to sign up for real. What had he given as a cover story? He was thin to the point of gauntness, bruises darkened the skin beneath his eyes, and a heavy shadow covered what Tara knew to be a strong jaw. In short, he looked as if he'd been living rough for weeks, even months.

Tara didn't believe that, either. Jake Nolan had money and smarts. Of course, he was also obsessively determined when he set his mind to something. She wouldn't put it past him to starve himself and sleep in a field for a week for an undercover job. Still, she couldn't help the twinge of concern over his appearance. Jake had taken leave from the FBI for a reason: his fanatical pursuit of answers had nearly destroyed him. What if he had strayed too close to the edge this time?

She didn't realize how often she'd looked at him until Joy startled her with a poke in the ribs.

"He's a handsome man."

"Y-yes." She felt a blush crawl up her cheeks. Well, better the woman thought Tara's interest in Jake was sexual than she realize the truth.

"Maybe the Leader will assign him to help you with the fencing."

"Oh no. I told you, I am doing fine." Plus, luck had never smiled on Tara, and she didn't expect it to start now. But Joy just winked, and Tara wondered whether the woman might be hatching some kind of matchmaking plan. Well, fine. If Joy had the Leader's ear and could arrange for Jake to work with her, so much the better.

All night, Tara fretted in her bunk in the twelve-woman cabin. She had seen nothing to indicate the Chosen were involved in anything that might bring them to the FBI's attention. Some separatist groups were dangerous, and many of the leaders were egotists if not worse, but she'd always believed the vast majority of members were simply average Joes and Janes trying to find a way through an overly complicated world. A bit credulous, maybe, but not bad at heart.

∽

THE MORNING HORN found Tara with gritty eyes and an aching head. Crawling out of her bunk took every drop of her energy. She brushed her teeth and scrubbed her face, then headed back to the dining hall for breakfast with three of the other women from her cabin, one of whom — Aurora — was six months pregnant.

Aurora had explained to Tara that she'd run from her abusive boyfriend the moment she realized she was pregnant, landing with the Chosen after six weeks on her own. She slept in the bunk below Tara's and chattered nonstop. Even, occasionally, in her sleep. Although she was probably only a few years younger than Tara's own thirty, she made Tara feel ancient.

The four women entered the hall together, but one of the door sentries pulled Tara aside the minute they were inside.

"The Leader would like to speak with you," he said. Tara's heart pounded. Please God, Jake hadn't betrayed her. Unable to speak, she nodded and followed the man, whose name she thought was Aaron, as he led her up to the front of the room.

"Serena," the Leader said in his mellifluous baritone. "Joy

has brought it to my attention that you could use a hand with the western fence."

"Only for speed, Leader. I would not want to take someone else from their duties." *There, that sounded appropriately humble.*

"Ah, but we would not wish you to suffer unduly in your service. You are precious to the Powers. Never forget that."

"Yes, Leader." *Puke.*

"Do you feel up to working with a new acolyte, being so fresh here yourself? It is a great responsibility, and one I do not request lightly."

"If you are certain you wish to entrust me with such an honor, I would take the responsibility most seriously."

"It is settled, then. This afternoon, you work with Jacob. Come after lunch and Aaron will introduce you."

That left the morning, during which Tara worked in the laundry. Whereas afternoon duties lasted however long they took—from a day to month—morning assignments rotated on a biweekly basis. Although the laundry wasn't fun, seeing as the camp had no air conditioning and the work made sweat roll down Tara's face and neck and pool at the base of her spine, it was still better than collecting eggs, which had been her first post-breakfast job. Eggs, rice, and beans were the standard breakfast fare of the Chosen and, while Tara found the food dull, she did admire the group's self-sufficiency. They raised their own chickens and had massive solar panels on all the roofs that provided the electricity for cooking and cleaning.

Not much else around the compound ran on electricity, though security lights dotted the area, each with its own solar panel. Someone had spent a small fortune outfitting the place, and not for the first time, Tara wished she'd had the resources to investigate the Chosen from the outside before coming in. But she'd given up her job with the Dobbs Hollow Police Department, and hadn't been inclined to renew contact with them. She'd used the Twin Oaks library's computer system to find what she could on the Chosen, but not much was available.

In the laundry, Tara switched wet clothes into the dryers, then sorted dirty things and stuffed them into the five large washers. Another woman took the dry clothes out and folded them, sorting them into stacks according to the laundry marks on them that showed which dormitory they went to.

They didn't talk much. By and large Tara had noticed that the Chosen weren't particularly chatty, with the exception of Aurora. The structure of the assignments, the rotation and separation, didn't encourage the formation of deep connections, and Tara understood this to be by design. Still, it frustrated her. The other laundress, Sarah, might or might not be a good source of information, but after another few days they'd be separated, each to take on a different morning activity, long before Tara could earn her friendship.

"How long have you been a member of the Chosen?" Tara asked, deciding to try anyway.

"Eight years."

"So you must have known the Leader practically from the beginning."

"His father was Leader before him."

Tara had known that much from her research, but she had to pretend she had just wandered into the compound without knowing the history of the place. Merely a friend Andrea had dragged along on several visits.

"You're lucky to have been here so long."

"Yes, I am."

"A friend of mine came here and she told me how

wonderful it was. She left, though, before I made up my mind to join her. She and her cousin, John."

"Of course. Pearl. She and John went on a mission. It was hard to lose them both like that, but after the rumors, it wasn't so surprising that she chose to go." The woman frowned.

"Rumors?"

"It's nothing. I am sure they weren't true."

The woman couldn't seriously leave her hanging like that. Not after the first hint of a clue Tara had heard in weeks.

"You know, I have a horrible admission to make." Tara kept her tone light despite her desperation.

"Nothing could be that bad," Sarah said.

"No, really. Here it is: I miss gossip."

That surprised a laugh out of Sarah. "Yes, well, you won't find much to gossip about here."

"I know. I think that's why I was so interested in whatever rumor you dangled about Pearl." Pearl, Tara thought, was an even stupider name than Serena. Andrea, with her red hair and flamboyant laugh, had been nothing like a pearl. A diamond, or a ruby, something glittering with the occasional sharp edge, but never a pearl.

"I didn't dangle anything," Sarah said with self-conscious dignity.

"Okay, okay. I jumped without you dangling!"

The older woman laughed again.

"It was nothing, really. Just some talk that she might have been having a romance."

"Ooooh, you call that nothing? That's the juiciest bit of gossip I've heard in the five weeks I've been here. Of course, it's the *only* bit of gossip I've heard, too, but still . . . Who was she seeing?"

Sarah shrugged. "I doubt it's true. Relationships have to be sanctioned, blessed by the Leader. It's probably just gossip created by people with too much time on their hands. It's better to keep busy so you don't have time to worry about trivialities."

But Tara wasn't so certain. For the first time, she had a tentative lead. If Andrea had been seeing someone, that person might know what had happened to her. Or might have caused it. And while she couldn't press for details without arousing Sarah's suspicions, the faint lead renewed her determination.

⸎

By lunchtime, Tara was drenched with sweat despite the fact that they were two weeks into November. Her hair, having escaped the confines of its French braid, frizzed around her face. At least the laundry building was closer in than the fence, so she had time between the first horn and the second to wash up a bit. Until she joined the Chosen, she hadn't realized how much she appreciated the simple amenity of a private bathroom and as much time as she wanted to spend in it.

Lunch was one of Tara's favorites—homemade tomato soup with grilled cheese sandwiches on the bread the women made. Tara herself had no talent for cooking, so she probably wouldn't ever be assigned kitchen duty, but she surely would like to learn how to make the breads and stews the Chosen ate at every meal. Of course, cooking for close to one hundred people was a skill she wasn't likely to need once she left the commune.

The kitchens were where she'd expected to find Andrea when she'd first arrived. After all, the two had met working at a diner in Twin Oaks, and Andrea, though only a waitress, had confided her love of cooking. Andrea had brought Tara to visit the Chosen a few times. She had a distant cousin who'd joined the Leader several years before. The Leader had invited both Tara and Andrea up to the main house, where they'd met with Andrea's cousin, John, who oversaw the sale of the goods the Chosen sold both on the Internet and in town.

Tara hadn't much cared for either the Leader—who'd insisted on being addressed as such even though he wasn't *their* leader, at least not yet—or John, who'd given her the creeps. But the house was lovely, and after lunch both she and Andrea had spent some time helping out around the place, appreciating the new scenery, the new people. They'd gone down to the gardens and pulled weeds and set stakes for various plants. Tara had enjoyed herself, and they'd gone back a couple more times to spend an afternoon relaxing in the sun.

That's all it had been for Tara. But when Andrea had stopped writing after joining the Chosen, it hadn't taken Tara long to decide to follow her. She hadn't even been certain she intended to convince Andrea to leave. Because according to what she'd gathered, members of the Chosen *were* allowed to leave. That fact alone suggested to Tara that nothing truly evil could be going on in the compound.

Leaving wouldn't be easy, of course, since the Chosen gave up their personal possessions to the Leader upon arrival, and lived a proscribed life that wouldn't exactly provide them with much to put on a résumé, but it wasn't forbidden. And guests were encouraged to come in, to spend a day in the gardens or the orchard. While they had to be checked in by guards at the gate and have their presence announced, they were not followed around the premises. On the surface, everything appeared to be on the up-and-up.

But when she'd arrived at the camp three weeks after Andrea, ostensibly to help in the gardens again, only to hear that Andrea and John had both gone on missions of self-discovery, every instinct she had rebelled.

A man like the Leader didn't just send away a brand-new acolyte over whom he hadn't guaranteed full control. John, maybe. Andrea, never.

And the longer Tara had stuck around, the more suspicious she'd become. Nothing about the way the Leader treated his flock gave the impression he'd let a single one out of his sight for longer than a day. And then there were the cameras. She'd noticed them almost by accident when the sunlight had glinted off a lens set just below the glass of one of the security lights. Why would a community farm and ranch need to spy on its members? So Tara had given notice at the diner and moved into the commune.

And now, Jake was here. What could it possibly mean? Both drugs and guns were possible activities for reclusive groups with charismatic leaders, but Jake didn't belong to the DEA or ATF. Kidnapping? No one in the compound seemed to be held against their will. In fact, they seemed quite happy overall, despite the hard work and restrictive living conditions. She hadn't made it into the ranch house yet, though, and there were acres and acres of land on which anything might be occurring.

The final dining horn rang, and Tara found Aaron at her side. He waited while she cleaned her plate and laid it in the bussing tub. Whoever had kitchen duty this afternoon would pick up the tubs, wash the dishes and silverware, and then reset the long tables in time for the evening meal.

Without speaking, Aaron led her over to the door, where Jake waited for them.

"Jacob, this is Serena. You will be working with her this afternoon." "Serena?" A spark of humor lit those dark eyes, and Tara had to squelch the instinctive urge to grin back. Finally, someone with a sense of humor about the ridiculous names. But laughter would draw unwelcome attention, so she simply nodded.

"We have to cut down a tree limb that's growing into one of the fences," she said. "Are you up to it?"

"Are you implying that I'm some kind of weakling?"

"Jacob," Aaron said, a note of warning in his voice, "the Chosen do not judge. Serena is merely concerned for your welfare."

"Of course," said Jake. "I'm just not used to anyone worrying about me." He cast his eyes down.

Damn, he was good. Even Tara believed him.

"You will become used to it in time. Serena, take Jacob out to the shed and get the tools. Don't allow him to overdo it today, though."

"I'll be careful," she promised, still astonished they'd let her take him out alone. It had to be some kind of test.

Jacob followed her silently through paths teeming with the Chosen headed to their afternoon duties. The western fence was close to the large area of empty soil from which beans had just been harvested. Unfortunately, three men were tilling the remnants of the plants into the soil, so she and Jake wouldn't be truly alone. Not that she'd expected to be.

At the shed, Jacob hefted the ladder and an ax with enviable ease, leaving her only the saw to carry. Regardless of what he'd put his body through, he remained strong, and she couldn't help staring just a tiny bit at the bulge of muscles in his arms. His physical presence had knocked her for a loop when they'd first met, and though she didn't want to remember the feeling, it was impossible to forget.

When they got out to the tree, he set up the ladder, took the saw from her, and climbed up to finish cutting away the branch while she stood below, steadying him. When she'd been working alone, she'd sat in the V of the branch, using the saw in front of her. It hadn't been particularly safe, but it had been the only way she could get good leverage, because without someone holding it, the ladder tended to sway alarmingly.

"What are you doing here, Jake?" she asked with a quick look around to be sure no one was close enough to hear.

"I came to find you. Now that I have, we're leaving."

"Like hell."

"You can't mean to stay with these . . . drones?"

"Not that it's any of your business, but yes. I do. You can leave any time, though."

"Why?" Sawdust rained down on her as Jake went after the limb with alarming aggression.

"Why what?"

"Why the hell would you want to incarcerate yourself in a place like this?"

"I'm looking for a friend."

"For crying out loud, TJ, I know you had a rough year, losing your family and all, but you have friends. And they're worried about you. They're the ones who sent me to find you."

She gaped at him. "You can't be serious. My brother was the scum of the earth and my father wasn't much better. You of all people should know that. I'm not here figuring out the existential meaning of friendship, I'm looking for one particular friend. This is the last place I traced her before losing her trail."

He digested that while he finished sawing off the branch.

Caught in the fence, it remained aloft even after it had separated from the tree. Jake yanked on it a few times, then climbed down the ladder.

"I'm going to have to take that off closer to the fence edge as well. Then I can chop the bigger part for wood while you re-stretch and reattach the chain link."

One of the men from the field wandered over, and Tara's belief that she'd been handed Jake as some sort of test intensified. The man's name was Samuel, and he was among the favorites of the Leader.

"Is everything working out?" he asked.

"It's fine." Tara managed a smile. "I don't think we'll need to replace this piece of fence at all. If Jacob can get all the pieces of the branch out, we should be able to just fix it."

"Waste not, want not," Samuel intoned.

"Exactly."

"And you, Jacob? The labor is not too difficult? You are handling it?"

"Yes, I am. It's good to be working again. Feeling useful."

"Excellent." The man nodded and went back to talk to the men in the bean field.

"They don't trust you yet. Be careful. I don't intend to let you get me kicked out of here."

"Do you have any idea who these people are, TJ?"

"Stop calling me that. Here you have to get used to calling me Serena, and I have to get used to answering to it."

"Jesus." Jake gave the tree branch a particularly vicious pull.

"And don't let them hear you say that or you will get a lecture from the Leader on how 'Jesus' is just a name the deluded masses of the un-Chosen give to one of the Powers."

"What cover story did you invent for being here?"

"I didn't need one. Andrea, the friend I told you about, she brought me out here a bunch of times. It all seemed harmless enough. Then one day she decided to move in. Soon after that, she stopped coming to town, and she didn't write. When I came to visit and asked to see her, I was told she'd moved on, gone on some kind of spiritual mission."

"And you don't believe that."

"Not a chance."

"Okay."

Tara couldn't deny the thread of warmth that snaked through her at his easy acceptance of her evaluation of the situation. She had little faith in her own instincts these days. She'd missed such important things when her friends at home had been in trouble that she'd almost gotten them killed. She wasn't naive; she recognized that part of her determination to find Andrea had to do with making up for having been unable to save Lucy. Jake's agreement based on nothing more than her word eased the constant burden of self-recrimination.

"What did you tell them?"

"I'm Jason Norman. They didn't ask for many details, but I'm sure they'll check, so I built myself a pretty solid cover. I told them I was a computer programmer who'd had a bad breakup from my girlfriend. She ran off, and I left my job to go look for her. I fell on hard times and landed in Twin Oaks, taking odd jobs."

"Why on earth would you tell them you were looking for a girlfriend?"

"Because if they asked around in Twin Oaks, they'd know I'd collected stories about Tara Jean Black."

"Shit!" Tara barely remembered to keep her voice down as she snuck a look at the field. Black was the name she'd used working in Twin Oaks. "You're going to get me kicked out of here!"

"No, I'm not. I told the Leader that I recognized you. I knew you wouldn't know what to say about me, so I told him you hated me and probably wouldn't even acknowledge my presence. I wouldn't tell him why, just said I deserved it."

"You do."

"Yeah, I do. But the fact remains that Tara Jean Black was involved with Jason Norman. You'll have to admit we know each other at some point, so here's what you need to know: We met while you were working in Dallas cleaning houses and I was a work-from-home computer consultant. I had to give us both jobs he couldn't check on easily. I hired you from a flyer you'd put up in a coffee shop, because I am a slob."

"Are you? Really?" Tara looked up at him with interest. She'd met him in Dobbs Hollow. They'd been brought together because a mutual friend had needed help from the law enforcement community, but they'd never been close, never had time to become friends. Tara knew more about Jake from a true crime book she'd read in which he was featured than she did from the time they'd spent together.

"Yeah, I kind of am." He grinned, and her heart leapt a little at the sight of the groove it carved into his lean cheek and the twinkle in his changeable blue-gray eyes. "I tend to leave papers out everywhere. That much is true." Serious again, he hurried on. "We started dating, fell in love, then you ran off. I followed you, and eventually heard you were here. That's the story."

"And I'll have to give a reason for not admitting it sooner. Thanks a *lot*." She glanced around to see who might be watching, but no one seemed to be paying them any attention. "Now they'll never trust me. You've screwed me up but good."

"Do you have any idea who these people are? Who that lunatic who calls himself the Leader is?"

"No. I didn't exactly have the resources of the FBI at my fingertips before I came looking for Andrea. I had to fly blind."

"Well, let me clue you in: His real name is Owen Stephenson. He inherited this ranch from his father, who died under extremely suspicious circumstances six years ago, when Owen was twenty-seven. His father had already set this place up to house his own ministry. He sent Owen to all the best schools hoping he'd follow in his footsteps but with a more modern twist. Little Owen went to the University of Texas as an undergrad and majored in biochemistry and psychology. Then he went to Harvard Medical School. But rather than going into an internship in a hospital, he came home one summer, his father died, and he stepped right into the top slot. Aaron and Samuel, he brought them with him when he came home from Harvard.

"Daddy Stephenson had close to two hundred followers, all of them living here. Owen stepped into his father's shoes, but not everyone liked the changes he made when he took over, and a good number of them left. Hal Stephenson was a live-and-let-live kind of guy. His son is most definitely not. He's a narcissistic sociopath.

"Nothing gets in Owen Stephenson's way, and some of the people who took off have said—though never publicly, never on the record—that others didn't make it out. People who knew too much about the inner workings of the ministry simply disappeared."

Jake's eyes slid to the side and he raised his voice.

"All I want is a chance, TJ."

"For what?" She slid smoothly into the role. "To screw me over again? I came here to get away from people like you. And my name is Serena. You can't convince me that you sincerely want to belong to the Chosen."

"I know I don't deserve—"

Aaron stepped into view. "The Leader wishes to see the two of you."

"Now?" Tara let her fear bleed into her voice to mask her anger. If Jake's appearance led to her being forced out of the compound, she'd kill him, but it was better to sound like a whiner among the Chosen than to allow her strength to show.

"Yes. Your tools will be put away for you. You are to follow me up to the main house."

"This is your fault," Tara hissed at Jake for Aaron's benefit as they trudged across the field. "All I wanted was a little peace and quiet, to make my life whole again."

"Running isn't the answer. We can make our lives whole together," Jake muttered, loud enough for Aaron to hear. "I'm just asking you to let me try."

"I'm staying, you're going."

"What about the Chosen not judging?"

"Maybe I'm not entirely settled in yet. But I'll get there. Faster, once you're gone."

"I'm not going anywhere, T—Serena."

They reached the ranch house and were ushered into a large, airy office, where the Leader waited in a leather chair. Aaron indicated that they were to kneel before the chair, and Tara did. Jake, she noticed, took longer to obey.

The Leader sighed.

"Serena, why did you not tell me you knew Jacob when you first saw him last night?"

Although she was prepared for the question, Tara stumbled through her answer. "I—I'm not really sure. I guess I thought . . . if you knew who he was, you'd send him away and I wanted him to stay because—Oh, this is so embarrassing."

"You have no need to be ashamed. Remember, the Powers are loving and forgiving."

"Of course. But I didn't live up to the best of what I can be. It was petty. I wanted him to be here, to see how good a life I had made for myself without him. I wanted him to know that I was one of the Chosen. When we were together, he made me feel small." That much was true; Jake *had* made her feel small. He'd spared her no quarter letting her know of her incompetence. "I wanted to show that I was better than he thought."

"What did he do to you?"

"I caught him with another woman." She'd decided to use the excuse about halfway through their trip to the house. It would explain their antagonism as almost nothing else could. Let him figure out what to say in his own defense.

"Is this true, Jacob?"

Jake shrugged, a movement as foreign to his body as the humble, kneeling pose. This man was driven, focused, never apathetic.

"I was drunk," he mumbled.

"You were drunk a *lot*," she spat, letting her anger fly free.

"I'm sorry, T—Serena. I haven't had a drink in weeks. I admit, when you first left, I got drunk and stayed that way. But then I realized I had to clean up. All this time, I've been looking for you. That has to count for something."

Tara didn't answer.

"Tell me, Serena, what you feel at this moment," said the Leader. Under his smooth, superficially considerate tone, she felt the fangs of an emotional vampire. He was enjoying watching her and Jake slap at each other.

"I wish I were strong enough to forgive him," she replied.

"I need to meditate on this. You will each go to your bunks and remain there until dinner. After dinner, we will speak again."

⸺

I N H E R B U N K H O U S E, Tara paced. Now that Jake had seen her, he could go home and tell their friends that she was fine. He had no reason to stay. But he would. She knew, just knew, he was going to stick around and cause a problem, and she didn't see any way of changing his mind.

At dinner, Aaron escorted Tara to the front of the room, where she and Jake were both placed at the newcomers' table to eat. Her gut churned, and she found it difficult to choke down the food placed in front of her. What did the Leader have in mind? The rest of the Chosen avoided her eyes when she glanced at other tables, leaving her no question something bad was about to take place.

When the Leader called both of them up to the stage and had them stand looking out onto the dining hall, dread roiled in her stomach, souring the meal.

"We have before us a question of judgment," the Leader intoned, and again Tara heard the tinge of malicious pleasure beneath his words. "Two of the Chosen have polluted their souls with lies. Jacob came in search of Serena, and while he admitted as much to me, he did not reveal the reasons for her flight. And Serena allowed us to believe she did not recognize Jacob, had not known him in their previous lives.

"Such pollution is a corruption that can spread, and we must drive it out or be infected ourselves."

Fury rose in Tara's heart, almost deafening her to the Leader's next words. How could she find Andrea if she were thrown out of the compound? She could not, would not fail another friend.

"Purification is necessary! The Powers have decreed that both shall suffer isolation for their lies."

The hiss of indrawn breath from the large room told her that isolation meant something more severe than simply having to do one's chores alone.

"Jacob shall be given three days' punishment." The Leader turned sad eyes on Tara. "Serena's corruption of spirit goes deeper, however, and the length of her sentence is as yet indeterminate.

"Aaron and Samuel. Take Jacob to the first shed. Joy, Jonas, and Crystal, take charge of Serena."

The five assigned jailers trooped up the stairs.

"Come now, Serena," Joy said, disappointment plain in her face and voice. "The sooner we begin, the sooner it will be over."

"What will? What is isolation?" But the older woman just shook her head and led Tara out a side door and around the back of the dining hall to where several sheds were set apart from the main group of buildings. When Tara balked at going into the farthest one, Jonas shoved her in the back. She stumbled inside.

The shed had no windows, but there was a bare, low-wattage bulb in a fixture hanging from the ceiling just inside the door that came on when they entered. The back part of the room was partitioned into a six-by-ten cell by iron bars. The floor was cement, and a thin mattress lay in one corner with a single sheet, a thick wool blanket, and no pillow. A large bucket stood in one corner with a roll of toilet paper on the floor next to it. Lovely.

This could not be happening. How had she lived among these people for five weeks and never heard a whisper about these rooms? She'd noticed the buildings, but from the outside they appeared abandoned and no one ever spoke about them, so she'd ignored them.

"Take off your clothes," Jonas ordered.

"Excuse me?"

"You have to," Joy explained. "You need to be purified and reborn. It's the only way to escape the corruption of your soul. Fighting will only make it worse. You can keep your panties." The woman sounded truly miserable, and Tara wondered how many times she'd witnessed this process, been party to it.

But she didn't dare ask. There was something in Jonas's expression that said he was eager for her to fight back. Heart in her throat, she stripped down to her underwear.

"In the cell." Jonas pointed.

For Andrea, she reminded herself, stepping into the cell.

Jonas locked the door behind her. "The light will come on for fifteen minutes every couple of hours. You will be brought water. Food will only slow down the purification process. The Leader will visit you to check on your progress."

With that, the three Chosen left, and she was alone. Her last thought before the light went out and she started feeling around in the blackness for the edge of the bed was that she'd get even with Jacob Nolan if it were the last thing she did.

⌒

JAKE SAT IN darkness worrying about TJ. She was tough, he knew. Even before they'd met, he'd heard great things about her from his friend Lucy. Lucy had told him all about Tara's strength of purpose, her gutsiness, her determination. But when he'd met the woman, all he'd seen was her pale skin, her fair hair, her stunning blue eyes. She did a good job of hiding her curvy shape with boxy clothes, but Jake was used to seeing beneath the surface, and Tara's outer shell hadn't fazed him.

And then, things had gone drastically wrong. He'd said terrible things to her, and before he'd been able to apologize appropriately, Tara had disappeared. She'd written and e-mailed a few times, but never with a return address. And then the letters had stopped, and Lucy—who wanted Tara Jean to be her maid of honor—sent Jake in search of her.

And he'd screwed it up again.

How would she handle the box? He didn't foresee the decreed punishment as being terribly difficult for himself. He'd spent time in isolation tanks by choice, had lived rough for weeks in pursuit of the worst kind of madmen the world had to offer, had few illusions left. He was good at meditation, and he'd studied mind control techniques. He had a pretty good idea of what the next three days would bring for him. Tara, on the other hand, had been a local cop in a small town. What were the chances she had any experience with the kind of monsters who would lock someone up indefinitely in a dark hole? Slim to none.

He hoped like hell the darkness and isolation were the only things Owen Stephenson, "the Leader," had planned for them. Others of his ilk employed beatings, rape, hallucinogenic drugs, whatever forms of torture might break a prisoner's spirit. Tara had to hold it together for three days. Then he could get her out. Whatever was necessary, he'd do it. He'd outsmarted and outmanipulated men like Owen Stephenson in the past, and though he was accustomed to having a team behind him, he could manage on his own if necessary.

And then, he'd make it up to Tara Jean if it were the last thing he did.

CHAPTER TWO

Tara had no watch, timepieces being the first things the Chosen were encouraged to donate to the cause. Their days were measured by the horns of the compound, and they had no need for external counts. Thus, she waited in the dark. If the light came on every two hours, she'd be able to count the time that way. Twelve lights-on periods each day. She just had to find some way to stay sane between the lit times.

But then, she had no idea how many days she'd be in this hellhole, so counting the hours wouldn't help much. The shed retained the heat of the day, and sweat trickled down from her neck between her shoulder blades. She wished she'd put her hair up after removing the braid to pick out the twigs and leaves before dinner. Of course, they'd probably have taken her hair clip. Assholes.

She sat on the edge of the mattress and stretched out her legs. They didn't quite reach the cell bars. The darkness pressed down on her, the still air rank with mildew and old sweat. How much longer before the light came on? She couldn't even see to make use of the bucket.

Had Andrea been punished in this same shed? Had something happened to her here? Jonas had said someone would bring her water, but how often? If Andrea had gotten sick while she was in isolation, would anyone even have noticed? But that didn't explain John's disappearance. Could he have objected to the punishment and been silenced for it?

The pieces didn't fit, though. Andrea had been eager to

join the Chosen. She had loved everything about the compound. The first day she'd brought Tara up to the commune, she'd been so excited. She'd shown her the fields, explained how the group collected so much solar energy that the excess was sold to the local electric company, prattled on about the ecological benefits of living the way they did and how happy everyone was there. They'd worked in the gardens together, and Andrea had paid close attention to every word the woman showing them around had said. Tara couldn't imagine Andrea doing anything that merited "isolation."

The bulb flickered to life, and Tara forced herself to use the bucket. Afterward she lay back on the mattress, trying to ignore the need to wash. How could they not even give her a sink? After a while, she started counting backward from a thousand by threes, a trick she often used when she had insomnia.

Somewhere in the middle of her third thousand, she slept.

Throughout the night, Tara woke every time the light popped on. Each time, the dimly limned scenery, or lack thereof, surprised her. Each time, she had to begin anew the counting trick to fall back to sleep.

After the fifth or sixth time, the door opened. Faint light came from outside the shed. Early morning, she figured, before breakfast horn. Aaron passed a large bottle of water through the bars and left without speaking.

How long did they intend the water to last? If she finished this, would more be made available to her, or would the Leader simply see her thirst as greed and try to "purify" her further by withholding that as well? She sipped cautiously from the bottle and sat cross-legged on the mattress with the blanket around her to ward off the chill morning air. She tried to keep her breathing slow and steady, to marshal her thoughts into some kind of order so she could create a plan for what she would do once released, but they kept drifting away from her, out of her control.

The lights came on again and she used the bucket. Would someone come to empty it, or was she supposed to live with that for several days, as well? In the far corner of the shed, something shifted in the shadow. A roach, she thought with a shudder. Insect companions: just what she needed.

When the darkness returned, she imagined she heard bugs. The scratchiness of the blanket felt like ants, and she found herself brushing imaginary critters from her skin. She stood and started to pace, hoping the activity would settle her somewhat, but her heart wouldn't slow and her mind created more phantom creatures to share her space. She drew deeply from the water bottle in an attempt to slow her heart. Something scurried along the wall in the corner, and she hurried back to the bed.

Okay, she thought. Two hours until the light came on. One hundred and twenty minutes. Seventy-two hundred seconds. She'd count it down if she had to. Then she'd see that the room was perfectly fine. Surely it had been at least a few minutes of that already. She could start with seven thousand. No problem. She drew herself into as small a ball as she could manage, pressed herself into the corner, and began counting.

The numbers wouldn't stick in her head, however, and she found herself constantly scrubbing at itchy spots on her skin. What was biting her? Where was it? She felt something buzz by her face, like a palmetto bug landing in her hair, and she jumped from the bed, shrieking and shaking her head. She ran her fingers through her hair, pulling at the knotted curls, searching for whatever had found a home there, but she detected nothing. Were the bugs in the walls? She should get away from the walls. She felt for the edge of the mattress and pulled it out into the middle of the cell, then seated herself in the exact center of the mattress.

The light popped on again, and she stared frantically around the space. Nothing. No rats, no bugs, nothing at all. Even whatever critter had moved in the corner two hours before seemed to be gone. Not that that comforted her. If he could get out, he could get back in. And bring friends. Sweat broke out from her hairline to the soles of her feet, and she clutched her arms to her body, which was when she realized she'd scrubbed raw spots in them.

Okay, Tara Jean, get this under control. You're not afraid of the dark. You're not even afraid of a few bugs. Your mind is playing tricks on you. But something touched her back, and she jumped. Even when she realized the blanket had merely shifted, she couldn't control the racing of her heart. For the first time, she wondered whether she could make it through the punishment. She'd counted on being bored but not scared out of her wits.

The bulb snapped off again, and she let out an involuntary whimper. *Shut it, Tara Jean,* she told herself. *You are better than this. It's just the effects of sensory deprivation.* But the bugs came back, and their crawling legs touching her skin, their squeaks and flutters, left her a sobbing and sodden mess. She rubbed her arms and legs, feeling for whatever was landing there, whatever was biting her, but her hands never came in contact with them. Without seeing them, she couldn't kill them, couldn't even stop them from touching her.

And when the light came on, they were gone, and the cycle of reason and terror began again.

When Jonas arrived with more water, she'd lost track of time. Was it the next morning already? Or merely evening? Her skin was red and raw where she'd thought the bugs were landing, and a couple places on her legs had deep gouges in them.

"Please," she said. "I'm ready. I understand my sins."

But the man didn't speak, just passed her the new water bottle and left. She poured what was left of the old bottle over the bloody spots on her legs, though it stung, and curled up on the mattress.

JAKE KNEW THE water Aaron brought him was likely tainted. A man like Owen Stephenson would leave nothing to chance. He'd want the punishment to break sinners, to leave them in the kind of pieces only he could put together. And then he would want them to testify, to tell the others about the great revelations they'd experienced while in isolation.

It was an effective strategy, allowing him maximum control over the largest number of people with the least effort. The majority of the Chosen, for whom the cult—or new religious movement, as he'd been trained to say in order to be more politically correct—satisfied some need, were perfectly normal, happy people, whose lives in the normal world weren't working out. And most of the ones for whom the Chosen was not a good fit were allowed to leave with no problems. It was only occasionally that an example had to be made. But when an example was needed, it had to be one that showed the complete dominance of the Powers over the Chosen.

So he figured the water was dosed with some kind of hallucinogenic. But dehydration would be deadly. He couldn't ignore the water entirely. Too, Owen would want a report on Jake's progress, which meant he had to react to the water appropriately. And without knowing exactly what was in it, he wouldn't know what the proper reaction was in order to fake it. He'd just have to drink it.

But there were ways to minimize the damage from hallucinogens, and one was to go into the "trip" with as positive images in mind as possible. And when he considered the road he most wanted to travel during his hallucinations, only one image came to mind: Tara. He had hurt her, and doubtlessly guilt would be part of his experience, but he was prepared for that. Besides, it would be totally in character for him to suffer guilt over the woman he'd supposedly cheated on.

He sipped slowly from the water bottle, remembering Tara as she'd looked when they'd first met and firmly closing his mind to what she might be experiencing now. He'd gone to her apartment, hoping to find Lucy. Tara had answered the door in sweatpants and a T-shirt, her face sheened with sweat, her fabulous hair slipping loose from its short ponytail and curling around her face. He'd barely even noticed the Glock she held at her side with careless competence. He'd introduced himself and she'd put the gun away, but the spark of interest he'd noticed in her eyes at first had disappeared.

His own fascination had just begun. During the days they'd spent tracking a serial killer in her hometown, he hadn't allowed himself any personal feelings whatsoever. He allowed them now. He pictured her as she'd been that day, then rewrote the scene, imagined her welcoming him into her home, imagined taking her into his arms, slowly stripping off her clothes.

The skin beneath her T-shirt would be soft, smooth,

white. She was, he guessed, a cotton-underwear type woman, but this was his fantasy and in his fantasy she was in silk. He would slide his hands over her warm skin, heating it further, then he would kiss her. Not on the mouth. Not yet. He would start with her jaw, her neck, dangerously close to the nipples pebbling beneath her silky bra.

His dick hardened and he shifted on the mattress. In for a penny, in for a pound. He took a long pull off the water bottle and, closing his eyes against the darkness, settled back into the fantasy.

THE FIRST TIME the Leader came to see her, he left the door open behind him. Midday light shone so brightly through the opening that Tara winced, her eyes unused to the brilliance. He was nothing more than a silhouette, but she recognized him. She stumbled to the cell's bars and held them.

"I'm sorry," she began.

"So am I, Serena."

"I understand my sins." He didn't seem inclined to let her out, though, and panic rose in her throat. What words did he need to hear? What would work? "I went against the will of the Powers. It was wrong. I should have told you immediately. It won't ever happen again." She knew she was babbling, but she couldn't seem to stop herself.

The Leader just shook his head, handed her another bottle of water, and left, closing her into the darkness, where the bugs waited. Tara wept.

By the time the Leader came again, Jonas had been in twice more. And something else had happened, as well. Somewhere in the darkness, she had dreamt of Jake, of his voice and his hands. And she'd remembered his analysis of Owen Stephenson. A narcissistic sociopath. When the man returned, she knew what to do. And it was easier than it should have been, easier than she'd ever want it to be.

Rather than approaching the bars on foot, she crawled to them, knelt before Stephenson, and begged forgiveness. Thank God she hadn't eaten in who knew how long, or she might have thrown up. But it worked. He opened her cell and laid a hand on her head, the first human contact she'd had since she'd been incarcerated. Jonas had always been careful not to touch her when he'd brought the water. She steeled herself against the twin emotions of relief and revulsion.

Joy waited for her outside along with Charity, whose eyes widened in shocked horror at the sight Tara presented. So this was the young woman's initiation. Tara doubted she'd disobey the rules anytime soon.

"Come on, now," Joy said, draping a sheet over Tara's shoulders and putting an arm around her waist. "We'll take you to the infirmary and get you all cleaned up. Then things will be better. You'll see."

Cleaning up would be a start, but in the sunlit afternoon, Tara could see the nasty scratches on her body where infection had begun to set in. And even here, in daylight, she could hear the insects chittering at the edges of her thoughts. No amount of bathing would help that.

As they made their way toward the infirmary, which was attached to the main ranch house, Tara saw Jake leaning heavily on Aaron headed in the same direction. So she had been in the shed for three days. It had felt much longer. She wanted to be furious at Jake for his part in her punishment, but rage took too much energy. Instead, she found herself worried about how he'd survived the isolation.

He and Aaron arrived at the ranch house before she did. They were moving faster, which Tara took to mean he'd managed to come out relatively unscathed. Even his limp seemed to be gone, though it might just have been masked by the Aaron's support.

⌒

"WHAT DO YOU think?" Owen Stephenson stood behind the one-way glass looking into the infirmary. At his side was Samuel, his most trusted lieutenant. Samuel always knew the correct punishment when the Chosen strayed. It was his Gift.

"She seems suitably chastened," Samuel said.

"Indeed. She was pathetically grateful to be released. She was on her knees. Very gratifying." Owen slanted a grin at Samuel, feeling almost as he'd done years before in med school, before he'd understood the meaning of the power that flowed through him, when all he and Samuel and Aaron had cared about was getting drugs and girls. "I almost asked her to take care of something for me while she was down there. But she was filthy."

"I still don't trust her. She came with Andrea. And look how much trouble that one caused." "Andrea was John's mistake; he believed she knew what he was, that she was ready to participate fully. Tara, on the other hand, is no better than the rest of them. And now that I've met *him*, I understand why she was so ready to join the flock. Look at her. She's not exactly beautiful. She probably thought she'd won the lottery with Jason Norman. He goes and cheats on her, and she runs off with her tail between her legs. No wonder she hooked up with Andrea. They had something in common. And then Andrea took off on her, too. We're all she has. She's not going anywhere. Especially now that her boyfriend's here."

Samuel frowned. "You really think he can replace John?"

"Absolutely. You're the one who told me that his background check turned up a couple scrapes with the law, but nothing serious enough to make anyone sit up and take notice. He's an excellent hacker with a little bit of a speed problem. He'll be easy to control."

"He asked Aaron if he could be the one to take care of her."

"Good. I'll set it up. It'll keep them loyal. A little responsibility will serve as a good test for him."

Owen let himself out of the viewing chamber and stepped into the infirmary. The girl was lying on her bed, curled into a ball beneath the blankets. He'd watched her shake the covers out before she got in, and had a pretty good idea what she'd seen in the shed. Datura always brought out the most interesting aspects of prisoners' minds. He only regretted that he couldn't watch the hallucinations in person. He'd considered putting night vision cameras in the sheds but hadn't gotten around to it. He didn't want word getting out. If people knew help was only a camera away, the isolation might not work as well.

Jacob lay on top of his covers, arms folded beneath his head. He stared at the ceiling, barely looking at Serena. That would be guilt working on him. Owen repressed a smile. He couldn't have created a more perfect situation if he'd designed it himself. He closed the door loud enough to draw their attention. Both sat up.

"Jacob. Serena. You have been purified and reborn. You can now undertake the work of the Chosen once again. Welcome back.

"You are weak. Deborah is in charge of the sickroom, and she will be by shortly with medications and some food for you. But you still have spiritual work to do. Jacob, you have atoned to the Chosen for your lies, but you have yet to make it up to Serena for your betrayal. Serena, you have also made reparation for your dishonesty, but the cause of it was your inability to forgive, and you must learn charity.

"So, Jacob, I am putting you in charge of Serena's recovery. You will take care of her and prove yourself worthy of her trust. Serena, you will accept Jacob's assistance without complaint and you will search your soul and drive out any anger you still harbor toward him."

Both of his renewed converts agreed to his will, and Owen left them alone.

⌒

"I'M SORRY." JAKE'S voice from the other bed jerked Tara's attention away from the itch on her toe she was trying to ignore. There were no bugs in this bed. She'd looked. "I shouldn't have . . . cheated on you, Serena."

The words confused her for a moment, until she realized what he was trying to tell her. He believed someone might be listening. That the room might be wired. She'd had the same concerns. She even thought the large mirror on the far wall might function as a window for anyone who wanted to watch them.

"Why wasn't I enough for you?" She played along, and

though her voice was more plaintive than Tara would have liked, it suited Serena.

"You were always enough." The sincerity in his tone almost had her believing he was talking about more than their fictional breakup. A lump formed in her throat, and she had to swallow it away. "If you hadn't been, I wouldn't have followed you here."

The door opened, admitting a woman Tara had never seen. Thick, dark blonde hair captured by a barrette, hung straight and smooth to her waist. Her skin was well tanned but unlined, and her green eyes were gentle. She carried a tray with two bowls of soup, bread, and an unlabeled bottle filled with pills.

"My name is Deborah," she said, setting the tray down on the table between the two beds. "I know you two must be hungry, but I want you to eat very slowly. After three days, your stomachs need to readjust." She took out one of the pills and put it next to one of the soup bowls. "This is for you, Serena. An antibiotic to stave off infection from your wounds."

She settled on the edge of Tara's bed. "Now, before we eat, we must give thanks to the Powers for their food, and love, and guidance." She reached out a hand to Tara, then leaned across and took one of Jake's hands as well. She bowed her head, so Tara followed suit. In the distance, the dinner horn sounded. The prayer was blessedly short, and then Deborah left them to eat in peace while she, presumably, went to get her own dinner.

Tara struggled not to gulp the hot soup, reminding herself of Deborah's warning. But nothing she'd eaten in any five-star restaurant in her youth had tasted as good as the simple vegetable soup and crusty, whole-grain bread. Even the water from the pitcher on the bedside table tasted cleaner, clearer, sharper than the water she'd been drinking in the shed.

Which was when it hit her. She nearly forgot about the listening devices and spoke aloud. They'd drugged her. The insects hadn't been real. No wonder they'd disappeared when the light came on. She'd imagined the whole thing. The slow burn of anger in her breast almost made her lose her appetite. Almost.

But she needed to get her strength back to take down Owen Stephenson. Before, all she'd wanted to do was find Andrea and be sure she was happy, get her out if she wasn't. When she'd arrived at the compound, she'd held no resentment toward the Leader. The beliefs of the Chosen didn't coincide with her own, but Tara considered herself a "live and let live" sort. If Andrea had wanted to stay, so be it.

That had changed with the transparently false story about Andrea leaving the community. Then Tara made it her mission to find out what had happened to her friend. Where she was being held. If she were even still alive. Her attention had still been on the single event of Andrea's disappearance. No one seemed to think it odd, and she hadn't heard about other members of the Chosen suddenly disappearing, so she didn't consider that anything more systematic might be going on.

With the realization of what had been done to them in the shed, however, Tara's focus changed yet again. She was going to bring down the high and mighty Leader and make sure he spent the rest of his life in a cell the size of one of his isolation sheds. Because, sure as God made little green apples, if he "purified" members of his congregation on a regular basis, he had a great deal more to hide than a bizarre view of the world and religion.

Stiff with anger, consumed by her own thoughts, Tara brushed her teeth and crawled back onto the bed. What she wouldn't give for her iPad, or even a pen and paper to map out her questions and plans. So many thoughts buzzed through her head that she could barely make sense of them. She had to find Andrea. John had been part of Stephenson's inner circle. If he'd revealed any clue to Andrea about the Chosen's activities, Tara needed it.

Jake tried to make conversation, playing his Jason Norman role, but Tara shut him out.

After about an hour, Deborah returned. "Time for lights out," she said, picking up the tray. "You sleep well, and I'll be by in the morning with breakfast." She flipped the light switch and closed the door behind her.

Slowly, Tara's eyes adjusted to the darkness. It was not as complete here in the sickroom as it had been in the shed, for illumination from the ever-present security lights leaked around the edges of the heavy curtains covering the single window. She could see the outlines of furniture and even make out the shadowy hollows of Jake's features when he turned his head toward her.

A curl slipped across her face, the sensation like an insect gliding by, and she jumped.

Not real, she reminded herself. But goose bumps covered her skin, and she couldn't lie still. After a moment, she heard Jake moving about, and then he came and sat on the edge of her bed.

"Move over," he said softly.

"What?"

He pushed her to the edge of the narrow bed and slid in beside her. Then he tugged her close, tucking her head into the hollow of his shoulder and curling one long, muscular arm down her back so that his hand rested on her ribcage just beneath her breast.

"What do you think you're doing?"

"My job. I'm supposed to be taking care of you, remember? And you're supposed to let me." A thread of humorous challenge lay beneath the words. How could he shrug off the experience of the shed so easily? Whatever visions the drugs had brought him, they had obviously not worked their way so deeply under his skin.

"What did you . . . think about . . . in isolation?" Would he understand what she was asking? That she needed to know what hallucinations he had experienced?

"You."

"Me?" Whatever she had expected, it wasn't that.

"I remembered the way you looked when we first met. You in those baggy sweatpants. All I wanted to do was strip them off you." Tara felt her heart speed up and her mouth go dry. She swallowed hard. "Of course, I couldn't do any such thing. You were"—*a cop, his friend's protector*—"my new maid."

Right. Silly Tara. He was playing his role. She'd almost forgotten the hidden eyes and ears. But he hadn't stopped speaking.

"And I remembered your eyes when I hurt you. They haunted me. That day. In the shed. Now. I live with them, with the knowledge I treated you unfairly." His arm tightened around her and under her palm she felt the muscles of his stomach clench. "I'll make it up to you. Just give me a chance to prove I'm a better man than the one you've seen so far. That's all I am asking."

Why did he have to sound so sincere? Tara could almost believe he was apologizing for his actual behavior rather than for the acts of his cover identity. And she, still weak from the

shed, still perilously close to falling apart, was all too sensitive to kindness, whether real or feigned. "Let's just go to sleep,
okay? We can worry about proving and forgiving tomorrow."

"Yeah, okay." He rubbed the top of her head with his
cheek, then took a deep breath and let his muscles relax.
Miraculously, she felt her own follow.

⤳

JAKE HOPED SHE could hear his honest regret. If she moved
her hand an inch or two, she'd certainly feel the truth of his
attraction beneath the loose scrubs they'd both been given to
wear as pajamas. Not that he'd mind that, either, though this
was neither the time nor the place to act on it. The sexual pull
he felt the moment they'd met had come out of nowhere at
a time he'd considered himself emotionally dead. His shock
and self-disgust had contributed to his harsh treatment of her.

She'd left before he could apologize properly. At first,
he'd been content to let her go, to retreat into the emotional
vacuum he'd inhabited prior to her appearance in his life. But
even before Lucy had called to tell him Tara had stopped
writing to her, that existence had begun to pale.

It hadn't been hard to track her. She wasn't some fugi-
tive carefully covering her tracks, merely a woman who'd left
behind a life she no longer wanted. He'd discovered the diner
she was working at less than a month after she'd left to join
the cult.

From there, things had become a little more complicated.

Jake had burned a lot of bridges taking leave without
notice from the FBI, but one or two people still owed him
favors. He'd created Jason Norman, had his pals supply

him with a minor record, and hacked his way into various social networking sites to give Jason a work history going back years rather than days. He'd also put Jason and Tara's breakup online—Jason would have used the Net to find his runaway girlfriend—and created some dummy accounts with "leads," one of whom sent him to Twin Oaks.

Regardless of the cutting comments he'd once made about her police work, Jake had known Tara would be able to pick up his cues, to take on the role he'd created for her. She was smart and savvy, even if she was in over her head. He just had to make her see that letting him help was best for all concerned. Not that he had high hopes for her friend Andrea. His FBI contacts wouldn't confirm that the Chosen were on any of the watch lists, but they wouldn't deny it, either. And after his experiences in the shed, Jake figured something fairly serious was going on around the compound.

He felt Tara's breathing slow into the regular, even pattern of sleep and let himself drift. For the moment, at least, they were safe.

CHAPTER THREE

The first thing Tara noticed the next morning was the warmth of the bed. She'd never been warm in the shed. During the day the air had weighed heavily in her lungs and the heat had beaten at her skin; at night she'd had to pull the thin blanket around her body. If she'd been herself, she'd have realized she could count the days that way, but of course, she hadn't been herself.

The second thing she noticed was that the warmth didn't come from quilts or heaters. It emanated from the very masculine, very muscular body sharing the bed with her. Jake Nolan. Sometime during the night, her leg had found its way between his, and now she felt the press of his morning erection against her thigh. Heat rose in her face, and she tried to shift away without waking him.

Instead, he pulled her closer. "Where you going?" Even the man's voice was sexy. Deep and sleep-rough, like chocolate-covered sin.

"I'm not going anywhere," she said. "You, however, are going back to your own bed. I don't know what you're doing here."

"Spoilsport." He pressed his lips to her forehead, then her jaw, then whispered in her ear. "Stay weak today. I want to keep us in the house as long as possible."

"Stop that. I want to get some more sleep before we have to get up." She pushed again, and he levered himself out of her bed and staggered over to his own. Tara couldn't help watching him go. What did he mean by kissing her like that?

Was it for any hidden cameras that might exist, to give him an excuse for whispering with her? And why did her traitorous body warm so insistently to his?

Despite her words, however, she couldn't fall back to sleep once he was gone. Without his warmth, the bed was no longer so inviting, and thoughts of Andrea's fate once again took over her mind. Jake was right. They'd been given an opportunity to be in the house by being in the sickroom, and they needed to take advantage of it.

Deborah came by with their breakfast and checked on Tara's wounds. She brought orange juice, as well, a rare luxury for the Chosen, who were usually limited to herbal tea for the women and coffee for the men. As before, she brought Tara an antibiotic, and clothes for both of them.

"Will we have assignments today, Deborah?" Tara asked.

"No. You should concentrate on regaining your strength. Maybe walk in the flower house. You know how to get to it? I can send a guide."

"No, no. No need to trouble anyone and take them from their duties," Tara said. "I am sure we can find it." And perhaps get strategically "lost" along the way.

The flower house was a large greenhouse next door to the main house. The flowers grown were sold in town at a small kiosk on Main Street. When Andrea had first joined the Chosen, Tara had seen her selling flowers a couple of times. The flowers brought in some of the money the Chosen needed to buy that which they could not produce for themselves. Anything else was bought with the funds they had turned over to the Leader upon entering the community, along with the sale of soaps, potpourri, herbs, and other natural products they sold in town and on the Internet. Andrea's cousin had run the web business.

Tara had handed over the hundred-dollar savings account she'd built up in Twin Oaks. She'd had no choice—she had the nasty feeling that the Leader checked to be sure you weren't holding anything back. That idea was confirmed the longer she'd stayed in the compound. The antibiotics showed he had doctors on his payroll. Bankers were a likely addition as well.

And cops? Anything was possible. If she did uncover what had happened to Andrea, who would she turn to? At the moment, she trusted precisely two people: herself and Jake. But that was a worry for another day. First, she had to find Andrea. Dead or alive.

After breakfast, Tara picked up the bundle of clothes Deborah had brought from her bunk and slipped into the bathroom to brush her teeth and change. The jeans rubbed uncomfortably against the scabs on her legs, but at least she'd lost a good deal of weight since joining the Chosen, so they weren't tight. She peered into the mirror and frowned. She'd scrubbed her hair clean the night before, but it was still dull and lifeless. She'd pulled out a couple of chunks in the shed, freaking out over the idea that something was nesting in it.

Oh well, nothing for it now. Deborah had brought a rubber band along with the clothes, and Tara brushed her hair until it had some semblance of its normal shine and then captured it in a high ponytail.

Time to go to work. The thought energized her, and she left the bathroom with a bounce in her step.

JAKE TOOK HIS time in the bathroom. Tara had come out looking revived, more like herself, for which he was profoundly grateful. He'd seen the kind of devastation an experience like the isolation shed could cause in a relatively short time, and though he knew Tara to be strong-minded, he'd been desperately afraid something fundamental might have broken inside her. She'd caught on to his hints about the place being bugged quickly enough, though, and he was certain she had the same idea he did about side trips on their way to the greenhouse.

Not that he didn't want to get out of the house, because he did. That was the only way he'd feel safe enough to have a real conversation with her, one not couched in misleading terms and covered in lies. He needed to know what she'd discovered about the Chosen in her weeks living in the compound and share his own information with her so that they could come up with a plan.

Of course, his own idea of a plan would be to get her the hell out of the compound entirely and let him figure out what the Leader and his lieutenants—for Jake was certain that Aaron, Jonas, and Samuel, the men in charge of taking them to the sheds, were involved in both the innocent *and* the not-so-innocent activities of the Chosen—were up to. Deborah and Joy were both high on his list of suspects, too, given the amount of freedom they seemed to have. The Leader didn't seem to hold women in particularly high esteem, however, so he doubted they would be in on the deepest of the Chosen's secrets.

Thanks to Google Earth and the FBI's intelligence network, he'd had a nice, long aerial look at the acreage owned by Owen Stephenson. Some of what he'd seen, he understood. The bunkhouses and main building, the laundry, gardens, fields, and now the floral greenhouse all made sense of parts of the map he had in his head. But there were huge sections that remained a mystery. Eventually, he'd have to get himself assigned to one of the jobs farther out on the property so he could examine the bigger greenhouses and corresponding storage units that seemed to take up the majority of land far from the house.

But for today, he and Tara would stick close to the ranch house and see what—and who—they could uncover.

When he left the bathroom, he saw her lying on her bed, one hand lying across her stomach.

"Are you feeling okay?"

"Yeah. Just still tired for some reason. I guess the purification really took it out of me. But I'll be fine. Shall we go find the greenhouse? I am sure the flowers will help to cheer me up."

Outside the sickroom lay a long, dimly lit corridor. The walls were whitewashed stucco, and Jake rapped his knuckles against it as they passed. "Look at this awesome plasterwork. I bet it's all original to the house. You don't see work like this anymore."

"Yes, it's lovely," Tara agreed. "When Andrea—Pearl—and I first visited, we ate dinner here with the Leader and a few others. We saw a bit of the house then. The whole thing is beautiful."

"Yeah? That office we met The Leader in was pretty swank, too. This place was probably the talk of the town when it was built. I bet a lot of people in Twin Oaks would love to see the inside. What else did you get to look at?"

"We ate in the dining room. Plus, we got a tour of the kitchen, and we got to see the front rooms briefly as well, since she wanted to visit with her cousin."

"It's a shame they're no longer here."

"Apparently, they both went on missions of some kind. I

wish they'd at least write to say they're well, but we have to trust the Powers to protect them."

Jake slanted a look at Tara, walking beside him. Damn, she was good. Her tone was so even, you'd never know she didn't believe a word of the crap she was spouting. For a bizarre moment, he wanted to grab her and plant a giant, smacking kiss on her lips. Something completely outrageous.

Could he possibly get away with it? Would Jason Norman do such a thing? Leading a double life was incredibly constricting in some ways, but in others, it was freeing. Jason was a lot more laid back than Jake had ever been, without nearly so many hang-ups. He was far less likely to worry about consequences.

Jake glanced sideways once more. Tara stared straight ahead as she walked, and he got the impression her mind was working furiously at some problem. If he grabbed her and kissed her, she'd probably smack him, which wouldn't do them any good at all.

They reached the end of the hallway, and he asked her if she knew which way to turn.

"No. I was kind of out of it when they brought us in. My gut says turn left, but I'm just not certain."

"Me, either. But I think I remember coming from that direction." He pointed right. He was lying. Left, he knew, would take them out of the house. But he wanted a chance to look around unsupervised, and he doubted they'd get many opportunities as good as this one.

Tara shrugged. "If you say so. Like I said, I don't remember much."

Tara followed Jake into a large, open room. They hadn't entered the house this way coming from the sheds. She knew it, and she suspected he did, too. But she'd been aching to get inside the main house since the moment she realized Andrea was missing, and though she doubted they'd be allowed much freedom, she'd take whatever she could get.

The airy room contained little furniture. At one point, it might have been a formal living room, but it clearly got little use in the ranch house's current incarnation. They passed through it quickly and entered another, more cluttered room.

And there, their luck ran out. A dark-haired woman with a prominent pregnancy belly was cleaning the furnishings with a dust cloth and a bottle of wood oil. The sight of two new faces startled her, and she clutched her supplies to her rounded stomach in a protective gesture. Tara didn't recognize her, but that was no surprise. After their seventh month, pregnant women were sequestered in their own bunkhouse and were relieved of the heavier chores. She'd never been certain exactly what duties they had, but cleaning the main house was probably considered light enough work for them. Too bad she, herself, wasn't pregnant.

"Wh-what are you doing here?" The woman asked in a voice heavily accented in Spanish.

"We came from the sickroom," Jake said in a soothing tone. "We're just passing through."

"Ah. You were purified." The woman's tension eased. "I heard." She rubbed her hand across her belly. "We don't eat with the others, so we don't see newcomers. It is best for the babies not to be exposed to anything until they have been brought into the Chosen officially."

"Of course," Jake agreed easily.

"When are you due?" Tara asked.

"In three weeks."

"Are babies delivered here?"

"Yes." The woman gave them both a curious look. "You are both new, aren't you? All babies are delivered in the sickroom unless someone is very ill and staying there and cannot be moved. Then both mothers and babies move to the nursery for a few months."

"Are there a lot of infants living in the nursery?" Tara thought of Aurora, with her wide smile and the belly that stuck out from her thin frame as if she'd hidden a watermelon under her sweatshirt.

"My baby will be the sixth, though Mathias and his mother are ready to move out. He is sleeping through the night. So she will go back to her bunk, and he will be moved to the infants' room. She can visit him there, and she'll take her turn in charge of the area as part of her duty rotation."

"I haven't seen children around the community," Jake remarked. "Where do they go?"

"When they're very small, they're in the nursery and in nursery school. They start actual school at age five in the big building behind this house."

"Won't you miss your baby if you have to move back to your bunk as soon as he can sleep through the night?"

The woman shrugged. "He will be my third. I see them enough, and they have a much better life here among the Chosen, cared for by the Powers, than they'd ever have in the outside world. I might see them more out there, but it would be selfish of me to consider that above their welfare."

Tara had to restrain herself from mentioning that perhaps spending time with their parents might be beneficial to the children's welfare. But then, maybe that was just her own prejudice, her own experience talking. She hadn't had much contact with her parents as a child, having been shuffled off with various nannies and housekeepers.

"Is your husband a member of the Chosen as well?" Jake asked.

The woman blushed. "I am not married. I am honored to have been chosen to carry one of our Leader's children."

Tara's skin crawled. Honored. She wanted to shake the woman. Were the other children she spoke of also Owen Stephenson's?

Jake shifted the conversation away from the awkward moment. "I didn't even realize there was a school here. Shows how much I know. But of course, it's obvious. The children need to be protected, so they can't get their education the way town kids do."

"Exactly. But, if you don't mind, I have to get back to work."

"Of course," said Tara. "We'll get out of your way." Rather than exiting through the door they'd entered, they took the door on the opposite wall. This led into the kitchen. The space had clearly been enlarged from its original design to become an industrial kitchen, where the meals for the rest of the Chosen were prepared. A familiar door at one end would lead to the dining hall, which was attached to the main house by a short, enclosed walkway.

As with the dark-haired woman, the occupants seemed shocked to see Tara and Jake, and all work halted. A woman who'd been shaping some kind of dough into fist-sized balls backed away from her work and stared as if little green men had materialized smack in the middle of the kitchen.

"Hi," Tara said. "Don't mind us, we're just passing through on our way from the infirmary. We were trying to find our way out to the flower house?"

"You can go out that door," the man said, his eyes narrowed and suspicious. Tara recognized him vaguely, but couldn't remember his name. He pointed toward a back door to the kitchen that led directly outside. Jake and Tara thanked him and headed out.

The greenhouse lay some hundred yards from the main house. Jake slowed his steps as they left the house, and Tara matched her pace to his. He laid an arm across her shoulders and asked, rather loudly, how she was feeling. Recalling his earlier instructions, she told him she was still under the weather, and that they should take things slowly.

He nodded. He waited to speak until they were about halfway between the house and the greenhouse.

"How are you doing, really?" He asked in a low tone.

"I'm fine. I was freaked out by whatever damned drugs they gave me in that shed. I don't know how you survived it so easily."

"It wasn't easy. But I have more experience than you do with that kind of thing. I knew what was apt to happen, I just didn't have any way to warn you. And, unfortunately, we both 'agreed' to the isolation, so there's no point in going to the cops and reporting it. Whatever drugs they used are long gone."

"I know. Plus, I'm not leaving here until I find out what happened to Andrea. That . . . ritual . . . convinced me more than ever she's in danger. Especially since Sarah—I worked with her in the laundry—said there were rumors Andrea was having an unsanctioned affair. If what we did merited three days in isolation, imagine what the Leader would do to someone who bucked the system that drastically!"

"If it's true. The 'unsanctioned affair' may have been the first idea about how to explain her disappearance. One of the easiest explanations for a woman's disappearance is always 'she ran off with her lover.'"

"Why would he change tacks and go for the mission story instead?"

"I don't know. But if her cousin had to go, too, then maybe the lover ruse became unwieldy. Or maybe he did send her away, but he did it because of the lover."

"That's a lot of maybes."

"I know. We need to stay in the house as long as possible. Delay recovery. Finding a way to do a comprehensive search of Owen's private quarters is the only way we have any hope of figuring out what's behind all this."

"They're not big on slackers around here." They'd reached the greenhouse, and Tara lowered her voice as they started to walk around the outside of the building, ostentatiously admiring the plants.

"There are cameras on the buildings," she murmured. "And in the lights. Don't be too obvious, but if you look at the security lights during the day, you can see the lenses just at the base, where the pole joins the lamp itself. I'd lay odds there's audio, too, so be careful what you say aloud unless there aren't buildings or trees or lights nearby."

He nodded. "Couldn't you, I don't know, pretend to have really bad cramps or something so we can stay in the infirmary longer?"

"Unfortunately, they even keep track of the women's cycles, and I've just had mine."

"How in the hell do they do that?"

"You have to go to the 'commissary' and ask for whatever supplies you need. Stuff like soap and razors are replaced in the bathrooms as they wear out or get used up. That's taken care of by whoever's in charge of bunk maintenance on a given week, and there's no reason they couldn't handle femi-nine necessities the same way, but they don't. I can't help but believe it's deliberate."

"Absolutely. It's another way of controlling you. Forcing you to ask for things you require, especially such personal items, is psychological trickery."

Tara shrugged. "One way or another, it means I can't play the weakling chick with cramps card."

He slanted her a grin that made her insides go hot and liquid. "I don't think the weakling chick card suits you par-ticularly well anyway."

She concentrated on planning, ignoring the spread-ing warmth. "Without any reason to stay in the infirmary, they'll probably give us the boot no later than tomorrow, and we'll be stuck back where we began. We have to take advantage of the time we have."

"I doubt there's any point in searching the more public areas. Look how many people seemed to be allowed to wander freely through the ground floor. If there are secrets, he'll keep them upstairs."

"No doubt. But he likely has some kind of secu-rity system up there. If he's hiding things, he'll have locks, possibly even cameras. How are we supposed to get by those?"

"Honestly, I don't think we can if all we have is tonight. We're better off trying to get invited back. A guy like this doesn't trust easily, but give me a little time to work on him. I bet I can get him to invite me in."

"You? What about *us*? You don't even know Andrea."

"I can't make guarantees. Everything I've seen and heard makes me believe he's far less likely to trust a woman, though he might think you were too stupid to worry about."

"Excuse me?" Tara ignored her own plan to convince the Chosen of her gullibility.

"I didn't say I agreed with him. It's who he is, what he thinks, that matters at the moment. This is a man who surrounds himself with people who literally worship him, then impregnates the women who follow him. That doesn't show a great deal of respect for them. Without respect, there can't be trust. He might not think you're smart enough to put one over on him, but he also won't give up his secrets to you."

"And he will to you."

"I didn't say that. I just said there was a possibility."

"We don't have forever here."

"You're telling me. Quite aside from anything else, if I don't bring you back before the wedding, Lucy will kill me."

"Wedding?"

"Damn, I haven't even had a chance to tell you. Lucy and Ethan are getting married. Lucy wants you as her maid of honor."

"But I—"

"Tara, I know you blame yourself for letting Lucy get into trouble, and I know the rest of your family made her life a living hell, but neither Lucy nor Ethan blames you. You're like family to them, and they want you at the wedding. When you wouldn't tell them where you were, it hurt them, but they understood you wanted your privacy. Until you stopped writing."

"And then they sent you."

"I volunteered to come. I had the time, the expertise, and I felt responsible."

Tara stiffened. "You're not responsible."

"Probably not. I've been known to have an overweening ego and to think people take me far more seriously than they actually do. But whatever the reason, here I am."

They'd reached the front of the greenhouse, so they entered. Along the left side, potted orchids grew in a row, long, pale green stems ending in pink-white blossoms. These would be taken only a few at a time to the cart in town for sale at the highest prices. Along the right side and the back, large beds housed a variety of flowers in bright colors. These were to be sold as cut flowers rather than as living plants, and they didn't bring in the same amount of money. Still, the Chosen did quite well with their flowers, especially the roses that grew in the central beds.

As well as flowers, the Chosen sold fruit from their orchards; quilts, sweaters, and socks made by the more talented stitchers among them; and both paintings and sculptures created by men and women during the free afternoons once a week. The money went for supplies — like the razors Tara had discussed with Jake — they could not produce themselves. Those who went into town to sell the items carried letters to be mailed and brought back anything that had come into the post office box the Chosen kept in Twin Oaks.

Tara and Jake left the greenhouse when they heard the lunch horn sound and headed back to the infirmary.

"When we get back," Jake ordered, "follow my lead, but be sure to be hesitant about doing anything without checking with the Leader first. I want to reinforce the idea in his mind that he has you totally cowed. That way, if I have a chance to distract him down the road a ways, he won't be worried about you betraying him."

Although Jake's bossy tone made Tara bristle, she had to admit the idea was solid, so she tamped down her frustration with his attitude and agreed.

When they arrived back in the infirmary, Deborah was not there, having gone for her own lunch, but she'd left two trays with hot soup and slices of buttered toast. One held an antibiotic pill for Tara, which she swallowed with a big gulp of water.

Jake reached for his spoon, but she put out her hand and prevented him from eating. "We need to say grace," she reminded him sanctimoniously.

"Of course." His dark eyes twinkled at her, and she hoped no cameras in the room could pick up the hint of a grin on his sharply carved lips. "Why don't you do it. You've been here longer. You understand more about the Powers."

"We should just do it privately. I don't have the right to lead a prayer. So just close your eyes for a minute and give thanks for what we've been given."

"That sounds like a good idea." They did, bowing their heads and folding their hands in a parody of prayer. Tara gave herself an extra minute so anyone watching would believe the isolation had worked its magic on her especially well. Then she raised her head and dove into the meal.

"What shall we do this afternoon?" she asked between bites.

"Well, after that walk this morning, we should probably stay inside. Maybe we can see whether we can help out in the house."

"We shouldn't interfere with the tasks assigned by the Leader." Tara injected a note of anxiety into the response and rubbed her hands up and down her arms. She didn't have to manufacture the fear. As much as she hated to admit it, Owen Stephenson scared her. This place scared her. The sooner they could find Andrea and get the hell out, the happier she'd be.

"Well, if you think you're up to more walking, we could go for another tromp outside. There are plenty of directions we could take where we wouldn't be in anyone's way out there."

"That sounds good. I want to go back to my bunk and get a sweater, though. It's a bit chilly out when you're not working."

"Sounds like a plan."

⌐

JAKE WONDERED HOW fast he could reasonably get Tara to move during their afternoon excursion without raising eyebrows and suspicions. He wanted a sense of the outer reaches of the compound. They couldn't get there today, as the place was close to four square miles in size. Not large by ranch standards, but far too big to search alone and on foot. He assumed the workers who maintained the orchards and the large, commercial vegetable greenhouses were bussed out to their jobs. But if they could get a look at any of the land and buildings, he'd be in better shape for later excursions.

He was anxious, too, to see Tara's living quarters. When he'd arrived at the camp, he'd been assigned a bunk in a barracks-like dormitory at the very front of the property. He'd assumed that to mean they didn't worry about him leaving. After all, at that point, as a new recruit, he wouldn't know anything that could hurt Stephenson. Six other men shared the cabin. The one who'd been among the Chosen longest, Ezekiel, had lived there a year. It had been Ezekiel who'd explained about the horns, the assignments, and the barest bones of the religion they followed.

"You'll pick the rest up quick enough," he'd said. "Just keep your head down and your nose clean and you'll do fine." Everything about the way the man spoke screamed "ex-con" to Jake. But then, he expected most of the Chosen had been broken in some way or another long before signing up to be part of Owen Stephenson's crew.

Tara's cabin, he discovered when they went to find her a sweater, looked much like his own, only the beds had both upper and lower bunks, allowing for twice as many occupants. The bathroom had been built to accommodate a few more people, too, but not twice as many. It would take the women a lot longer to clean up. Deliberate? Quite possibly. But Jake had noticed the ratio of women to men at dinner. Perhaps they'd had to put in the bunks because there were simply too many women.

Tara sorted through a trunk at the foot of her bed and pulled out a heavy cotton cable-knit sweater. She pulled it over her head and slid her hand beneath her hair to pull it out of the neck. As he watched the curls bounce back, his fingers itched to slide through the silky strands. He'd caught her looking at him a couple of times when she thought him otherwise occupied and had high hopes the crazy attraction he felt might be returned, but until they found her friend and got out of the compound, he couldn't very well explore the question.

"Ready?"

She nodded, and he led the way to his own bunk, where he pulled on a ratty sweatshirt with a *Star Trek* logo on it that he'd brought as part of his cover persona. She looked around, obviously as intrigued by his dwelling as he'd been by hers.

"Only six of you live here?"

"Yeah. I guess there's a shortage of men."

"Or not." She started to say more, then seemed to think better of it, obviously concerned about listening devices. He doubted Stephenson would bother bugging the bunks. Much easier, generally speaking, to rely on people's innate fear of being turned in by their peers to keep them quiet. Under normal circumstances, he'd never be alone in the cabin. But it didn't pay to underestimate one's opponents, as he'd learned to his cost in the past, so he didn't press Tara for her meaning. He'd get it out of her outside.

When they left, he led the way back toward the ranch house. The property was a rough trapezoid with the bunkhouses and vegetable gardens in the front, at the southern edge. After the gardens, mostly fallow this late in the year, they passed to the right of the bean field beyond which he and Tara had worked his first day in the compound. Then came the ranch house, the dining hall, and the greenhouse they'd visited that morning. Beyond that lay open fields and then the orchard.

And past even the orchard were the commercial-sized greenhouses and storehouses he'd seen on the aerial maps of the property.

"Has anyone mentioned what's in the big buildings at the far end of the property?" he asked Tara once they were well away from the cabin.

"No. I checked out the area online when I was researching the Chosen and noticed them, but when I asked a couple of women, I was told they were insulated and used for storing potatoes and other produce. Seems like a lot of potatoes, but whatever it is they keep out there, I sincerely doubt they're holding prisoners, so I dismissed it as having nothing to do with Andrea's whereabouts.

"I know the FBI and various other branches of law enforcement look askance at separatist groups for having guns and drugs, but I haven't seen any evidence of either here apart from the weapons the guards carry. The Chosen aren't a militia group. Maybe Andrea did discover what they were hiding out there, but it doesn't help me figure out what happened to her afterward."

Jake had a pretty good idea what would happen to anyone who uncovered something Owen Stephenson didn't want them to know, but he figured Tara had been in law enforcement long enough that he didn't have to spell it out for her. Instead, he reached out and took her hand, twining their fingers together.

In the distance, a white picket fence beckoned. He tugged Tara in that direction. A few minutes later, however, he was almost sorry he had when they arrived to find the fence surrounding a small cemetery.

"What the hell? Jake—"

"Just hold your horses. Remember, this place probably existed as a working ranch for a hundred years before the Chosen took it over. It could easily have had a cemetery on the property for that reason."

"And the fence? The gate? They aren't centuries old. They don't even look a decade old."

"So Stephenson modernized when he took over the place." He kept his voice down. He didn't necessarily believe the graveyard held nefarious secrets, but if it did, Stephenson would have some kind of security set up. And to tell the truth, although he enjoyed playing devil's advocate with Tara, the gated cemetery gave him the heebie-jeebies.

"Let's go in," Tara suggested. "Maintaining the graves must be part of the weekly chores, because the whole place is meticulous."

Jake raised the latch on the gate—unlocked, which argued for the spot's innocuous nature—and ushered her in. Tara hadn't exaggerated the perfection of the spot. Living plants covered the graves, their leaves turning brown with the change of weather. Someone had planned well, however, with cacti and other xeriscaping, so the maintenance would be minimal.

Most of the graves seemed quite old, with weathered stones dating back to the mid–nineteenth century up through the nineteen fifties. The only thing out of place was a large round brick building at the corner of the cemetery. About twelve feet tall, it had a single bank of windows ranging the entire circumference just below the peaked roof.

Tara tried the door, which opened easily. Jake followed her in.

Sunlight shone through the western windows, slanting through dust motes and illuminating the eastern quarter of the building. Rectangular niches were carved one after another in rows and columns all along the rounded wall. Boxes filled some, others were empty. After a moment, Jake realized what he was seeing.

"It's a columbarium," he said, whispering this time out of respect for the dead rather than fear of discovery.

"A what?"

"It's where cremains are stored. That's what's in the boxes. I guess the Chosen aren't big on burial. Cremation keeps the flock together after death rather than being farmed out to whatever cemetery has room for them."

"Cheaper, too," Tara muttered. "Wouldn't want to waste money on the dead that the living yet need."

Jake picked up one of the boxes. "Someone's used a wood-burning tool to burn a name and date into this. 'MATTHIAS 2007.'"

Tara lifted a box near her. "'DAMARIS 2009.' These are definitely the Chosen."

"They must be cremated in town and then brought back

here for . . . interment. I can't imagine the Leader running a crematorium here on the property." He watched as Tara wandered among the boxes, which didn't seem to be stored in any particular order that he could make out, peering at each in the dim light.

She stopped abruptly and pulled one from its niche.

"Pearl," she whispered. "Goddammit."

"*Serena,*" he reminded her.

"She was my *friend.*"

"Are you sure it's her?"

"You think two women named Pearl died this year?"

"No, I suppose not." He gave in to the impulse driving him and pulled her into his arms. Let her believe it was an act for Stephenson's benefit if she liked. The forlorn expression on her face tore at a heart he'd believed numb to such emotions.

"They've been lying to me," she said into his shoulder. "All of them. Not just him. Everyone said the same thing: she went on a mission. But someone's keeping up the graveyard. Someone knows she's in here. Probably lots of someones."

"I know, sweetheart." The endearment came naturally, and he found himself rocking her gently, the action completely out of character for him. Usually, he liked to keep his relationships with women simple: plenty of sex, little emotion, no commitment. He called it his rule of three and, given how little of himself he'd had left after the work he'd done for the Bureau, it had seemed the perfect combination.

He wasn't particularly anxious to give up the rule that had served him so well, but he couldn't see applying it to Tara, either. He shifted her away from him, pressing his lips quickly to her forehead before letting her go.

"Look, I am sure there's a reasonable explanation. Why

don't we go ask the Leader about why you were told Pearl had taken a trip instead of that she'd died?"

"Yeah." She nodded, and before she turned quickly away, the glimmers of light from the windows caught the sheen of tears in her eyes. She had to have known the likelihood that her friend would turn up dead. Missing women cases rarely ended well, and Tara of all people would know that. Obviously, despite her suspicions, she'd managed to hang on to hope.

They left the columbarium, and Jake blinked hard against the afternoon light. They walked around the side of the building and saw Owen Stephenson waiting for them at the gate. Jake felt Tara tense beside him.

"Serena. Jacob. You've walked quite a ways today. I assume you're feeling better?"

"Why did you tell me A—Pearl had taken a trip when she's actually dead?"

Jake tried not to wince at the aggressive question. Hand at the small of Tara's back, he gave her a quick pinch to remind her who she was dealing with.

But Owen didn't act upset. He merely frowned in a thoughtful manner. "I didn't say she'd taken a trip. I said she'd gone on a mission. I'm sorry you misunderstood."

"I'm afraid I still don't understand, Leader," Jake hurried to speak before Tara. "We believed Pearl and her cousin had left the compound."

"They have." Stephenson shook his head sadly. Jake wanted to strangle the man. He was being deliberately obscure.

"By dying," Tara said.

"I'm afraid it was more than that." Stephenson measured his words like a master tailor, revealing glimpses of the truth while hiding far more. "We don't like to speak of suicides, and we so rarely suffer them, but even in this community some have problems they are unwilling to turn over to the Powers. And when one does not submit entirely to the will of the Powers, one cannot be truly happy. A long time ago, we decided it was easier not to remember that people had taken their own lives, and agreed to consider them merely choosing to go on in search of a better place.

"No one here meant to deceive you. We simply don't speak of suicides. We refer to them as you've heard us refer to Pearl."

"Pearl killed herself?"

"Yes. But no more on the subject. As I said, it is better not to remember the fallen in such a way. Let's walk back to the house. You'll want to clean up before the dinner horn sounds. Perhaps one more day in the infirmary, then you can go back to your bunks and resume duties."

Stephenson strode ahead, simply assuming they would follow him. Much as Jake would have liked to have hung back for no reason other than to spite the man, he grit his teeth and obeyed for Tara's sake. Their stroll was more in the manner of a forced march, and Stephenson didn't speak another word to them. Whenever Jake sped up to draw even, Stephenson would speed up even more.

"Could we possibly slow down?" Tara asked after a few minutes. "I'm not quite myself yet." Although she gasped the words out, Jake didn't believe her heavy, irregular breathing for a minute. The woman was in phenomenal shape. He'd felt all those muscles beneath her skimpy scrubs when they'd shared a bed.

Once they'd adopted a more relaxed pace, Tara called out to Stephenson, "Do you cremate all the Chosen?"

"Assuming they haven't made other arrangements themselves," he replied. "Usually, once a person has been a member of our community for a while, he will decide that he prefers to remain a member even after death. At that point, we ask that you make a will stating your wishes."

"I see. So Pearl made a will?"

"No, she didn't. But John was her only relative. Since she was a member of our community, we made arrangements for her. Had we realized how close the two of you were, someone would have contacted you. But after she moved onto the ranch, she never spoke of you, so we presumed you were mere acquaintances."

Jake could feel Tara's frustration like a physical presence among them. He would get an earful about this later, he was certain. But with a little luck, he could convince her to leave. Her friend was dead; her reasons for joining the Chosen had dissolved.

Owen led them to the front of the ranch house where hard-eyed, hard-muscled men with guns nodded to him and glared at them as they followed him inside. A similar pair kept watch on the front entrance to the compound, the excuse being that the Chosen needed protection from Outsiders. Jake had noticed the men spread out at various tables during the few meals he'd taken with the Chosen, but nothing could convince him that they were devoted to Owen Stephenson's safety because they believed he was a religious leader. Nor did he imagine they served in any other capacity than as guards. No way did they pick beans or plant tomatoes. But even without putting such men in the fields, in order to keep up any kind of rotation there had to be at least a dozen of them. Bought and paid for, and hired muscle didn't come cheap.

Inside the ranch house, Owen led them directly back to the infirmary.

"Serena and I were noticing how amazing this building is," Jake said as they passed down a long hallway. "Did you grow up here?"

"I did."

"And now you get to live in it again. Lucky. My folks sold the house I grew up in the second I went to college. Couldn't wait to get divorced."

"The Outside world can be a harsh place."

"This'd be kind of lonely, though. It's beautiful, but so big. You live here alone?"

Owen glanced at him, probing. Jake kept his expression bland.

"There are others. The disciples live in the satellite wings, and Deborah lives here as well. Up until recently, John also shared the house. And, at various times, members of the Chosen attend me here. But I must be alone a great deal to meditate and open myself to the Powers."

"Oh, of course."

"Jacob's a true child of the city," Tara interjected, sounding eager to smooth things over. "He doesn't know what to do with himself without all kinds of distractions. At home he went to sleep with the television on, and when I'd turn it off, he'd flip it back on first thing when he woke up."

"Outer peace leads to inner peace," said Owen. "The quiet of the compound will seep into your heart if you let it, and you will find all that you need right here."

He opened the door to the infirmary and stood aside to let them enter. "Dinner will be in another hour. Relax here, and Deborah will bring you food."

TARA BARELY RESISTED the urge to spit curses after Owen. With a few words, he'd effectively locked them inside the infirmary, putting paid to any idea of further exploration of the ranch house. And she could practically feel the electronic eyes and ears pressing on her skin and forbidding discussion. A frustrated shriek rose in her throat, and she stuffed it down.

Jake settled on her bed and pulled her down next to him. "I'm sorry."

"I knew. I just didn't want to believe it."

"Without your friend, are you sure you want to stay? Is this the life you're choosing, or was it just the one she wanted?"

What was he asking? Did he really think she'd abandon her investigation? She couldn't prove these fuckers had killed Andrea—not yet—but she knew it. The fact that the Chosen refused to discuss suicides would make her job more difficult, but not impossible.

"Why don't you take a shower," Jake suggested when she didn't answer immediately. He reached over and poured a glass of water from the pitcher on the nightstand between the two beds. "We need to remember to stay hydrated."

She took the glass and sipped at the liquid, which cooled her throat but not her temper. *Men.* The lot of them should take a long walk off a short pier. Jake might be playing the part of the skeptical boyfriend for the cameras, but his voice and the look in his eyes dug deeper. He wanted her to leave. To take off without finding the truth, without bringing those responsible for Andrea's death to justice.

And they were responsible, despite Stephenson's pious crap about suicide. But Jake wasn't likely to believe her without proof. Why was it acceptable for any of her male colleagues to "go with his gut," but when women had no hard evidence to support their intuitions they were accused of "operating on emotion"?

She drained the glass, then stood and smacked it down on the table. "A shower sounds good." If the bathroom door slammed a bit too loudly behind her, well, perhaps it was just a draft.

She'd left the scrubs they'd given her on her admission to the infirmary hanging on a hook on the back of the bathroom door that morning, but now they lay neatly folded on the edge of the vanity. Just more evidence that nothing in the com-pound—let alone inside the house itself—was private. A little more psychological manipulation. Tiny terrorism at its finest.

Could there be cameras even in here? She gritted her teeth. If she started poking around in the light fixtures and behind the mirror, she'd arouse suspicion. Assholes. So tempting to give them the finger. Of course, that would blow her cover faster than searching the room for video equipment.

Well, screw 'em. They'd seen her close enough to naked in the shed. She'd handled that; she could handle this. There might not even *be* cameras.

Her jaw ached and, despite the film of sweat on her body, she cranked the water as hot as possible to create steam before stripping off her clothes and stepping into the shower. The water pounded on her, stinging in her scabs and scrapes. She soaped, shampooed, and rinsed as quickly as she could, then wrapped herself in a towel before stepping out of the steamy shower.

Even in the infirmary the luxury did not extend to a hair dryer, so Tara carefully maneuvered the scrubs over her damp and scabbed-over body and then carried the comb from the vanity out so she could sit on the bed while she braided her hair for the night.

"Shower's all yours," she said to Jake. But he didn't move. Instead, he reached out and tugged on the comb in her hand.

"Let me."

She backed away. "What?"

"C'mon, sweetheart. You know I love your hair. Let me do it." His voice was low, rough, persuasive, hypnotic. It slid through her, weakening her resolve, and her fingers let go of the comb and the towel. He took both, then positioned her on the edge of the bed while he took up a spot behind her, his knees on either side of her hips. He shook out the towel, then draped it over her head and began to massage her scalp.

Oh my God. The man had magic fingers. She'd never considered her head an erogenous zone, but clearly she lacked imagination. She held back a moan of pleasure only by sheer force of will.

He dropped the towel to the side and picked up the comb. At home, when Tara had kept her hair to a practical law-enforcement length, she had still used an expensive conditioner to detangle her curls and keep them under control. When she left Dobbs Hollow and went off to find herself, she'd quit with haircuts but had kept up the conditioning. Since joining the Chosen, however, all that had ended. Her hair looked and felt like a haystack. Dragging a comb through it after showers generally involved cursing, and the only reason she hadn't cut it all off was that she couldn't imagine how much worse it would be if she couldn't tie it back.

Jake, however, didn't seem to care about the straw-like qualities. Rather than forcing the comb through knots as she did, he patiently teased out each one, stopping now and then to run his fingers through the damp mass and to rub her neck and shoulders.

By the time he was done, Tara's anger had dissipated and

she had relaxed to the point that she was half-asleep. She felt the gentle tugs as he partitioned her hair and braided it, then tied it off with the rubber band that had been around the handle of the comb.

And then Deborah opened the infirmary door, and every muscle and nerve awoke once more.

"I'll be in with dinner in a minute," she said. "But I've brought your pills, Serena. And I wanted to check you over after your first day. How are you feeling?"

"Tired. But I'm okay. If the Leader wants us to go back to work, I'm ready."

"Not yet." Deborah handed her the antibiotic pill. "Keep drinking plenty of water. The sheds are hot. Tomorrow is soon enough to talk about going back to work."

"Okay." *Docile. Stay docile.* But Deborah's appearance had resurrected all her seething anger. If Deborah could get antibiotics to treat infection without Tara seeing a doctor, what would have stopped them from getting some drug to poison Andrea and John and simply claiming they'd killed themselves? It wasn't as if the compound were crawling with investigators—if Owen announced that John and Pearl had "gone on a mission," the Chosen would accept it as fact.

Deborah stepped out and came back a moment later with their dinner. She led them in prayer, then left them to eat. Tara could feel Jake's gaze on her, but she kept her own on the food as she ate. "I didn't mean to walk so far or fast today that I wore you out," he said at last. "Maybe tomorrow we should stick closer to the house." She shrugged. "Maybe. We'll see what morning brings."

JAKE HEARD DEBORAH clearing the trays as he stepped out of the shower, which was just as well. The way Tara tensed whenever the woman entered the room knotted his gut and his fists. He'd just gotten her nice and relaxed after the traumatic revelations at the cemetery when Deborah had spoiled things. Of course, relaxing Tara meant putting his hands on her, which had exactly the opposite effect on him, but he didn't even mind the fact that he'd become a walking Viagra warning label.

He'd thought about taking the edge off in the shower, but with Tara right outside the door, the idea held little appeal. He didn't want his own hands; he wanted hers. Hell of a thing to be thinking about right now, but there it was.

He scrubbed his hair as dry as he could and combed it out with considerably more force than he'd used on Tara's. He considered shaving—when he'd been with the FBI, he'd often found himself shaving twice a day to stay presentable because his stubble came in so fast, but here fastidiousness would earn him a strike. Owen Stephenson had a shaggy beard, and his lieutenants tended toward the scruffy.

He slipped into the scrubs some faceless acolyte had folded and placed on the vanity for him while they were out—he'd left them laid out on his bed that morning when he changed into his jeans—and went back into the infirmary.

Tara lay flopped on her back on top of her bed, staring at the ceiling. Her whole demeanor spoke of exhaustion. Not physical—though the olive green short-sleeve top she wore showed the oozing and scabbed evidence of her nights in isolation—but emotional. The light and electricity that always surrounded her, the force and magnetism of her personality, had fled.

He stepped back into the bathroom and grabbed the

toothbrushes off the vanity, then flourished them as he entered the room. "Hey, dragon breath, time to clean the fangs."

"What?!" Tara bolted upright and glared at him. Ah, there she was. *Welcome back, sweetheart.* She stomped over and snatched the toothbrush from him before storming into the bathroom, and he suppressed a grin.

He didn't bother to hide the laugh that surfaced minutes later when she held up her hand to stop him from crawling into bed with her for a second night.

"I'm fine. I don't know what was the matter with me last night, but I don't need company tonight."

He opened his eyes as wide as possible. "But don't you *want* me to sleep with you?" He watched her struggle for an appropriate response. "Remember, the Leader said you need to forgive me." He eased under the covers before she could come up with a valid objection, then slid his arms around her and hung on despite the unwelcoming stiffness of her limbs.

Gradually, she relaxed. The single bed gave her no choice but to press against him. She lay half atop him, and every breath pressed her breasts more firmly against his chest and side. Another sleepless night for him.

"Jacob," she said at last, the words sleepy and slurred, "we're staying. At least, I am."

"I know we are, baby," he replied, giving in to temptation and stroking her hair, curling the braid around his fingers. "I know we are."

CHAPTER FOUR

THE MORNING HORN, though only faint inside the main house, woke Tara. In the weeks she'd lived at the compound, her body had become attuned to the sound. But seeing how it was only the second time in her life she'd awakened in a tiny bed wrapped around a large man, she'd made no such adjustment to *that* circumstance. During the night, her disobedient hand had managed to slip beneath his pajama top and now rested on a truly spectacular pec.

Holy hell, how did that happen?

She tried to lift her hand off his skin, but the material of his shirt had twisted, so that to free herself she would have to slide her hand all the way down his torso.

She flicked a glance at his face, but he appeared not to have heard the morning horn. Thick black lashes rested on his cheeks, and his mobile lips showed no hint of expression.

Slowly, she began to inch her hand down, careful to disturb him as little as possible. Just when she thought she might escape unnoticed, his voice sounded above her head.

"Well, now things are getting interesting."

She snatched her hand away, almost falling out of the bed in the process.

"I thought you were asleep."

He had the audacity to grin at her. "I was. But I woke up when you started groping me."

"I wasn't!" She started to punch him in that lovely pec, but he grabbed her hand in one of his and brought it to his mouth. With his other hand, he pried open her fingers. Then he pressed a hot, sweet kiss to her palm.

"I'm just teasing, sweetheart."

Blushing fiercely, she escaped to the bathroom. Playing girlfriend to Jake Nolan might overtax her acting skills. It was certainly overtaxing her hormones.

JAKE WISHED HE could afford to examine the pills Deborah brought for Tara with breakfast. Not that he knew diddly about black- or gray-market prescriptions, but he'd love to get the pill number and see if he could find out whether the damn things were even sold in America. The pills had sparked a memory. He'd spotted a familiar face among the Chosen his first night with them, though he hadn't been able to place the man. The sight of Tara swallowing the antibiotic, however, triggered full recognition: He'd met the guy years before at a task force meeting. He was DEA.

The Chosen hadn't landed on any official watch lists that he'd been able to track down, but every agency had official and unofficial investigations.

He needed to talk to Tara, and it wasn't going to happen inside the house. Or anywhere close to it. When she'd told him about the cameras in the security lights, he'd felt a chill he hadn't experienced in all his years chasing serial killers. He'd heard victims of stalking describe the sensation of being watched, had sympathized as he'd interviewed them, but had never expected to be able to empathize. Owen Stephenson had the whole place wired for sight and sound, and Jake felt the surveillance like spiders crawling over his skin.

After breakfast they tried to walk around the house again, but once more they were shuffled outside.

"Shall we walk out to the orchard?" Jake suggested. The orchard lay fairly far from the main house. They might not make it there, but it would take them out of the range Stephenson probably considered dangerous enough to monitor.

"That sounds nice."

As they left the house, he took her hand. "How are you feeling today?" "Better. Stronger." She slanted a look up at him, letting him know she meant it.

"You're a strong woman."

Her brow wrinkled as if she might protest, so he picked up the pace a bit. They left behind the buildings and passed by the field workers. When he could breathe, when the spiders stopped crawling over his skin, he brought up the subject of the cemetery.

"What do you think happened to Andrea?"

A muscle popped in Tara's jaw. He'd never thought about a woman's jaw before, but hers fascinated him. Square, yes, but also utterly feminine.

"They killed her. Don't ask how. If I knew that, I'd have the police out here already."

"Think like a cop, Tara, not like a friend. Suicide means autopsy, and the crematorium would have required a death certificate. It's not like Stephenson could murder two of his followers, toss their bodies into a truck, and haul them off to the mortuary and have them cremated."

"I *am* a cop, Jake, but I was also Andrea's friend, regardless of the line of bull we were fed about Andrea not talking about me. Maybe you can turn off your friendships, your family feelings, but I can't."

Well. There it was. He should have expected her to bring up Lisa sooner or later. God knows, he never forgot her. He swallowed hard and counted to ten before he spoke. "Lucy asked me whether she could put that into her book before she wrote it," he said at last. "At the time, I thought it only fair. I let Lisa die. My only sister, the only family I had left. I let the heroin take her."

"You can't help an addict unless they want help." Tara touched his face, her tone soft, all the accusation gone.

"I could have worked harder at it. Been there for her. I wasn't. When Lucy met me, when she was covering the Paxton case, I'd already seen the road my sister was traveling. She'd been on it for years. I'd given up on her the way I've never in my life given up on a criminal.

"So, yeah, I let Lucy write about me and Lisa. I even encouraged it. It's a cautionary tale for workaholics."

"No, it isn't. It's a public flogging you think you deserve."

"Excuse me?" He stared at her.

"What I said to you about the loss-of-family feeling, that's what you wanted. You told Lucy to write about you so people would hate you. But it doesn't work that way. Especially with Lucy. Nothing she wrote encouraged that perception."

"She was too kind in her evaluation."

"How many times had you tried to save Lisa before the Paxton case took you out of town?"

"What do you mean?"

"Had she gone through rehab?"

"Yeah. Look, it happened, okay? It's history. Let's talk about the present."

But Tara wouldn't let it go. "How many times?"

He shrugged.

"How many times, Jake?"

"Three."

"And who paid for it?"

"The first time, she was only seventeen. She was on my parents' insurance."

"And the other two times?"

"Look, I don't even know how we got on this topic. We were talking about Andrea, not Lisa."

"Just answer me. Who paid for your sister's last two stints in rehab?"

"I did. She didn't have any money."

"So you did try to save her. Even knowing, better than most, how unlikely it was that she'd make it after her relapses, you kept on trying."

"I paid for rehab, but I didn't give her what she really needed. I didn't support her enough, care enough. I wasn't *there* for her."

"Did she ask for help?"

"What does that matter?"

"You want to play the martyr card, that's fine with me. Just don't expect me to buy into it. I saw how you behaved when Lucy was in trouble. If you'd believed you could do anything at all for Lisa, you would have."

"Fine. We'll just have to agree to disagree. Now, before we get interrupted by one or another of the Chosen, can we get back to the question of your friend and what happened to her?"

"She didn't kill herself. I can't explain how he convinced everyone here that she did it, but she didn't. All that crap about never talking about suicides . . ."

"That part's probably true. Cults have languages of their own. It's a portion of what ties people into the group, makes it so hard for them to even envision leaving."

"Fine. So they have a creepy way of referring to people

who kill themselves. And maybe they all believe that's what she did. But I don't."

"Tara, face it: You only knew this woman a couple of months. She joined the Chosen of her own free will, even you admit that. So there was something peculiar about her."

"She liked the idea of living off the land, of making a difference in the world. There's nothing peculiar about that. Yes, she could be moody, and maybe an overly cautious shrink would have diagnosed her as bipolar, but her depressions were never very serious. She thought being part of something bigger than herself would help her. If it hadn't, if she felt worse instead of better, she would have just left."

"You're certain."

"Absolutely."

She was completely convinced. Whether he believed or not made no difference — he'd never get her to leave until she knew what had happened. And ever since he'd found out about the cameras, he'd known he could never leave her alone inside the compound. "Okay," he said. "I'm in."

"In?"

"We stay until we figure out what happened. And given that, I should tell you that, last night at dinner, I saw an old acquaintance . . ."

⌐

As she listened to Jake's story about seeing a man he recognized among the Chosen at his introduction dinner, Tara tried to match Jake's description to one of the Chosen. Jake knew the man as Kevin Reasoner, a seasoned DEA agent.

"So maybe Andrea discovered that the Chosen are into drugs, and that's why Stephenson killed her."

"If he killed her—and I'm not convinced he did—and if Kevin is here on a job, then yeah, it's a possibility. Remember, he probably took one look at me and assumed the FBI had an eye on Stephenson, which they don't. Until I can talk to him alone, I can't say for sure he's on assignment."

"Dammit." Tara scuffed the dirt. "I hate the uncertainty."

"I can relate. Where do most of the men work during the afternoons? Maybe we could walk in that direction after lunch, see if we can find him. I don't know what name he's going by here. He wouldn't have used his own name to join, and they'd have changed it even if he did."

"Three separate names to keep track of. Undercover work takes a special kind." She hadn't bothered to change anything but her last name when she left Dobbs Hollow. But then, she hadn't been looking for criminals, just for herself.

"It does indeed."

"Everyone scatters for chores, though. Since we walked out behind the house yesterday, shall we try heading toward the berry patch? Though I think berry picking is usually women's work. There are the greenhouses and the drying sheds, but the greenhouses are too far, and we have no reason for us to be in the drying sheds. It's funny—I don't see the men much during the day. I hadn't thought about that before. I believe several of them are framing out a new cabin on the far end of the bunkhouses. We could go there."

"Sounds good. But for now we should probably head in for lunch." He led the way. "I'd like to meet up with Kevin in a casual way so people see us getting to know each other. Otherwise, I have no idea how we'll arrange it, since he's not in my bunk. This way at least we have an excuse to talk to each other at dinner and such."

"There is some free time. You're supposed to use it, of course, but we get Sunday afternoons off. It's when the artsy types do their thing."

"And what do you do?"

"I'm learning to knit. Not very well, mind you, but it gives me a chance to talk to the women."

"Interesting."

"It's the only socialization you get. It's where you learn the rules, where you learn about the Powers and the Leader. Once you're over the age of fifteen, and out of their school, there's no real education here."

"Okay. Jason Norman isn't exactly the crafty type. You said the women knit; what do the men do?"

"Well, no. Not all the women knit, but all the knitters are women. There are quilters, woodworkers, artists in all media. I think it's also when the fancier cooks do their cooking."

"Can't see Jason doing much of that, either. The man's a total geek."

"Hey, watch your mouth. Tara Jean Black fell for this guy. He had to have some good qualities. And I've known plenty of geeks who were fabulous cooks."

"Yeah, well, I can burn water, so that's out. Maybe I'll volunteer to check out the Leader's computers on Sunday. Streamline the Chosen's website."

As well as selling their goods locally, the Chosen shipped them across country. John, Tara had learned when she and Andrea first visited, had supervised the website and packed and shipped items people bought. The sago palms they grew were particularly popular.

"He might go for that. It would be great if you could get a look at his computers."

"If the guy's smart, and he is, he won't have anything incriminating on the computer he lets me see. But it will give me freedom in the house, and that's something."

⌒

TARA FOLLOWED JAKE back to the main house, where they were escorted back to the infirmary by one of the goons at the front door, who didn't want them wandering around unsupervised. Tara had asked Joy about the guards at one point, and the woman had told her that the government had tried to kill the Leader, so he kept those of the Chosen with military or law enforcement training as guards. Tara believed that like she believed in the tooth fairy.

Joy, however, seemed convinced by the story. When Tara pretended shock and fear that government agents might try again, might harm the Chosen in a raid, Joy assured her that the men had snuck in for an assassination attempt, only threatened by the Leader, not by the Chosen.

She could only imagine Jake's response to such a story.

Once again, Deborah brought them lunch. Jake tried to engage her in conversation, but the woman shut him down, citing the need to get to the dining hall before prayers. Nor did she return to retrieve the trays. Instead, the pregnant woman they'd seen cleaning the previous day came to pick them up. What did Deborah do when the infirmary was empty, and how had she earned so much freedom? She looked to be in her late twenties, close in age to Owen himself. Had she been a part of the group when his father had been in charge? Might she have administered the drugs Owen needed to simulate the heart attack that had allegedly killed Stephenson senior?

She wished she could ask Jake, but if they were looking for his DEA friend, they'd have to stay within the area surveilled by cameras. And despite his assurances that he would help her, she could still feel his doubts. He'd probably scoff at the idea that Deborah had earned a spot in the main house by

helping to murder Owen's father.

She and Jake took a meandering route toward the bunks. They stopped to visit the berry patch first, where three women wearing long sleeves to protect themselves from thorns plucked raspberries and strawberries.

"Hot for that," Jake remarked.

"It's not that bad," said Tara. "Believe me, I'd rather deal with thorns than beaks. If I never have to go back to collecting eggs it will be too soon."

They heard the sounds of construction as they rounded the bunkhouses. About a dozen men measured, held, sawed, hammered, and generally stood around looking masculine. Tara had to admit, the sight impressed her. These guys worked out in the fields, not in gyms, and the Chosen never got junk food, so a fair number of muscles were on display. Still, none of them turned her on like the brief glimpse she'd had of Jake's lean body fresh from the shower, or the feel of his arms around her as they lay in bed.

She shut the door firmly on the memory.

"Is he here?" she asked quietly as they stood about thirty feet from the group and watched them.

"Up top. Dark hair."

"Oh yeah. Here they call him Caleb. I've met him a couple of times."

Three men stood at various places on the top of the framed rectangle of the building, hammering trusses into place. The work would be boring and backbreaking since it was all done by hand, but at least the weather was cooperating.

"Hey, y'all," Jake called out. Several of the men looked up from their work. Although they appeared mildly surprised to see Tara and Jake, they didn't evince the same shock as those working in the house had.

Jake walked up to one of the men and introduced himself and Tara. The man, a tall, thickset brunet, introduced himself as Tobias. When Jake asked if he could help in any way, Tobias shrugged and told him to jump in wherever he felt comfortable. Rather than heading toward Caleb straightaway, Jake introduced himself to a couple other men. Tara understood the tactic, but still her frustration grew.

Tobias asked her if she'd like any water. She accepted a glass from the large canteen set up on the back of a pickup, then sat next to the canteen to watch the men work. The Leader had sent her out with a saw to deal with the branch caught in the fence, but none of these men would even consider letting her at their tools. She bet she could outshoot every one of them, with the possible exceptions of Jake and Caleb. She was a damned good marksman, so odds were she could even take *them.*

Too bad that wasn't a skill prized by the Chosen. At least among women.

Jake approached two men who stood at the corner of two of the walls. He chose them because he figured he could do nothing to help them and they'd send him on up Caleb's way. He was right. After asking whether he could handle himself on the beams, one of them handed him a hammer and pointed out the ladder at the back of the structure.

At first, Jake couldn't even be sure Reasoner recognized him. The man didn't so much as blink when Jake introduced himself.

"Caleb," he said.

"What are we building and how can I help?"

"Couples housing. Take this end and attach it over there." As Jake began to hammer, Reasoner caught his eye. "This your assignment from the Leader?"

Jake translated: *FBI operation?* and answered accordingly. "No, I don't have an assignment today."

"Well, we can always use the help. Maybe you can get assigned to our crew for a while." Reasoner's eyes shifted to where Tara leaned against the truck. "Your girlfriend—or whatever the outside world is calling them these days—partner?"

"All of the above," Jake said. "We can just go with 'mine.'" The words struck him as fundamentally right, truer than anything he'd said publicly since entering the compound. Reasoner lowered his voice. "Keep her close." Raised it again. "Maybe you guys will be in couples housing yourselves soon."

"How does that work?" Jake moved slightly away and began to hammer another beam into place.

"Well, once the Leader sanctions a relationship and it is formalized in front of the community, you can move out of the bunkhouses. The couples units are two bedrooms with a shared bathroom. So two couples live together."

So even private housing wasn't truly private. No real surprise. Still, it would be easier to get out at night for a good look around sharing with only one other couple than sharing with five guys. Or, in Tara's case, with eleven other women.

"My girl and I live over there." Reasoner gestured toward one of the smaller dwellings. "Tobias and Astrid were living with us, but Astrid passed while giving birth, so he moved back to the bunkhouses."

"And your girlfriend? What's her name?"

"Bea. She mostly works in the kitchens. She was given to me by the Leader when already four months pregnant." Reasoner moved to a new position. "You'll find life among the Chosen is much less stressful than what you had before. In the outside world, I fought all the time. Here we work together."

Jake figured Jason Norman, even post-purification, wouldn't be quite so accepting. "You don't mind raising some other guy's kid?"

"Children are blessings from the Powers. They don't belong to any individual. Bea's child will be raised with the others, after which Bea will move back into the regular roster of duties with the other women."

Very damn convenient if you were Owen Stephenson and given to impregnating your followers. Claim the kid belonged to the whole community, that no father had to take responsibility, and all the women went around feeling blessed rather than used. He glanced down at Tara, who had wandered a little ways from the truck, and a sudden surge of protectiveness nearly knocked him off the beam. He was going to bring down this damned den of plague dogs and then he was taking her back to civilization.

Jake had played a part in grinding Tara down. He was going to play a part in building her back up.

As he watched, Jonas approached Tara and leaned in close as he spoke to her. Jake could see the tension in her shoulders as she held herself in place, kept herself from flinching. Jonas had been among those who had taken her for purification. What had happened to her in the darkness of that cell?

His fingers clenched so tightly about the nails he held that, before he realized what was happening, one of the other men shouted that he was bleeding.

"Damn. Guess I'm not ready to be doing construction yet," Jake said, passing the nails to the man who'd come to his side and swinging down off the frame of the house.

"Are you okay?" Tara took his hand and ran her finger across the bloody gouge.

"Yup. You know me." He gave Jonas his most earnest look. "If I am focused on a computer, the rest of the world disappears. Otherwise, I am kind of an airhead. Too bad the Chosen don't have any use for a programmer."

"You will find your place. For the moment, it would be best not to overdo. Tomorrow after breakfast you will rejoin the others, and tomorrow evening you will return to your bunks. Serena, you will remain in the laundry in the mornings for the next cycle. In the afternoons, you will join those repairing the bed linens. It is not strenuous work. Joy will show you what to do."

Jake couldn't imagine a job less suited to Tara's temperament. Lucy had told him long before he'd met Tara how she'd been a crusader since childhood. A girl—and then a woman—of action, constantly striving to make things better for others.

"And me?"

"You will be working in the drying sheds in the morning. Aaron will show you the ropes."

"Drying sheds?"

"The Chosen sell dried herbs and potpourri," Tara explained. "The flowers that don't sell in town get hung in bunches to be turned into potpourri. We also make soaps and small batches of essential oils.

It's all organic. The income from the sale of those things helps to pay for the community's needs."

"I see."

What he saw — what he expected Tara saw as well — was that the compound abutted the border to Mexico, where one very specific kind of "herb" was grown and dried for sale. Was that what Kevin Reasoner was investigating? Did the DEA suspect the Chosen of being involved with the cartels?

THEY WERE ASSIGNING Jake to the sheds. Tara had wondered about them — it was impossible not to with a law enforcement background — but only men worked there, so she'd had no way in. She'd never had a chance to look at the shipping operation, either. According to Andrea, that had been John's purview. But John was gone, so who oversaw shipping now? And why did she never hear anyone being assigned to help?

Of course, John had lived at the main house. Maybe the pregnant women who worked inside on "light duty" tasks packaged up the Chosen's products. Nothing they sent out was particularly heavy or bulky.

"And what about in the afternoon?" Jake asked Jonas.

"The Leader has not given me your afternoon assignment yet."

Of course not. Too much security in knowing what tomorrow would bring. But Jake merely nodded, his anxious geek persona firmly in place.

"Sure. Whatever I can do."

Jonas left and Tara felt her muscles relax. Damn. She'd been trying so hard to stay calm, stay loose, even though the minute she'd seen the man approaching, her mind had flashed back to his greedy eyes watching her undress in the shed. And he'd wanted her to remember, too. He'd taken his own sweet time surveying her as he walked over.

"Come on, sweetheart," Jake said, draping an arm over her shoulders. "Let's get moving and leave these guys to their work."

Once they were out of range, Tara expected Jake to let her go, but he didn't. Instead, his arm tightened around her as he paused, turning her to face him.

"What did he do to you?"

"Who?"

"Jonas. In isolation."

Naturally he had noticed. He was, after all, a trained observer.

"He didn't *do* anything. He just gives me the creeps."

Jake flashed her a grin. "Everyone in this place gives me the creeps." Serious again, he tipped her chin up so she couldn't avoid his eyes. "But it's more than that with him."

Tara swallowed the bile that rose in her throat as she recalled Jonas's behavior in the shed. "He got off on it. The punishment. For the others, it was duty. They were just following the Leader's orders. But he enjoyed the whole process: the stripping, the humiliation; it gave him a thrill."

A muscle flexed in Jake's jaw and anger flashed darkly in his eyes. He took a deep breath and let it out slowly before replying. "Nice. So the Chosen are a power trip for Jonas. Not terribly surprising to find a man like that among the top echelon. I wonder what the others get out of it?

"How many of them are there? The Chosen of the Chosen, as it were?"

"Four. Jonas, Aaron, Francis, and Samuel."

"I don't think I've met Francis."

Tara considered the little she knew about Francis. "He's the youngest of the lot. Only in his late twenties. He spends most of his time out at the big greenhouses where they grow the tomatoes and stuff. It's part of chore rotation — everyone goes out there sooner or later, and it's coed. At least when they bus you out. I haven't done it yet, so I don't know whether they segregate you once you're there or not."

Jake took her hand as if it were the most natural thing in the world, and they resumed their walk.

"Who's been here the longest? Among the regular people, not the special acolytes?"

"Well, there's Joy. She joined when Owen's father was still the head of the Chosen. She's not the only one who's stuck around, but the others I've met don't seem as . . . dedicated to the cause. They're just living day by day, escaping from the rest of the world."

"So in your opinion they don't know what's going on behind the facade?"

"No. Joy I am not so sure about. And that woman Deborah from the infirmary. If she's allowed to wander around in the house, she must be close to Owen. But what do you think *is* going on?"

Jake shook his head. "I'm not sure. But I can tell you one thing: this place is more than your basic religious commune. Despite their alleged open-door policy, in the past ten years there have been no 'insider accounts' written. No one blabs on blogs or writes books or headlines the talk show circuit talking about how they were once a part of the Chosen and telling the 'true story.' That's not just odd, it's a statistical anomaly that makes my every nerve itch. There are plenty of older accounts, and really wild tales of the stuff Owen did when he first took over, but nothing recent. Has anyone left since you've been here?"

"No. But right when I arrived a guy was rejoining."

"He left and came back?"

"Yeah. He was pretty crazy. Looked . . . rough. When you want to come back, apparently, you have to go spend a week in the desert with Aaron waiting for the Powers to speak to you. Like a Native American spirit walk or something. If you make it through that, you can come back. According to Andrea, some people decide they don't want back in after all. It's a test of dedication and determination."

"If you see the guy who came back, point him out. I want to hear about his trip. And his return."

"I will. His Chosen name is David. I had the same thought, but he wouldn't talk to me. Maybe you'll have better luck. There's not a lot of mixing of the sexes here."

"Speaking of that"—Jake paused, so Tara stopped, too—"how do we go about getting into 'couples housing'? We'd have a better chance of getting out at night to explore if all we had to worry about was two other people."

"Yeah." Tara's heart sped up, but she squelched her immediate, utterly inappropriate excitement at the idea of sharing Jake's bed every night. It was a *job*. An undercover assignment, nothing more. She forced herself to think practically. "But first our 'union' has to be 'blessed' by the Leader and given that we just fucked up and had to be purified, I'm not sure he'll go for it."

"How do we ask?"

"I don't know. Hooking up with one of the Chosen wasn't part of my plan. We can ask Deborah tonight if she brings our dinner. Or we can ask around at breakfast tomorrow."

"Okay. Are there searchlights at night?"

"No, just the ones that look like streetlamps. They're solar powered, come on at dusk, and shed pools of light but leave plenty of shadow. I wouldn't put it past him to have triggers or night vision security cams that are monitored up at the house, though. I suspect the lack of searchlights is to keep it from looking too much like a prison, to keep the 'uninformed governmental authorities' as he calls people like you and me, from having an excuse to invade. He frequently goes on at length about how jealous they are of our freedom from the ties that keep them bound to their miserable lives and of our closeness to the Powers. Essentially, as you will no doubt hear on Sunday morning, the religion of the Chosen is government-as-terrorist."

"Sunday. That's the free day?"

Tara nodded.

"And today is . . ." Jake shook his head. "Thursday?"

She had to shut her eyes and count backward to figure it out herself. "I think so. Assuming we were in isolation for three days. You joined on Friday, we went into isolation Saturday. Got out Tuesday afternoon."

"Okay. Then for the next couple of days we'll likely be separated, but everyone will expect us to want to spend Sunday together. Alone. If we can't make a move on the couples-housing front until then, we'll figure something out. But your idea about asking Deborah is a good one. I bet anything she hears goes right into Owen's ear, so he'll be prepared."

He ran a finger down her cheek, the calluses on the pad sending shivers down her spine.

"Have you ever done undercover work before?"

"No. I mean, not until I joined the Chosen."

"And since you've been here, you've still mostly been yourself. But I am going to ask you to change that."

"What do you mean?"

"We have a better chance of getting behind the scenes with a two-pronged approach. I'm new. And I'm a hacker. I also gave myself a minor criminal record. I'm going to play the doubter. As far as Owen is concerned, I'm only here because you are. But that means you have to be utterly convinced that staying is the right thing to do. You have to play against type, as if the isolation experience made you a complete convert. Obey all the rules, be eager to please."

Tara's stomach sank. "I'm not sure I can do that."

"Of course you can. Just remember, it's for Andrea. And when in doubt, say nothing. These guys like their women seen and not heard."

"No kidding."

"You can do it. I have great confidence in you."

"You do?" *Wow, way to sound pathetic.*

"I do." He cupped her face in his rough hands and Tara shivered again despite the lingering heat of the afternoon. "Listen, Tara, this is me, Jake. Not Jason Norman. When things fell apart back in Dobbs Hollow, I said a lot of harsh things about your abilities as an investigator and your dedication as a friend. Even then I knew they weren't true. I lost control, and I apologize. You're a good cop, Tara Jean Dobbs, and a good friend. No matter what name you're going by now."

Tara had to clear her throat before she could respond. "Thanks. I appreciate that. But I let emotion—shame—get in my way in Dobbs Hollow. It won't happen again. These assholes don't have the faintest idea what's coming down on them."

"Good. Hold that in your heart, but keep your outward demeanor all sweetness and light and devotion to the Powers. One way or another, we'll dig out the Chosen's secrets.

Together." He dropped his hands, but laced the fingers of his left with her right.

Together. That sounded good. And not just because it was Jake saying it. The Dobbs family had gone down under a landslide of scandal. Her parents and brother were dead. Not that they'd ever been close—and the elimination of the family name was all to the good as far as Tara was concerned—but it still felt peculiar to be out on her own. The police force had been her family, and having a partner again would be good. Even if that partner made her imagine a type of relationship strictly forbidden in any police department.

⌐

As THEY APPROACHED the main house, Tara made to slip her fingers free of Jake's grasp, but he held tight. He wanted Owen—or his lookouts—to see a romance between them. Plus, he liked the way her hand felt in his: small but capable, rough skin showing her to be unafraid of hard work. That had been the worst of what he'd said to her in Dobbs Hollow: that she wasn't capable.

And it wasn't true. He'd been so freaked out by the sight of one of his few remaining friends in a hospital bed, and so overwhelmed with his own guilt at not protecting her, that he'd simply lashed out at a convenient target.

Deborah from the infirmary met them at the front door.

"How was your walk?" she asked.

"It was lovely," Tara said, as if they'd been to a garden party rather than doing reconnaissance. "I feel quite restored."

"Excellent. Jonas tells me you are ready to rejoin the community tomorrow."

"Yes," said Tara. "He has already given us our assignments. It will be good to be working again."

Jake tugged her closer and slid his arm around her waist. "Deborah, before we came here Serena and I were engaged to be married. I admit I don't understand how everything works here yet, but do you have something similar? A way to formalize our commitment to each other?"

The woman frowned, and Jake could practically feel her gearing up for a lecture.

"Your first commitment is to the Powers and to the Leader as their representative. Then to the Chosen. Any personal commitment follows those."

"Okay, but—"

Tara, perfectly in character, put her hand on his chest. "Jacob, you'll get used to it. In time, we can ask the Leader to bless our relationship."

Deborah nodded in approval. "The Leader knows you were together in your previous lives. Once you have adjusted to our ways, you can speak with him regarding a union."

A cold day in hell, then. Nope, Jake wasn't planning on waiting.

CHAPTER FIVE

Jake's chance to talk to Owen Stephenson came sooner than he expected. Thursday night in the infirmary, he again crawled into Tara's bed. She curled into him and, though he knew that for her it was all part of the act, for him it felt real and right. Her head rested in the hollow of his shoulder, her blonde curls tickled his chin, and her small hand lay on his chest, just over his heart.

He'd lain awake most of the night, trying to plan. He needed to talk to Reasoner about what the DEA believed the Chosen were doing. He'd find a way to approach the man on Sunday without raising suspicion. And once he found out what Kevin knew, he had to get out of the compound and contact Ethan, who was doing a more thorough investigation of the Chosen than Jake had had time for. Plus, Ethan and Lucy would be worried. Jake needed to reassure them that Tara was okay.

Friday morning, he and Tara joined the others for breakfast. At the door to the dining hall they separated and Tara went to join the same woman he'd seen her with the first night. Jake found himself a place at one of the men's tables next to a sullen, dark-haired man in his thirties.

"Jacob," Jake said, extending a hand.

"Ezra." A spark erased the sour expression on the man's face for a minute. "You're the new one, aren't you? The one who went through isolation."

"'Fraid so."

"What was it like?"

"Believe me when I tell you that you don't want to find out."

"Pretty much what everyone says."

"Everyone?" Jake tried to keep the horror from his voice. "I figured it was reserved for fairly serious transgressions. How often does the Leader have to punish people?"

The guy cocked an eyebrow at him. "Punish? It's not punishment, it's purification of the soul."

Jake shrugged. "Yeah, well, my daddy called it beating out the Devil, but it felt like punishment back then, too."

"I hear ya, man." Ezra studied him. "So you got roped into the Chosen because of your girlfriend?"

Jake didn't hide his surprise. "I could almost believe you don't like it here."

"It's not so bad." Ezra shifted in his chair, looking around the room. "Compared to some places I've lived, it's damn near paradise. It's just that nothing ever *happens*."

"How'd you wind up here?"

"Got sent up in 'Bama when I was seventeen for driving the getaway car when my older brother robbed a convenience store and shot the clerk. He got life, I got ten-to-twenty-five. Got out at twenty-seven, couldn't find a job or a place to live. Wandered around for a few years till I heard about the Chosen from a guy at a shelter in San Antone. He had a sister living here. They're not judgmental, don't give a flip about your past. Can't say I care much for the religious aspect, but I pretty much let it roll off my back. Obey the rules and it's not a bad life."

"Good to hear." Prison made sense. A guy who'd spent his whole adult life in the system would probably find the structure of the compound comforting. Especially since it came with decent food and the security of not constantly looking over your shoulder.

The Leader took the stage at the front of the dining hall and all conversation ceased. He yammered on about the quality of life provided by the Powers to those who believed and how every new believer strengthened them all and brought forth goodness tenfold.

Finally, they were allowed to eat. Platters of eggs scrambled with vegetables and cheese and baskets of thickly sliced bread were passed down the tables. Jake had read about the dairy operation that helped to keep the Chosen self-sufficient, had even seen the buildings on aerial surveillance photos. The Chosen raised both cows and goats for milk, butter, and cheese, as well as chickens for eggs. Whatever illegal activities the compound hid, it was also a fully functioning farm that he couldn't help but admire.

After breakfast, Aaron led Jake to the drying sheds. Again, the size and efficiency of the operation impressed him. Two huge barns were dedicated to drying and packaging the herbs and flowers. Rope pulleys hoisted beams on which the plants were hung for drying. Solar panels on the roofs ran giant fans that kept the humidity to a minimum so the herbs didn't discolor or mold while drying, but didn't do much to alleviate the oppressive heat that hit Jake like a fist when he entered the first barn.

Aaron put him to work on one of the beams with a man named Paul. Together, they lowered the beam until the herbs hung within reach, then tied it off to anchors on the wall. Paul showed him how to detach the herbs, place them in a designated basket, and get more fresh ones to be hung. Then they raised the beam once more. Each time they moved to a new beam, they stopped for water from the large tank at the front of the room.

They had completed four beams when the door to the

shed opened and a man Jake recognized as one of Owen's lieutenants stepped inside, followed by one of the men who had been constructing the new cabin the previous day. Paul stopped working and nodded to them.

"Samuel."

"Paul. Zeb is going to take Jacob's place for a while, as the Leader wishes to speak with him."

"That's fine." If being taken to visit Owen Stephenson in the middle of a workday was unusual, Paul showed no sign of it. Zeb came over and took Jake's gloves without a word.

Samuel ushered Jake outside and began walking toward the main house at a fairly good clip.

"I don't think we've met," Jake said, catching up to Samuel as they got to the front door. "I'm Jas—Jacob."

The man's blue eyes were positively arctic despite the Texas heat. Here was a true enemy. Jake had to force himself not to tense up as he held out his hand.

"I know who you are." Samuel's gaze deliberately dropped to Jake's outstretched hand, then back

up to his face.

Fuck. Did he? Not that it made any difference. If Owen and Samuel had figured out his true identity, both he and Tara were screwed. But for the moment, there was nothing to do but brazen it out.

He dropped his hand and shrugged.

"I guess word gets around."

Without another word, Samuel led Jake through the atrium at the front of the house and the big room he and Tara had found while exploring to a study where Owen Stephenson sat behind a heavy, old-fashioned wooden desk. Owen gestured to a chair in front of the desk, and Jake sat. Samuel went to stand behind Owen.

"Jacob. I see you've met Samuel."

Jake wouldn't so much call it a meeting, but he nodded anyway.

"Good. Samuel is my strong right hand. He manages the earthly concerns of the Powers."

Jake didn't respond. He'd found through years of interrogations that he got a lot further letting others fill the silences.

"Despite your purification, Jacob, I still sense within you an unwillingness to become a part of our community."

Jake leaned forward and rested folded arms on the desk.

"Look. I'm willing to work. But I was up front with you when I got here about the fact that I came for my girlfriend. If I could get her to leave here tomorrow, would I? You bet. I asked her to come away with me while we were out yesterday, but she wouldn't go."

Owen smirked, and Jake's gut clenched. "She won't be happy anywhere else." There was something entirely too self-satisfied in the man's expression.

"She was happy with me before."

"She won't be. Not since she has been one with the Chosen. This is the only place she will ever be content."

What the fuck? He tamped down the urge to lunge over the desk and strangle the truth out of Owen.

Stick to the plan.

"Maybe, maybe not. I'm just trying to be straight with you. I'm not easily convinced about stuff like your Powers. I can see how some people might find this lifestyle to their liking, but I can't promise I will. I haven't slept in a bunkhouse since I went to camp when I was twelve. And I haven't been without a computer in twenty years."

"That is part of why we make you change your name

when you come to us," said Samuel. "So you leave behind the past. But you didn't come to us the way most of the Chosen do."

"Samuel is not yet convinced you were truly Chosen," Owen said.

No shit. "Neither am I."

"I have meditated upon this, asked the Powers what to do. I believe you were brought to us for a purpose. I cannot think it is coincidence that we lost the one who managed the Chosen's Internet presence so shortly before you arrived."

"You need an Internet guy?"

"This would bring you some measure of peace?"

"Well, yeah. I could help you out with that for sure. Boost your SEO, get more traffic to your sites, sell more product. I can do all of that."

"Deborah tells me you were asking about having your relationship with Serena blessed so that you might move in together."

"Like I said, bunks are for kids."

"And you're sure it's Serena you want? After all, there are many women here. We are not so conventional as the outside world. Many men here do not choose a single mate."

So the men got to choose, and the women just went with whoever asked? No wonder Kevin had warned him to hold Tara close.

"I'm sure."

"Then it can be arranged. We will have the ceremony Sunday morning. Aaron will find housing for you to move into once the ceremony is complete."

"Just like that?"

"Life among the Chosen does not have to be difficult, Jacob." A horn rang in the distance. "Ah. Time for lunch. Clean yourself up and go to the hall. After lunch, Francis will take you out to the greenhouses."

It was a dismissal, and Jake obeyed. After all, he'd gotten more than he could have hoped for out of the meeting.

⁓

"ARE YOU SURE it's a good idea to give him access to the computer?" Samuel asked, checking the hallway to be sure Jake was gone. "He's a hacker. He's going to want to go beyond what we tell him he can do."

"We don't keep anything on that computer. John may not have understood people, but he did understand security." Owen relaxed back into his chair, enjoying the hot rush of energy from the verbal fencing with Jacob. It had been too long since he'd had to be careful what he said. The Chosen were children to be managed and his apostles understood the mission, so there was no need to mince words with them.

"And what if Jacob uses the computer to contact someone on the outside? To tell them about the Chosen? What if he's a reporter out to expose you?"

"What would he say? He won't know anything until it's too late. Plus, he has a weakness. He's not going anywhere without his girlfriend and she's not leaving." As usual, the reminder of the control he held over his children brought a surge of sexual excitement. After lunch, he would find one of the women, bring her in for a private tea, and enjoy himself. But which one? The new girl, Charity, had caught his eye, but she might not be ready for him yet.

"But he doesn't know that." Samuel paced the room, drawing Owen back from his fantasies. "We can't let him find anything out until we're absolutely certain of him. I don't like that you even hinted at the truth. Did you see his eyes? He's suspicious. A lot of those hacker types are conspiracy theorists—who knows what he's imagining now? Especially since the purification. Even if all he told people about was that, he could bring a world of hurt down on us."

"Relax, Samuel. Jacob and Serena both accepted their punishments. What would he say after the fact? That they'd willingly gone through something they now regret?

"Besides, I do believe he was brought to us for a reason. We've never been betrayed by anyone we've vetted. Once you and Francis feel you can trust him, we'll tell him the truth about why he can't take his girlfriend away from us. For the moment, keeping him happy is easy. We watch what he does on the computer and we watch his movements around the others, and we decide whether we can bring him into the inner circle."

"And if not? If he tries to contact some of his buddies on the outside?"

Owen shrugged. "Then he dies."

TARA ENTERED THE dining hall on the heels of the two other women from the laundry and immediately sought out Jake. He'd seated himself toward the head of one of the men's tables and was talking to a man she didn't recognize. As if he felt her stare, he looked up and gave her a quick grin.

How did he look so good after all morning in the drying sheds? She was pretty sure she'd sweated out half a gallon in the laundry, her hair was sticking out in a frizzy halo she could see in her peripheral vision despite the tight French braid she'd made that morning, and any energy she'd woken with had disappeared.

Aurora plopped down next to her along with one of the women who'd been introduced the same night as Jake.

"This is Mary," Aurora said. "She's been assigned to our bunk."

"Welcome," Tara said. "I'm Serena." The name still choked her, but she forced a smile. "Mary worked with me making soaps this morning," Aurora said. "This afternoon she's going to be selling flowers in town."

She has the face for it. Mary's sweet, shy demeanor would drive sales. Tara had never been sent to town. Not a surprise, but she wished she'd had the opportunity to get out of the compound and send a message to Lucy. Did Jake have a means of contacting the outside world? Or had he simply assumed he'd be able to convince her to leave and wouldn't need to join up for long himself?

She glanced across the gradually filling hall. No, Jake was not a man who assumed. He strategized, prepared, investigated. And when situations changed, he remained flexible. He might not have come into the compound with a concrete plan, but he would have put a framework in place before setting foot on Owen Stephenson's land.

"Where are you from, Serena?" Mary asked.

"Here and there. Most recently right in Twin Oaks. A friend of mine moved from town to the community and she seemed really happy so I decided to join, too." Bringing up Andrea was a calculated risk. It could piss off Owen if he heard about it, but she needed to keep the conversation alive if she hoped to learn anything.

"You have a friend here?" Mary asked as if Tara had scripted it. "Who?"

"She's not here anymore. Her name was Pearl."

"Not here? Where did she go?"

"She . . ." How to put it? Tara certainly wasn't going to use the crap "gone on a mission" expression. "She passed away."

"Oh, that's terrible." Mary reached across Aurora and patted Tara's hand. "But at least your boyfriend is here now."

"And he's *hot*." Aurora grinned.

Tara felt a blush crawl across her cheeks. "He is, isn't he?"

"It's totally romantic that he came all this way to find you," said Mary. "None of the guys I know would cross the *street* for a woman."

"You just haven't met the right kind of men," Tara said. "There are good ones out there." *Look at me, giving relationship advice. What a joke.* And then she remembered that Jake was supposed to have cheated on her. "Of course, none of them are perfect. Jacob drank too much, but I am hoping now that he's away from that temptation, we can get our lives back on track."

"Booze and drugs can destroy even the best of them," Aurora agreed. "Jimmy—my ex—he never hit me when he was straight. Course, he wasn't straight much."

Mary put an arm across Aurora's shoulders. "At least your baby won't grow up afraid or exposed to those influences."

What would happen to these women if she and Jake were right and criminal activities underlay the Chosen? The whole compound would be shuttered. What then for the Marys and Auroras? Could any kind of honest community grow in the soiled ground?

Owen took the stage to lead them in prayer, and Tara caught Jake's gaze once more. One thing about their cover— no one would be surprised to find them looking at each other, meeting up, whispering in corners. With a little luck, even Jake would believe her covert glances were all part of the act.

⌒

JAKE HELD TARA's gaze until Ezra jabbed him in the side with his elbow and muttered, "Ogling your girlfriend during the Leader's sermon isn't cool."

"Sorry." But he wasn't. Tara no doubt interpreted his stare as part of their cover, and that was fine for the moment. They could explore the reality and limits of the attraction between them once they were out of danger.

When they'd finished eating, he hurried to put his dishes in the tub at the same time she did.

"I spoke to the Leader," he said, grabbing her hand and tugging her out of the crowd of the Chosen bussing their tableware. "He said he would bless our relationship on Sunday."

"That's wonderful." Tara grinned up at him, her wide smile open for the public, but a second, secret one in her blue eyes just for him.

A surge of pure lust surprised him and he pulled her forward to plant a quick kiss on her soft lips.

"Jacob," she admonished, pulling away. Her cheeks were pink.

"Sorry, baby. I'm just excited."

"Me, too. But it's time to go to work."

"I know." But he couldn't resist pressing his lips to her palm and closing her fingers around the lingering heat. A promise, even if he himself wasn't sure of what and she didn't recognize it as such.

"Where are you working this afternoon?"

"Francis is taking me out to the greenhouses."

As if summoned, a slight, dark-haired young man who

had been at the head table with Aaron, Samuel, Jonas, and the Leader, appeared at Jake's elbow.

"And here I am," he said. "Jacob, we haven't met. I am Francis."

"Then I guess that's my cue to go." Jake followed Francis out of the dining hall and back to the main house, where they picked up a Jeep.

"Those assigned to the greenhouses generally leave by bus after breakfast and come back for dinner," Francis explained. "They eat lunch there because it's wasteful to drive back and forth in the middle of the day."

"Why are the greenhouses so far away?" It had nagged at Jake ever since he'd checked out the aerial photographs of the property. The bunkhouses were clustered on top of one another—which made sense now that he saw that the Chosen were putting up their own buildings, because if they had to dig the plumbing lines by hand they'd keep everything close—but the greenhouses were a good two miles away, separated not only by the dairy buildings but also by a cluster of fruit trees and a large, open area.

"The Leader inherited this land. The orchard was already in place, as was the foundation for the building that became the first greenhouse. He placed it close to the river for irrigation purposes. It is no trouble to us that they are some distance, and being well inside the perimeter means that none will sneak onto our land and steal from us."

"Do you worry about that from the Mexican side?"

"You believe Mexicans to be less honest?"

"No. But I do believe the average Mexican is hungrier than the average American. And your greenhouses are so close to the border, I can see them being a tempting target."

For a long time Francis did not speak as they bumped

along the narrow, rutted track around the fruit trees. Jake recognized peaches, apples, pears, and a couple of kinds of citrus. Some doing better than others, but all carefully pruned and set at a good distance from each other so they'd bear maximum fruit. An odd selection, but one he could imagine Hal Stephenson planting as he attempted various uses for his land, various crops to feed his people. By all accounts, the elder Stephenson had been a decent man, though he'd held a strong grudge against the government, whose regulations he'd blamed for his failure as a cattle rancher.

"Good fences make good neighbors," Francis said at last. "And we have very good fences along our border."

"I imagine it's a pain dealing with the US Border guys. They've gotta always be in your business. Government types always want more authority than they should have."

The bait dangled there for a bit while Francis considered his answer.

"This land has been in the Leader's family for generations. Government officials have no cause to be on our property. Their concerns are with cities far more than the open land. The river provides a natural barrier, and we have nice, high fences should anyone get to this side."

He examined Jake. "What's the most complicated thing you ever hacked?"

"Huh?" It was so out of left field that it took Jake a minute to adjust.

"The Leader says you're a computer specialist. I figure that means you hack. Do you?"

"Some," Jake admitted. "Mostly gaming software. To make it work the way I want."

"So you've never tried to, say, hack into a database to erase your criminal record?"

They had checked him out. Good. "How'd you know?"

"Just a guess. Many of the Chosen have records. Comes from being misunderstood by Outsiders."

And I am the king of fucking Siam. But he kept his expression neutral and shrugged. "You can't hack human memory or paper. Even if I could get into the database, the chances someone would remember the arrests is too great. I'd be in way deeper if I got busted and they found out I'd erased my rap sheet." He was pretty sure none of the inner circle had a sense of humor, but he tried for a joke anyway. "Why, you got a record you want taken down?"

"Not at all," Francis said as he circled the greenhouses to park behind them. "I am just curious about your apparent dislike of authority."

Jake shrugged. "I never thought about it. It kind of goes with the territory. If you get into computers, you get an up-close-and-personal look at how much control corporations—and the government is the biggest corporation around—exert over you. They can—and do—track all kinds of stuff they have no business knowing."

"Well, you don't have to worry about that here. Many of the Chosen come to us specifically to get away from that kind of oversight. Here the government doesn't tax you, doesn't spy on you, doesn't shackle you."

No, the Leader does. With your help. But Jake just nodded as he got out of the Jeep.

"Between the greenhouses and the plantings we do outside, we can grow a great deal here." He gestured to the short green plants with feathery leaves dotting the land around them, and some staked plants in the distance that Jake thought might be peppers.

"We grow vegetables for our own consumption, but we

grow the flowers to sell, and we also grow sago palms for various nurseries around the state. They bring in good money, but they're a long-term crop—slow growing and the nurseries don't want them until they're a good size. But they are hardy and require little enough care, just trimming and caring for the pups."

Surreal. Jake could be talking to any of the many farmers he'd known over the years instead of to some possibly criminal whack-job. He followed Francis inside the first greenhouse. Immediately, he was smacked with the humidity and the sweet, green scent of the place. It was late enough in the year that they were growing tomatoes and cucumbers inside, rows and rows of them, the vines staked up taller than Jake could reach. Two men were making their way down the aisles—the floors of which were steel plates with large drains cut in—carefully plucking the ripe tomatoes and placing them in baskets. Parts of the greenhouse were open to the air, and large fans like the ones in the drying shed circulated air through the plants.

Francis led him through the massive greenhouse and out the other end.

"We generally have the same crew working out here for up to three months at a time. People have to be trained. Not so much for the tomatoes—most people know how to take care of them—but the root vegetable and lettuce and herb houses take more skill. What can be pulled, what can't, what they should look like, when a supervisor needs to look at a plant."

"Okay. Umm . . . not that I don't appreciate the knowledge and all, but am I going to be assigned up here tomorrow, or why am I getting the tour?"

"The Leader says you are taking over John's position running our website."

"I guess I am."

"John was very conservative about the site. It was just product, price, details. I think we need more than that. I want to put pictures of the greenhouses up. Use the site to explain why our products are so good. How they're grown, cared for. It could help people understand how the Chosen fit into their lives, as well. Ease any animosity the Outsiders feel."

Was this guy for real? Maybe he was so into the whole organic-farming aspect that he just hadn't noticed how fucked up everything else was and honestly believed they needed to do more to bring the green-living message to the rest of the world.

Francis kept up his narration as he walked Jake through both of the other greenhouses and then drove him back to the main house.

They arrived in time for Jake to go back to his own bunk and check on his things before dinner. Whoever had gone through his possessions had been thorough and had made no effort to hide their presence. But why should they? They had the excuse that they'd had to bring clothes to the infirmary for him, and the invasion of his privacy was intended to reinforce the communal nature of the place. And if it served as a warning not to step out of line, so much the better.

⌒

AFTER DINNER, JAKE caught up to Tara as he had after lunch, and though she'd expected him to continue his eager-lover act—even prepared herself for it during the mind-numbing hours repairing worn bed linens—still, a little shiver of pleasure went through her when he took her hand.

"Let's take a walk." His eyes fixed on hers, shadowed and intense.

"I have to get back to the bunk. It will be dark soon." The bunkhouses had no electricity. Solar-powered water heaters provided hot water, and plenty of ambient light from the compound came into the bedroom through the unshaded windows, but the bathrooms got very dark once the sun had gone down. Tara didn't care, but Serena would.

"It's not dark *yet*," Jake coaxed. "Just a few minutes. We'll take the scenic route back to your bunk."

"Well, okay." She let him tug her along after him out into the gloaming.

"They're going to put me to work on the website," Jake said as soon as they were clear of the building and sure no one would overhear. Even so, he kept his voice low and glanced around, deliberately taking a rambling path that kept them in the open, away from buildings, lampposts, or fences where listening devices might be installed.

"With Internet access, I'll be able to get rudimentary messages out to Lucy and Ethan. I won't get into detail because I don't know what kind of computer skills anyone else here has, and it's virtually

impossible to completely erase electronic tracks."

"What if they installed a keystroke tracker on it?"

"Oh, I fully expect they have. I have no intention of sending e-mail or the like. I'll be accessing a protected server site. Ethan and I have a code system that depends on the day, date, and time of access. The password changes the same way. If it's Monday, even date, odd hour, the code works one way. If the hour is even, it's different. A keystroke recorder will record what looks like gibberish."

"And what if they confront you about the gibberish?"

"That's why I want to keep the message short. I can blame failed code attempts for short strings of gibberish, but long documents attract more attention and are harder to explain away. The real advantage to the system is that Ethan and Lucy have been using all their contacts — and mine — to dig into the Chosen. So with a little luck, there will be fresh intel on the server. I can pick it up as long as there aren't any eyes on me."

"Eyes? You think there are cameras?" Tara's stomach clenched.

"I've seen three for certain: one in a knot in the oldest of the trees by the dining hall, one inside that big room where the women were cleaning, and one in the dash of the Jeep Francis and I took out to the greenhouses."

"I scoured the laundry and my bunkhouse pretty thoroughly and didn't find anything. I figured there might be ears I couldn't see, so I've been careful about what I said, but I didn't find any video in the actual rooms, just outside for surveillance."

"They probably only have cams in places they consider high risk. But you can bet they will either have a camera or a human in the room with me when I have Internet access. Even with whatever kind of firewall they've set up."

"You think giving you access is a test?"

"Wish I knew. I can't figure these people out. Owen is crazy. You can see it in his eyes. You

gave me your assessment of Jonas, and I'm sure you're right. Samuel's a thug, but a smart one — I'd like

to know what he's getting out of this. Likewise Aaron. What keeps them here? Surely they don't buy into the religious crap. And Francis . . . Francis seems completely dedicated to his plants."

"Francis has been here a long time. Since he was a child,

I think." They were pushing the time, so Tara turned in the direction of her bunk.

"That may be why he's more interested in farming than in Owen's agenda. That could work in our favor, if we can be certain."

"It would be nice if that were true. For all the creepy cultness, there are a lot of people living here who probably couldn't function in the real world. I can't imagine some of them paying bills, keeping a normal job, coping with the distractions and stresses of daily life. That's what Andrea found so attractive. Well, that and the built-in sense of community. She once told me that she felt out of step with life. John was the last of her family left alive, and she didn't have many friends."

"She had you." The sincerity in his voice warmed her. "You're a good friend. You always have been."

Back in Dobbs Hollow, he'd accused her of being a bad friend and a bad cop. She wished she could ask him what had changed his mind, but they'd reached the bunkhouse. To her surprise, Jake stopped by the door and pulled her into his arms.

"I can't wait until Sunday when we can begin our lives together."

Just an act, Tara Jean. Don't lose your head. "It's only two more days."

"It's not the days that worry me, it's the nights." He slid one hand over her cheek and tilted her face up. Her breath caught and her heart skipped a beat.

"Jake—"

He kissed her, and her mind shut down. Logic, plans, all sense of time and place deserted her. Her world consisted of the heat of his mouth, the scent of his skin, the hard, masculine strength of his body against hers. His tongue traced the seam of her lips and she opened to him eagerly, desperate to taste him. And, God, he tasted good. Better than burgers, better than chocolate, better than any of the luxuries she'd been denied since joining the Chosen.

"Ahem." The cough from behind her startled Tara out of the moment, and she pulled away from Jake.

"Sorry," said Aurora, who'd appeared at the door. "I thought you might appreciate the reminder that you had an audience."

Indeed, through the bunkhouse windows, several women watched. And when Tara remembered the cameras, a blush crawled up her cheeks.

"Thanks, Aurora."

"Nice kid," Jake said as Aurora popped back inside and shut the door.

"She thinks you're hot."

"Yeah?" In the semidarkness, Jake's teeth gleamed as he grinned. "She's got good taste."

Tara laughed. "Nothing wrong with *your* ego."

"Nope. But you like that about me." His smile faded. "But cute or not, there's only you for me, baby."

Tara's throat went dry, and she reminded herself once more that Jake was just acting. "Get back to your own bunk," she said, giving him a little shove. "I need to shower and get my beauty sleep." Without waiting for a reply, she escaped into the bunkhouse.

⌁

JAKE TOSSED IN his bed, the loud discomfort only partially feigned. Kissing Tara had been a terrible idea. A wonderful, terrible idea. He'd wanted her on a purely physical level from the moment he'd first seen her, which had shocked him — lust had gone the way of every other strong feeling in the months after his FBI flameout. And she was just as beautiful inside. At the age of thirteen, she'd gone up against her own bullying brother to rescue a school friend, and that strength of character had never wavered. Here she was again, taking on forces far greater than herself in defense of a friend.

But that kiss . . . it had been more than he could possibly have imagined. Hot, sweet, as energizing as pure electricity shooting through his body. He could get lost in her, forget his purpose entirely. Hell, he'd been damned close to taking her up against the wall of the bunkhouse with God alone knew how many people watching.

And he hadn't been able to give himself any relief in the shower, either, not with a half dozen guys in the next room.

He sat up and stretched, deliberately making noise so others in his cabin would notice.

"Chill, man," said one.

"Too antsy. Is it against the rules for me to take a walk?"

"Do what you gotta do. But the morning horn sounds early, so do it quietly."

"Gotcha."

Outside, he did some stretches and a few calisthenics for the cameras, then began a Tai Chi routine. Owen's sentinels needed to become accustomed to seeing Jake wandering around the grounds after hours. Programmers had a rep for being night owls and insomniacs that would work in his favor. The trick would be to maintain his insomniac status while getting up at the crack of dawn every day to work in the sheds.

He lay on his back on the hard, cooling ground and stared up at the sky. The moon, the stars, the tiny extra-bright glow at the base of each of the lamps lighting the night, showing where the cameras hid.

Yeah, exploring this place was going to be a bitch, no matter how much at ease he tried to put the guards.

Jake rose and walked for a bit, keeping to the obviously "safe" areas of the compound so as not to set off any alarms. Just your basic sleepless dude wandering around.

Still, he wasn't surprised when Jonas appeared from the shadows.

"Trouble sleeping?" The man might have been aiming for friendly, but the words came out as a challenge.

"Yeah, well . . . I've never been good at resting. My mind just keeps going until I pass out." That much was true. "At home, I used to get a little . . . chemical assistance . . . when I needed to close my eyes. But I gather that's not going to happen here, so I'm just trying to work off a little excess energy."

"After a few days with the Chosen, your body will no longer need drugs. Fresh air, hard work, they contain transformative properties." In direct conflict to Francis's enthusiasm for the greenhouse work, Jonas sounded as if he were reciting a lesson. And beneath the recitation, Jake could swear he heard a smirk. An "I know something you don't know" taunt. Was Jonas on something? None of the disciples had the skinny, strung-out look of junkies, but Jake had seen plenty of functional users in his life, indistinguishable from the general population except via blood or urine tests.

"But you can't sleep either?" he asked Jonas.

"I am assigned to this shift. The Leader knows that in the darkness doubt can assail even the Chosen, so he makes sure someone is always walking the grounds should they need to talk. Just as there are always guards at the gates in case

Outsiders should try to interrupt our peace, so must we be alert to the needs of our people inside."

"Does that happen often? The Outsiders thing?"

Jonas shrugged. "Occasionally. People misunderstand us. They send in their 'deprogrammers' to kidnap the Chosen, as if we were brainwashing them. They cannot understand that for the Chosen, this is the best way. They are miserable taken from us and return as soon as possible.

"You should go to bed. At least rest if you cannot sleep. After lunch, Samuel will take you up to the computer room."

Jake trotted off like an obedient child, but he lay awake for a long time mulling over Jonas's words.

CHAPTER SIX

MORNING WAS A serious drag, and Jake's lack of sleep didn't help. There was nothing to do while tying off the blasted plants but think, and his thoughts were not productive. He needed to get a message out to Ethan and find out what information the man had for him.

After lunch, Samuel led him to an office off the large central room in the main house. Nowhere near as elegant as Owen's office, this room held a small desk, probably four feet long and two feet deep, that could have come from any online office supply company. A Macintosh computer sat on the desk. Not ideal—Jake was far more comfortable programming on a PC, but luckily the newer Macs allowed you to get down to a command-line interface, which he could handle—and a combination printer, scanner, and fax machine rested on a stand in the corner. A pad of paper and a pencil lay next to the computer. On the top sheet, someone had scrawled three websites.

Samuel pulled out the chair for Jake and then leaned against the wall next to him.

"That top one, thechosen.org, that's our main website. It tells about who we are, some basic tenets of our beliefs, and it has products for sale on it. The server we host that site on is right below it. We also sell through the online outlet Etsy. That's the last address there. You'll have to keep renewing stock as it falls off their listing system."

"What about orders?"

"For the moment, you don't need to worry about those. Eventually, once you get comfortable with the sites, we'll move you into billing and shipping, too. But for now, we need this taken care of. I had the hosting site and Etsy send us the passwords for the two log-ins." He handed Jake a slip of paper out of his wallet.

"Great. First, though, I think I am going to try to clean this computer. This room is kind of dusty. Do you have any canned air? And some tools so I can crack the shell?"

"That won't be necessary. The computer is fine."

"It's not good for them to get all dusty inside. And that reminds me, do you have any kind of backup going?"

"We don't need backups. The computer doesn't serve a purpose to us except to access records maintained on external sites."

"Really? Wow. That's so . . . retro. Do you do your accounting by hand? Or, like, with an abacus?" No fucking way was Jake buying that they didn't have digital records. And Owen was far too paranoid to store everything in the cloud somewhere. No, they kept their information on a local computer; it just wasn't this one.

"The Chosen have what they need."

"Well, uh . . . okay. If you're sure."

Samuel nodded.

Jake turned on the computer and logged on to the first site. His first thought was that they couldn't possibly be doing serious business from it. The user interface was not just butt ugly but a complete clusterfuck. He could see why Francis thought it needed updating. Plus, John, or whoever had written the copy, skated the edges of literacy.

He pulled the pad toward him and began making swift notes.

"Whatcha doing?"

"Making a list of the things I'm going to have to change and fix. I know you say the Chosen have what they need, but with this website, I am not sure how. It could bring so much more business, so many more people your way. You could get the word out about what kind of place this is, bring others into the fold."

"So you're going to rebuild the whole thing from the bottom up?"

"Well, yeah. That's what you want, isn't it?" *And it's going to take forever, so get out of here and leave me to it.*

"Of course."

Samuel pushed off the wall and headed for the door. "I'll be back later." His eyes flicked up to the corner of the ceiling as he spoke and, though Jake carefully didn't let his own follow, he knew there was at least one camera on him. That was fine. He could work around a camera.

He started by accessing the Chosen's main site, logging on to the back end just as they would expect and downloading the index file. Then he printed it out and brought it back to the desk to give himself an excuse to get up and walk around the room. A couple of big stretches gave him a full view of every corner and hidden camera.

He opened several documents on the computer screen and began typing a bit into each. Whoever was watching the camera pointed at the monitor was going to get pages and pages shuffled through. With any luck they wouldn't notice an extra when Jake downloaded it from the server he and Ethan had set up.

He left a bunch of the pages open while he worked on paper with notes for CSS code for a bit. Then he came back to the screen and brought up the password window to allow him to access the server. It appeared, as it was designed to, in the lower right corner of the screen. Small. Unobtrusive. Hardly noticeable among the profusion of windows Jake already had open. He checked the time and entered the appropriate password. Another tiny window popped up. It had an up arrow, the letter O, and a down arrow. Next to the down arrow was the number 1.

Ethan had information. But Jake didn't dare download it, so he hit the O instead. The little window disappeared. The window with the information Ethan had coded would appear beneath everything else on the screen.

Jake stretched again and sat back in the chair, waiting for any indication that someone had noticed anything odd on the computer screen, but no one came. He looked back at the pad of paper and made a couple more notations before popping the window with Ethan's document to the front on the screen. He made it small and kept it down in the corner where it could be hidden or closed in an instant.

Something is seriously off there. Couldn't find anyone who had left. DEA sent someone in undercover last year. He came out after nine months, said he couldn't find anything wrong, then ate his gun. Likewise, two young women in the past five years who were brought out by deprogrammers took their own lives.

Jake remembered Owen's words about Tara: *This is the only place she will ever be content.* What the fuck were they doing here? The DEA agent's death had to be why Reasoner was on the property.

Not much on the various members. We talked about Owen and Samuel. The one who calls himself Aaron did time for armed robbery and meth dealing. Jonas has a sheet for possession of oxy. Haven't been able to find anything on Francis, though there's a good possibility he was actually born on the property. A couple who left when Hal died remembered him as a baby.

Coding the words in his head, putting the date and time at the top so Ethan would know which code to use, Jake replied.

There's a DEA guy here. Kevin Reasoner. See if you can find out what he's looking for. Tara and I are okay. Staying until we can figure out what's going on. Chosen swallowed a friend of hers.

He closed the window, automatically logging him out of their server, and turned his attention back to the Chosen's web presence.

⌒

In the sewing room, Tara deliberately sat next to Joy. Until Jake could get in touch with Ethan, they were on their own and needed to find out as much history of the Chosen as possible.

"You've been a member of the Chosen for a long time, haven't you?" she asked, squinting as she held up a needle to thread.

"Oh, yes," answered Joy. "This is where I belong. I hardly remember the time before this land and this work."

"Have you ever been—I hope this isn't too rude—have you been part of a couple? Like a blessed union?"

Joy laughed. "In my day, we didn't bother with such things. If you wanted to be with a man, you were."

"Where did you live, then?"

"If you wanted to make it permanent, or semi-permanent anyway, you moved into an empty house. If none of the houses were empty, you could wait for one to open up or you could move into one of the rooms in the main house if one was available."

"The main house? Really?" So whatever secrets Owen hid there had come into being after Hal's time.

"Oh, yes. It was very democratic in those days." Joy stitched steadily, without looking up, as if her words were not a complete indictment of Owen's lifestyle.

"What changed?"

"The old Leader sent his heir to be educated in the Outside world so that he might return better equipped to help the cause. The information he gathered was useful, but when the old Leader passed on, our current Leader made changes based on what he had grown accustomed to Outside."

"Wasn't that difficult for you?"

"Of course. Change is always hard. But the work, the mission, remain the same and that is what matters. The trappings are irrelevant." She looked up from her sewing.

"Are you nervous about your bonding with Jacob?"

"I'm not really sure what to expect. I mean . . . I was ready to marry him in the Outside. And I love him. But I'm barely settling in here and I am not sure he's really ready, despite what he says."

"Pledging yourself won't change much about your life here. And should things turn sour, it's easier to walk away. It's not as if you have to 'choose friends' the way couples on the Outside do. You will remain part of the community. You won't even fight over children because they, too, belong to the community as a whole."

Tara choked. "Oh, I am definitely not ready for children yet."

"You'd best be. They're inevitable."

"I—I thought that since I went off the pill when I joined, Jacob would use condoms?"

"Children are blessings from the Powers. We do not try to prevent them."

Well, hell. Was everyone going to be watching her for signs of pregnancy now? Because they were going to be sadly disappointed. She and Jake needed to close this damned case before Owen or one of his lieutenants began to wonder why a couple as hands-on as they were in public somehow couldn't conceive.

⌒

BY THE TIME Sunday morning rolled around, Tara didn't even have to act nervous. As she sat in the dining hall waiting for the Leader to finish his sermon and announce that he was uniting her with Jake, her stomach rolled and twisted. They'd been out walking Saturday night, and Jake had filled her in on what he'd learned from Ethan.

He'd also passed on the information that two separate women had been to visit him in the office as he worked and tried to seduce him.

Tara had stopped dead when he'd told her about the woman who'd slid into the room on the pretext of offering to bring him coffee or water and proceeded to stroke his arms and massage his shoulders. He'd sent her away, reminding her that he had a commitment ceremony coming up, but then another woman had arrived.

"The first one was dark, this one blonde, like you. I think they're testing my dedication to you."

"Why?"

The look in his eyes . . . Tara couldn't ever remember being so chilled by anything.

"Back when I talked to Owen the first time and he told me I could work on the computer, he mentioned that you couldn't leave, that you wouldn't be happy anywhere else. I didn't put much stock in it then, figured it was just the kind of narcissistic nonsense you get from these guys. But the news from Ethan about the suicides . . . I'm getting a very bad vibe. I think they want to be sure that as long as you can't go any-where, I won't, either."

"So they test your commitment by sending hot chicks to try to seduce you?" *Try not to sound so pathetic, Tara Jean.*

"I didn't say they were hot."

"Wouldn't be much of a test if they weren't."

He shrugged. "Honestly, I didn't notice. I was too busy trying to figure out why they were there, what was the right reaction to have."

At that, she laughed. "You know, I believe you."

"Why should I look at another woman when you're right here?" he asked. And her foolish heart had trembled.

And now they were to be united, whatever that meant in Chosen terms. Tonight their walk would not end with him kissing her good night in front of an audience at her bunk-house. Tonight they would share a bed.

She shivered. When they'd been in the infirmary, she'd slept against him, entwined with him, but she'd been so tired, so weak, that she hadn't had the energy for nerves. She'd needed the comfort of his strength so badly after the isola-tion cell. This would be different. Entirely.

At last the sermon ended and Owen gestured for her and Jake to come to the stage. They climbed the four stairs together and stood beside him, hand in hand.

"Unity of all kinds is our strength, our bulwark against those who would defeat us, trample us down, and force us into the world of the Outsiders. Just as our earthly community mimics the perfection of the community of the Powers, so our terrestrial unions bear shadowy witness to the pure love of the Powers.

"Today, Serena and Jake are to be united, their bond with each other blessed by the Powers. This does not lessen their bond with the rest of you, as so often happens to couples in the Outside; it merely indicates that they have moved to a new stage of life.

"Serena, Jake, you will be moving into the empty side of the house shared by Caleb and Bea. They will show you where it is."

Caleb and Bea. Kevin Reasoner, the DEA agent, and his girlfriend. Coincidence, because half their house was empty, or was it another test? Did Owen know about Kevin? Kevin had been "given" Bea. Was she there to watch him, and to watch them, too?

And then it was over. Owen put his hands on their shoulders, turned them to face each other and then out to the crowd. He gave them a little shove forward toward "their new lives as one."

Not so different from a traditional wedding, though without the kissing. And thank whatever powers there were for that, because kissing Jake always took her places she had no desire to go in front of a crowd.

Kevin and Bea came up to the stage and offered to help them move their things to the cabin.

"I usually quilt on Sundays," Bea said. She was a petite blonde whose hard, round, pregnancy belly looked as if she'd stuffed a basketball up her shirt.

"When are you due?" asked Tara.

"Oh, not for another month. I can't wait, though. I feel so restricted. Just wait and see. It's enough to drive you mad, not being able to move right."

"Won't you mind giving your baby up? That's the part that scares me. That the baby just becomes part of the community."

"Oh no. I'll still see him. And he'll have so much more opportunity as a member of the community than he would as the child of just one parent. All the children are raised that way, so it's a tremendous benefit. Even the Leader's children don't get special treatment. He decided that based on his own experiences. Because he was sent away, singled out as a child. When he came back, he said he would never do that to his own child, that he would want his offspring raised as part of the community, too."

Bile rose in the back of Tara's throat and she swallowed it down.

"So is your baby one of the Leader's children?"

A frown crossed Bea's face. "No ... I'm not—Jonas is the baby's father. It was just a night of ... you know ... fun."

Sure didn't sound fun. In fact, it didn't sound as if Bea particularly remembered it, which set every nerve in Tara's body on fire. She'd been drugged in the isolation cell; what other drugs were they using here?

She patted Bea's back, feeling the bones shift beneath her hand as she flinched slightly. "We all have nights like that. But it looks as if you're doing better now, if you and Caleb are a couple. He seems like a good man."

"Oh, he is." She nodded rapidly. "He's amazing. So kind and understanding and helpful. I couldn't believe my luck when he chose me and the Leader blessed our union. And your Jacob seems much like him. I am sure you'll be very happy together."

They arrived at Tara's bunk and collected her belongings. Tara didn't have much experience with pregnant women, and she was pretty sure if she allowed Bea to carry more than a toothbrush and a T-shirt, the woman would pop.

They arrived at the new bunk just after Jake and Caleb. Jake had brought his trunk from the bunkhouse and sat it by the door. In the women's bunks, they had industrial-size chests of drawers, so Tara had been forced to bring her few possessions loose. When she arrived, Jake opened the trunk so she could put her things in with his. It felt . . . intimate.

"I'll put the toothbrush in the bathroom," Bea said, disappearing through a door.

"Help me move the bed," Jake said to Tara. "You know I can't sleep with my feet facing the door."

Caleb raised his eyebrows. "What?"

"Oh, it's this ridiculous superstition he has," Tara explained, just as they'd practiced on their walk. Wherever the bed was when they got into the house, Jake was going to insist on moving it. And Tara would find a reason. "Some stupid thing about how if the bed is set so your feet face the door, you'll die quickly and they'll carry you out in it."

"We can just put it up against that other wall," Jake suggested. "No problem."

"Well, yeah, it's a problem, because the bed's bolted down," Caleb said.

"Bolted down?" Jake's eyes flicked from the bed to the ceiling and back to the bed. "I am going to go talk to the Leader."

"It doesn't work like that," Kevin said. "You can't just 'go talk to the Leader.' You have to make an appointment."

"Well, then, I'll find one of his guys. I saw Jonas the other night, and he said there's always someone around if I need to talk, and I do."

Tara saw Bea flinch at Jonas's name and held back her rage by sheer force of will. When they brought down the Chosen, she was going to take special pleasure in destroying him.

Jake stalked out, and they followed him.

"Bea, honey, why don't you go find your quilting friends," Caleb said gently. "I think Jacob and Serena can settle in well enough from here. And they probably want some time alone, anyway."

"Would that be okay with you?" asked Bea.

"Of course! Maybe some week, you can teach me to quilt. I'm not a very good stitcher, but I would love to learn."

Bea's face lit up. "I certainly will. It's easy once you get the hang of it. And very satisfying to make new quilts out of what would otherwise be nothing more than rags." She hurried away toward the dining hall.

Jake, too, was speeding along, his long legs making quick work of the distance between the cabin and the main house, but Tara held Caleb back. "Let him go. He'll be fine. He'll talk it out. It's his way.

You should go on and do whatever you usually do on Sundays, too. I'll wait for Jacob."

"Are you sure?"

"Positive."

She watched Caleb take off toward a barn where they kept carpentry tools, then turned and reentered the cabin. She lay on the bed and closed her eyes, pretending a complete lack of concern, when in fact every muscle remained almost painfully tense.

AT THE FRONT door to the main house, Jake was stopped by two men who were standing as sentries. He'd never spoken with them, though he'd seen them eating at a separate table with others of their ilk: big muscles, suspicious eyes. Former military or mercenaries. More of the hired help.

"Where do you think you're going?" asked Muscles One.

"To speak to the Leader."

"Not without an appointment," said Muscles Two.

"Then get me an appointment."

"Talk to Samuel or Aaron," said Muscles One.

"Fine. Where are they?"

Muscles Two shrugged. "Around."

The door behind them opened and Samuel appeared. "What's going on?" The muscles twins didn't precisely salute, but Jake had a pretty good idea who they answered to.

"Man says he needs to speak to the Leader," said Muscles One.

"I'll handle it. Jacob, come in. Let's talk."

Jake followed Samuel across the main hall and back into the office where he'd met with Owen originally. This time, it was Samuel who sat across the desk. Owen was nowhere to be seen.

"So what's the problem? I would have thought you'd be enjoying yourself with your girlfriend."

"You know my background. You know what I do—did—all day before I came here. I spent eighteen hours out of every twenty-four online. Which means that I saw more than my fair share of Internet porn. So I am sorry if my brain's not been purified to the point where I can consider a bolted down bed anything but positioned for a camera."

Samuel placed his palms flat on the desk and rose to lean

heavily on them so he loomed over Jake. "You are accusing the Chosen, the *Leader*, of making sex tapes?"

"I'm not accusing anyone. The Leader knew when he brought me in that my mind didn't work the way other people's does all the time. Maybe it's not about sex tapes. Maybe it's about control. I don't know. But I don't want Serena to see anything like that. She believes a lot more than I do. So I am going to take her for a nice, long walk this afternoon, and when we get back I am going to climb up on that bed and check every nook and cranny for video. I wanted to give you a heads-up so you could get rid of anything that might be there before she saw it and decided you weren't what she thought you were."

"You are free to leave. You know that. If you don't like it here, if you don't trust us . . ."

"This is my punishment. I fucked up in the outside world. I cheated on her. I can't leave until she's ready to, and I have no intention of having her lose faith in her own judgment again the way she lost it when I screwed her over. She doesn't deserve it. So, yeah, I'd like her to see me find a camera because then we could just leave, but it would destroy her. She's fragile, doesn't believe in herself. I'd rather she just outgrew the need to be here, and I am content to give her time to do that."

Samuel nodded. "And if she never wants to leave? Most people don't. And if they do, they come back. Part of what they like here is the stability. That's why the bed is bolted down. We don't allow personalization in the houses. That leads to discontent, the perception of inequality.

"But you take your girlfriend for that walk. Figure things out. You haven't been here long, so it is to be expected that our ways still seem strange to you. I think the women plan to do a "welcoming surprise" anyway. They usually do, but I don't know whether they've had time to put anything together yet, given how quickly the two of you got to your bonding ceremony."

"Sounds like a plan," said Jake.

He took his time heading back to the cabin, stopping to talk to various groups of people out enjoying the cool weather and sunshine.

When he arrived back at the cabin, Tara was lying on the bed, eyes closed. He knew she was awake, could feel her tension, but to anyone else she would appear utterly relaxed.

"Hey, babe," he said. "It's beautiful out. Let's go for a walk."

"Did you talk to the Leader? Ask him about the bed?"

"No, but I chatted with Samuel. I think what we can do is maybe make up the bed backward, just so our feet are against the wall. Would that be okay with you?"

"Of course. You know I only want to make you happy."

"I know." He pulled her into his arms. "I love you, baby." He bent his head and took her mouth. She rose to her toes and wrapped her arms around his neck, opening to him so sweetly he had to remind himself three times of the damned cameras in order to stop from pulling her down on the bed and taking everything she offered.

"Walk," he groaned at last. "Let's go for that walk."

Instead of letting him go, however, Tara tucked her head beneath his chin and clung for a long moment. Could she possibly be as affected as he by their kiss? He let his hands wander just a little, up and down her spine, feeling knotted muscles and taught tendons. He slid his fingers through her soft curls and massaged her scalp for a minute, and her moan nearly undid him there and then.

Sucking in a deep breath to firm up his resolve, he stepped

away. But he couldn't let the connection go entirely, so he took her hand. He'd become accustomed to the sensation of her small palm resting against his over the past few days, and now it felt . . . right.

⌒

I love you, baby. What she wouldn't give to hear those words for real. But she followed Jake out into warm afternoon sun without, she hoped, giving away her thoughts. She'd taken the kiss as far as she reasonably could, using the excuse that there might be cameras. When they returned from this walk, video surveillance would be over, and there would be no reason for Jake to treat her like a lover in private.

At least there was only one bed. She'd discovered in the infirmary that she liked sleeping with Jake. The logical part of her brain was certain the security she felt wrapped in his arms was an illusion, that neither of them would be safe as long as they were inside the Chosen's territory, but some base, chemical part of her refused to recognize that truth, simply shut it out the minute his body curled around hers.

Jake hadn't found anything in the drying sheds or at the greenhouses, which left the odd storage buildings at the far edge of the property to search, assuming Kevin hadn't discovered anything. Between them, they'd covered almost the entire compound and were still no closer to finding out how or why Andrea had died. Maybe she should just give up. Nothing about the way Owen and his pals behaved seemed right to her, but intuition could take her only so far. Keeping the investigation going, putting Jake in danger without any real evidence, was unfair.

Of course, there was the creepy thing Owen had intimated about her not being happy if she left. She shivered, and Jake dropped her hand to slide an arm across her shoulders. Pulling her close, he pressed a kiss to her temple.

"You okay?" he murmured in her ear, and she nodded.

Other people were clustered into small groups here and there, taking advantage of the free time to socialize, even to flirt. Tara pointed out David, the man who'd returned after leaving the Chosen, and she and Jake circulated among the various groups until they could approach him without being obvious. He was standing with Aurora and Mary, so Tara let them make the introductions.

"You left for a while, right?" Jake asked.

"Yeah." The man shifted, his eyes quickly surveying the area. They lit for a minute on Jonas and Joy, who stood talking a few yards away.

"What made you come back?"

David shrugged. "Wasn't much out there. I thought I'd be happier. I was wrong."

"Was it hard? Coming back?" Tara did her best to keep the question from sounding too desperate.

"That trip to the desert with Aaron, yeah, it pretty much sucked."

"What did you see? I mean, did you commune with the Powers? Did they touch you?" Aurora's innocent face lit with curiosity.

"Touch me?" His laugh was bitter. "I guess you could call it that. Felt more like a whipping. I thought I might die out there. With the fasting and the drinking of the herbs. But I came back. And when I did, I felt better again. More like myself than I had after I left."

"Harsh," Jake observed.

"Yeah. I guess the message is that you don't turn your back on the Powers."

"Why would you want to?" asked Aurora, just as Jonas and Joy sauntered up to their little group.

"I guess I felt like I needed a change. But it's out of my system now." His eyes flicked to Joy and then to Jonas.

"Lives change," Joy said placidly. "People grow and in the peace of our community they sometimes forget how little the Outside has to offer. They think there was some lack in themselves that has now been cured and they can be happy Outside. It doesn't take too long for them to remember why they prefer living here." She tucked a few loose strands of her salt-and-pepper hair back behind her ears.

"Have you ever tried leaving to see whether it suited you?" Jake asked her.

"I had my time Away. Once I came here, I knew I'd found my place."

"But you've been here how long?"

"Twenty-eight years."

"So you were just a kid. Aren't you even curious about what the world looks like now? So much has changed."

"I get what I want right here. I don't need to look outward. You will see. You just need to let yourself adjust."

"I suppose. I admit, it seems foreign to me. Not even to go into town for a day or two at a time."

"I've sold flowers at the market. Gone in to buy supplies. It's not as if I am unaware of how things are done Outside, but I would not want to live there."

"Well, that makes sense."

"I told you, Jacob," Tara said. "You just need to give it some time."

He looked down at her, his gray eyes hooded and lazy.

"You know I'd do anything for you, baby. You just gotta let me move at my own pace."

"I will. I promise."

"Having each other will make the transition smoother," Joy said. "Serena is well adjusted to the Chosen. She visited with Pearl before signing up herself, and she's lived among us for more than a month, so she can help you with any issues that may arise." She cocked her head and looked at him as one might an odd, inexplicable animal. "But you cannot let the Fear drilled into you Outside ruin your life among the Chosen. We know what is out there; we just don't let the fear of it oppress us."

"I know the bad stuff, but there's some good stuff, too. Don't you miss . . . I don't know . . . chocolate?"

"For the first few weeks it's hard. After that, you don't even notice. What do you miss most, Jacob?"

"Computers. I mean real ones, not like building websites, which is nice, but the rush of beating a game that's been programmed to beat me. Solving the final puzzle and gaining the treasure, beating the speediest guy on the track and taking home the trophy. That kind of thing."

"And it doesn't bother you that none of those things are real? The treasure, the trophy?"

He flashed a grin that—even though it wasn't aimed in her direction—weakened Tara's knees.

"Nah. I just like to win. I don't care about the prize."

"You're not in competition with anyone here," Jonas said. "The Chosen work together. In harmony."

Except when they don't. Tara desperately wanted to punch him. Jake must have felt her tension, because his thumb began making slow, lazy circles on her neck.

"Well, right now, I figure I'm in competition with

everyone else in the world trying to sell organic products like ours. It gives me a goal—to make our website so rocking that keeping up with the orders will be tough.

"And speaking of that, do you guys have a camera? We need to get better product photographs as well as some shots of the greenhouses and the orchards and stuff. People *love* to see how things they are considering buying are made. Plus we should really start a blog. You know, "what's happening in the gardens of the Chosen" or the like that would have weekly pictures of what was coming up, what was being harvested, things like that. Keep people coming back."

"I believe there is one in the Leader's office," said Jonas. "I'll ask him whether you can use it to improve the website."

"I have a pretty good one on my cell phone," Jake said. "If he doesn't want me to use the one from his office. But I gave that up when I came here, so you guys would have to dig it out."

"All cell phones are donated out for recycling," Jonas said.

"Oh. Then the camera it is." Jake shrugged, but Tara didn't believe his casual response any more than she believed the cell phones turned in by all who took the oath of the Chosen were sent out of the compound. Certainly not without being thoroughly mined for any and all information first.

"There is one other thing I miss," Jake said, tugging Tara even closer. "And if you don't mind, I think my new bride and I are going to go remind ourselves what it is."

Tara felt her face flame, but it was obviously the right thing to say, as the others virtually pushed them away.

WHEN THEY RETURNED to their cabin, Jake proceeded to climb on the bed and search for cameras while Tara harassed him about his paranoia.

"The government has drones the size of cockroaches. You don't know who might be spying on us," he said, poking into a shadowy corner. He came away with spider webs on his fingers and grimaced.

"The government isn't interested in you anymore, if they ever were. You're a member of the Chosen. They don't even know where you are." She was about to launch into the part of the script where she extolled the virtues of the community over life Outside when she heard a sound from the bathroom. Without considering the consequences, she wrenched the door open.

On the floor, Bea sat curled into a ball, her arms around her knees, rocking slightly.

"Bea! What's the matter?" Tara looked over her shoulder. "Get Caleb." Jake took off and Tara lowered herself carefully to the floor beside Bea, making no quick moves that might startle the girl. "Is it the baby?"

A shudder rippled through Bea's body, but she shook her head.

They hadn't checked the bathroom for listening devices, so Tara got up and turned on the shower full hot. Steam would also cloak any cameras in the room, though she sincerely hoped Owen hadn't stooped so low as to put them in the bathrooms.

"You need to get warm," she said loudly. "Breathe in the steam slowly and see if it helps."

Moments later, Jake and Kevin burst in. Kevin dropped to the floor immediately and took Bea into his arms. "Hey, now," he said gently. "What's this?"

Bea shook her head.

Tara leaned close. "With the shower going, no one outside this room will know what you say. You're safe here, with us."

"They always know," Bea whispered. "They know everything." She stared at the shower, then fixed her gaze on Tara. "You should get out. Now." She looked up at Kevin. "All three of you. You're good people. You don't belong here."

"You're a good person, too," Kevin assured her.

"You don't know what I've done."

"What you've done—what you've been made to do—isn't who you are," Tara assured her.

"It doesn't matter." Fat tears rolled down Bea's pale cheeks. "I can't ever leave."

"Why not, honey?" Kevin stroked Bea's hair, wiping it away from her face.

"He filmed it." Bea's voice was tiny, so frail and far away it took a minute for her words to penetrate, but when they did, Tara's stomach revolted and a rush of pure rage sliced through her. "He put it on the Internet. Millions of people have seen it."

"None of that matters," Kevin said. His tone was gentle, but in his eyes Tara saw fury warring with devastation. Clearly, he cared for the woman the Leader had "given" him. "If you're scared of people recognizing you, you can get plastic surgery. A little change here, a little change there, and no one will ever know you're the same person."

"That's expensive. If I left, I'd have no money, nothing. I'd be alone. I wouldn't know where to start."

"You wouldn't be alone. And I have money. I'd get you the plastic surgery."

"Why?"

"I—"

Tara took pity on Kevin's inability to speak. Here, now,

wasn't the time to try to explain his feelings. Perhaps he hadn't even thought them through himself. "I wish we didn't need to ask this, to bring up something so painful again," she said to Bea, "but how do you know about the videotaping and the Internet? Did Jonas tell you?"

Bea looked from one to the other, searching each of their faces from the haven of Kevin's arms. Whatever she saw gave her the courage to tell her story.

"He came for me one Sunday. Said he wanted a quilt for his room and would I come look at the bed, the decorations? I shouldn't have gone. He always made me feel strange. But he's one of the favorites of the Leader, one of the apostles. When we went to his house, he offered me a cup of tea."

Bea paused and Kevin pressed a kiss to the top of her head.

Behind Tara's back, Jake shifted position slightly so he could take her hand. Tara twined their fingers together and held on.

"I don't remember anything after that until I woke up n-naked in his b-bed." Tears dripped steadily down Bea's face, but lost in the past she didn't notice them. "He had a l-lap-top. And he showed me the s-site. Where men paid to watch me. There were c-close-ups of my f-face. I was d-doing th-things . . ." She broke down completely, and Kevin rocked her and stroked her hair and murmured in her ear.

"So you s-see," she said when she'd regained a modicum of control, "it wasn't exactly rape. I did those things."

"It *was* rape," Kevin growled. "Exactly. Precisely. And that rat fuck bastard will pay for it."

But Bea wasn't hearing him. "And you don't have to stay with me," she said. "I'll understand if you want me to go."

Tara watched Kevin's biceps bunch beneath his T-shirt as he held Bea in place. Simultaneously, she felt Jake squeeze her hand.

"Do you want to leave me, sweetheart?" Kevin asked.

"No, but—"

"I think we get along pretty well."

"But we haven't even—"

"Plenty of time for that. I wouldn't expect you to be interested living here where you have to see that rat fuck every day."

"Bea," Tara jumped in before Kevin's understandable fury could lead them off track, "can you tell us how you came to join the Chosen, and about your life here before?"

"And your real name," Kevin added. "I don't want to think of you with the name these assholes assigned you."

Was that why Jake never referred to her as Serena? "Baby," "babe," "sweetheart"; always endearments, never a name.

"Elizabeth," Bea said. "Elizabeth Addison. My mother called me Lizzie. There was only ever me and her. I never knew my father. She got sick—breast cancer—and I dropped out of college my sophomore year to take care of her. It took her three years to die, but she did despite the fact that I used every penny we had to try to keep her alive. So I was alone, broke, and without any skills or a degree.

"I heard about the Chosen in a grief support group. A guy was considering coming out here because he thought being closer to the land might help him heal, but he was afraid it was just running from his grief rather than dealing with it. But he had ties I didn't—a job, a family—so I didn't care whether it was just running or not; I took off the next day and hitched out here.

"It was hard at first, but I adjusted. And I did feel better, I missed my mother, but the pain seemed . . . distant, less pressing, I guess is the best way to describe it. Not so all-consuming. I felt secure for the first time since she got sick. And then . . ."

"And then Jonas raped you and took it all away." There was murder in Kevin's voice.

"Elizabeth, was the video the only reason you stayed?" Jake asked.

"What the fuck kind of question is that!" Kevin half turned his body as if to protect Elizabeth from Jake.

"Chill!" Jake hissed. "And keep your damned voice down. We're all on the same side here." He raised his voice. "I know pregnancy is a personal thing, but it's not like I'm asking about your sex life." He paused, then returned to his careful whisper. "Look, something more than threats is keeping people here, and killing them when they leave. Your partner wasn't the only one."

"Partner?" Elizabeth's head came up and she looked around, her tear-filled gaze coming to rest on Tara. "You're police?"

"Law enforcement," Jake confirmed. "Different branches."

"No wonder," Elizabeth breathed.

"No wonder?"

"This afternoon, when you were out, the Leader called me into his office. I was so scared. You asked me why I stayed. Well, there was the video. But I was also just kind of dead inside. I didn't do chores or anything for days. Didn't even eat or drink, just huddled into a ball in my bunk. But Deborah, who runs the infirmary, kept after me with soup and tea and vitamins. Day in and day out, soup and tea and vitamins. And eventually it seemed like escape or even suicide was more effort that it was worth, more effort than just getting back to work. After all, work had saved me before.

"And then, when I found out I was pregnant—" She sat up straighter and squared her shoulders. "Well, then I did try to kill myself. I stole a knife from the dining hall and tried to cut my wrists. But one of my bunkmates found me in the bathroom, and Deborah bandaged me up and it all started again. Soup and tea and vitamins. Because," her lips twisted bitterly, "*I might not matter, but children are 'blessings of the Powers,'* and I couldn't damage myself without damaging that baby.

"I was in the infirmary for almost a month, and I was never left alone. Not ever. Eventually, the numbness came back, and I just went back to doing what I was told. It was easier than fighting."

She looked up at Kevin. "And then they gave me to you. And I was terrified. But it was the best thing that ever happened to me." She frowned. "Why did they do that?"

"At a guess," Jake said, "to separate you from the rest of the group in case you said anything about what had happened to you. You'd be less likely to confide in a man."

"Especially me," Kevin agreed. He held out his arm, and Tara noticed a crude tattoo drawn inside his forearm. " My cover. Two years for domestic assault. When I came here, I wouldn't give them a name, wouldn't tell them anything about myself, but I left enough information for them to find it out if they wanted to. Apparently, they did."

Elizabeth nodded. "For the past, I don't know, month or so, I've been feeling pretty good again. But when the Leader called me into his office, all the stuff I'd managed to push away came back. We sat there in his office drinking tea, and he said—" she shuddered. "He asked me whether I liked living with you."

"And do you?" Kevin asked.

Elizabeth nodded again. "And he said he didn't like to dissolve unions, but that another man had expressed an interest in me."

"Jonas," Kevin growled.

"He didn't say, but I knew who he meant. He told me this other man might be a better fit for me because he—the Leader—wasn't sure I'd truly devoted myself to the will of the Powers as I should, and that I might need a man more established in his service than you are. Or I could prove my dedication and stay here, with you."

"What did he want you to do?" asked Jake.

"I am supposed to keep an eye on you two. He didn't think your purification had taken. I'm supposed to befriend Serena, teach her to quilt, that sort of thing. Try to listen in on your conversations. Be sure you are truly dedicated to the Powers and the Chosen."

"Spy on us." Tara's mouth tasted sour. At least it meant Owen had probably removed electronic bugs from their bedroom—if he had those, he wouldn't need human ears.

"I didn't want to, but—"

A knock at the door of Jake and Tara's side cut her off. Jake pressed a finger to his lips and went to answer it.

CHAPTER SEVEN

Jake swung open the door, prepared to shove whoever was outside away with an excuse that he and Tara were settling in, only to find Samuel waiting for him. *Shit.* Clearly, Owen was already suspicious of them, but Jake couldn't see what they might have done differently if they hoped to gain any kind of traction in the investigation.

"Samuel," he said with a nod. "How can I help you?"

"I just stopped by to be sure you didn't find any hidden cameras in your new home." A decided smirk crossed the man's face as he stepped inside without invitation. His eyes went to the bathroom door. "What in the name of the Powers? Are you trying to turn this place into a sauna? That's an inappropriate use of our resources!"

He stomped to the bathroom and pushed the door wide. Tara looked up at him from the floor. "Bea wasn't feeling well," she said calmly, and Jake felt a surge of completely unwarranted pride. *God, she's good. Strong, smart, beautiful.*

"We thought the steam might help her feel better," Kevin added.

"You're sick, Bea?"

"Yes. No. I c-can still do what is needed of me."

Samuel leaned in and shut off the shower. "Perhaps you ought to come to the infirmary and let Deborah have a look at you."

"No! I mean, I'll be fine. I just need to lie down." Jake could see the panic in her eyes, and he felt an echo of it in himself.

She knew who they were. If Deborah got hold of her and plied her with drugs, it was all over.

Tara, bless her, completely ignored Samuel. "Let's get you into bed," she said to Bea. She and Kevin helped the woman to her feet and hustled her out the opposite door.

"Perhaps Deborah could come here," Jake suggested.

"I will ask her. Though her medicines are there."

Where were they getting the damned medicines, anyway? It had bothered Jake from the moment Deborah had brought antibiotics in the unlabeled container for Tara. Was some doctor in town on the payroll? Or were they importing from Mexico, where prescriptions were unnecessary?

"Look, Bea's just pregnant, for crying out loud. She probably doesn't need any medicine anyway. You know how pregnant chicks are. I'm surprised she didn't lose her lunch all over the bathroom."

Samuel pursed his lips and cocked his head. He stared for a long moment before nodding slightly and turning to go.

The minute he was out the door, Jake grabbed Tara and, with a brief nod to Kevin and Elizabeth, pulled her back into their room where he could be sure they would not be overheard. "We're going to need a plan," he said, keeping his voice low. He wanted to pace, but then he'd have to talk louder, and he just wasn't sure how deep Owen Stephenson's paranoia ran.

He scrubbed a hand through his hair. "We can't trust Bea. Now that she knows the truth, all they'd have to do is threaten her or drug her and we'd be blown."

He glanced down at Tara and saw that she'd wrapped her arms around her body and was shaking slightly. "Tara? Baby? What's wrong?"

"It's the tea."

"What do you mean?"

"When Elizabeth was depressed, she didn't eat or drink, and she got worse. Until they made her drink the tea, then she got better again."

"Well, yeah, but not just because of the tea. Calories, attention, all that factored in I'm sure."

"Listen to me, okay? People are allowed to leave, but when they do they get so depressed that they either come right back within a day or two or they kill themselves. No one survives out in the world."

"But men don't drink the tea."

"Unless they're leaving. The whole reason women aren't allowed to drink coffee is that caffeine supposedly muddles the mind and women are too easily confused. Men can handle it. But when one of the Chosen wishes to leave, the assumption is that he or she is confused, so before they go—which no one stops them from doing—there is a ritual. For a full day, they fast and drink tea and discuss their reasons for dissatisfaction with the way of life here with the Leader. Only the following day are they permitted to leave, provided they're still certain of their decision."

"Fuck." He wrapped his arms around her, tucking her against his chest, reassuring himself that she was there—solid, well—as his mind ticked through possibilities. "It fits with what Owen said about you never leaving. But what about the ones who come back? If the tea is a distribution method, and men come back, what do they do?"

"It must have something to do with the reintegration ceremony, the trip they take with Aaron in the desert."

"So there's an antidote, a way of losing the addiction, defying the withdrawal that causes the suicides. Has to be. But given that not everyone makes it back from that little ceremony, the antidote either doesn't always work or it's sometimes fatal."

He slid his hands up Tara's arms, over the taut tendons of her neck and into her hair. He tilted her head back so he could look directly into those bottomless blue eyes. "We're going to find it. We're going to get it. That's our plan. We bring these assholes down and we get you and all the rest of the women here off the damn drug."

"And if we can't?"

"We *will*."

"Jake . . ."

He couldn't think of anything to say, so he did the next best thing. He kissed her.

It was meant to be comfort, promise, assurance that he wouldn't let anything happen to her, but the minute his lips touched hers all such altruism went out the window. Her mouth opened beneath his, hot and sweet, and all he could think was *More*, followed quickly by *Mine*. She wound her arms around his neck, and he felt the press of her small, firm breasts against his chest, the heat of her skin through her clothes.

He tugged the elastic off her braid and combed his fingers through the pale silk of her hair. He'd fantasized about that wavy blonde fall more often than he should have. Right from the moment they'd met, when it had been considerably shorter than it was now, he'd imagined it spread out across his pillow, wrapped around his hands, tickling his cock.

He slid his hands down her back—feeling her ribs moving erratically with each ragged breath, her passion driving his own even higher—and cupped her ass. She made a small sound and pressed impossibly closer, spearing the fingers of one hand through his hair and gripping the strands so tightly it might have hurt if the rest of his body hadn't already been on fire.

And then she stepped back, drawing him with her, until they hit the bed. The movement gave his brain enough room for a single strand of coherent thought.

"Christ, sweetheart, tell me to stop."

In answer, she sat on the edge of the bed, tucked her fingers into the waistband of his jeans, and began to unbutton his fly.

"Oh, fuck, baby, you're going to kill me." He tipped her backwards, certain that if he remained standing with her head, her mouth, on level with his cock, he'd go off before he could get her naked. And that was unacceptable. He needed to see her, touch her, taste her everywhere.

<hr>

WHEN JAKE FOLLOWED her down onto the bed and slipped his hands beneath her T-shirt, Tara almost crowed in triumph. For a moment, she'd thought he might balk, and her heart had dropped into her stomach. But from her position, his erection was unmistakable. He wanted her. *Her*. It was mind-boggling, and gave her the strength to push on when she might otherwise have chickened out. She'd heard her own death in Elizabeth's words that afternoon, and she wasn't going down without finding out what it was like to have Jake as a lover.

His long legs tangled with hers, frustrating her attempts to open his jeans.

"Slow down, sweetheart," he said when she tried to wedge her hand between them, "we have all night."

"Only until the dinner horn." And what time was it anyway? How long *did* they have?

"Fuck dinner." Jake's eyes went storm-gray with desire. "The only thing on my menu tonight is you."

A wave of pure heat shot through her, and she couldn't prevent the little mew that escaped. The left side of his mouth kicked up in a ridiculously sexy grin.

"You like that idea, do you?"

"Yes," she squeaked.

"Excellent." In a quick, smooth move, he divested her of her tee, leaving her exposed to his sight in her well-worn cotton bra. But if his low groan was anything to go by, he didn't care about the state of her lingerie or even that her breasts only barely filled the B cups. He ran a reverent finger along the picot trim of the cotton, following almost immediately with his tongue. Her whole body trembled, and he lifted his head and stared down at her.

"You are so goddamned beautiful," he whispered. "From the moment I saw you, I imagined you this way."

"You did?" Was he still acting? They'd swept the room thoroughly for bugs.

"Lucy told me to stay the hell away, but I couldn't. I can't."

The pain of that statement pierced the sensual fog surrounding her. "She knew I would be bad for you." She'd tried to help Lucy, and Lucy had almost died. She'd tried to help Andrea, and Andrea *had* died. And now she'd pulled Jake into the cesspit of the Chosen. She *was* bad news. She just hadn't realized that one of the few women she considered a friend knew it, too.

"You're joking, right?" Jake propped himself up on his hands waited in silence until she met his eyes. "It wasn't me she was worried about. She loves you and wanted to be sure

I didn't hurt you. I don't have a good track record, and you deserved better than a one-night stand." He lowered himself over her, biceps bunching, and pressed a kiss to her forehead. "You still do. So I promise you right now, we're getting out of this place and we're getting you well."

Tara wasn't going to argue. Not tonight. She reached up and pulled him down so his full weight rested on her, and he caught his lips with her own. He sank into the kiss, running his hands over her body, every touch setting fire to her skin.

His kisses stole her breath. Deft fingers unsnapped the front clasp of her bra, and the cooling air slid over her skin. He lifted her slightly to slide the garment off entirely, and Tara took the opportunity to grasp the hem of his tee and pull it over his head. Hot. The man was bone-melting, blood-boiling hot. Wide shoulders heavy with muscle, a broad chest sprinkled with crisp, golden hairs tapering to a narrow waist, not an ounce of fat anywhere. Just sleek, sinuous seduction, like a giant jungle cat. And she was his prey.

He didn't give her much time to admire, however, as he ducked his head and swept a stubbled cheek across one of her nipples, sending a streak of pleasure and pain straight down to her core. The next moment his tongue soothed the same pathway. She gripped his hair in her fists, trying to pull him up to meet her mouth, but he pried her fingers loose and continued his exploration of her breasts. How had she never known they were so sensitive? Every caress of his fingers, swipe of his tongue, scrape of his teeth set her to squirming beneath him.

"Please," she sobbed. "Jake . . ."

"Off," he said, rolling them over so she sat atop him, his fingers going to work on the fly of her jeans. She scrambled out of them, pulling off her soaked panties at the same time, but he made no move to remove his own, so she tugged at them.

"Your turn."

"Baby, I can't."

"Can't?"

He groaned. "No protection. Just let me—"

She laid a hand across his mouth. "Three little letters, Jake: *I. U. D.* And I'm healthy if you are."

His eyes blazed hot and dark, pupils expanding so only a tiny rim of color remained, and he yanked her down onto the bed with him. Once again he reversed their positions, this time wedging a leg between her thighs as his hands swept over her, memorizing.

"Are you sure? Be sure, sweetheart."

She slid her hands down the back of his jeans, pulling him harder against her, grinding her body against his. The rough denim against her tender skin had its own appeal, but she was done waiting, done with foreplay.

"Positive," she said.

In a minute, he'd shucked jeans, underwear, and socks, and stood before her fully naked and perfect as any man she'd ever seen. Ever imagined. This time when he joined her on the bed, he lay beside her, propped up on an elbow, and ran a long finger down her body from the hollow of her collarbone to just below her bellybutton. Back and forth, back and forth, as if they had all the time in the world, in direct contrast to the urgency she felt, the urgency she saw mimicked in the thrust of his erection.

She reached for him, tried to pull him over her, but he held himself away.

"Just let me look for a minute, baby. I need . . . a bit of control . . . or things are going to be over way too soon."

But she couldn't resist touching him, leaning up to sweep her hands over that chest and feel the tiny, springy hairs and the smooth skin beneath. She pressed her mouth to one flat nipple, and he groaned.

His hand cupped her hip and his thumb slid into the crease of her thigh. Reflexively, her muscles tightened. He used the grip to flatten her once more onto her back while he bent to press a hot, open-mouthed kiss on her belly, then lower, teasing, tempting, brushing against the curls covering her core with the bristles of his chin.

And then his tongue found her center, where she was hot and wet and ready. She cried out before she remembered that they were not entirely alone in the cabin and pressed her lips together.

Jake grabbed her ankles and bent her knees so her feet rested flat on the bed and she was completely open, completely exposed to him. He tasted her again, light, repetitive strokes of his tongue like a cat licking cream, but it wasn't enough and she squirmed beneath him, her body begging for more.

And he gave it to her, sliding first one finger, then two inside as he suckled her. His fingers curved up and slid across a spot she'd never found on her own, a spot that sent shivers of reaction out through her nerves and had her thrusting against his hand. And when his teeth scraped oh-so-gently over her throbbing clit, an orgasm like nothing she'd ever felt ripped through her, and she buried her face in the pillow beside her to muffle the scream she could not prevent.

She was mortified, but he didn't seem to mind at all. He licked and sucked his way up her body, stopping to pay full attention to each breast in turn before meeting her lips. She could taste herself on his tongue, the sour-sweetness undeniably erotic. It was not her first experience with oral sex, but it was the first time a man had brought her to climax with nothing more than his mouth and his hands.

"You doing okay?" he asked, grinning at her with that lopsided grin that was both boyishly endearing and dead sexy.

She reached down and slid her fingers over the smooth, velvety skin of his cock and watched the grin disappear. His mouth came back down on hers and in a single long glide, he was inside her.

"Oh God." She locked her ankles behind his waist and shuddered helplessly against him.

"Hang on, sweetheart." He sucked the lobe of her ear, blew on it gently. "This is going to be fast. I apologize for that."

But he'd already been talking too long for her. She was ready, more than ready to fly again. She dug her heels into his back, urging him deeper, and he obliged. She could feel his tension mount, feel the throbbing of his cock deep inside her, the racing of her own heart. Each thrust drove her higher, higher, until she felt him stiffen and his thumb found her clit, and she bit down on his shoulder to stop from crying out as she went over the precipice.

He collapsed on top of her, his arms sliding around her back as he tipped them both to the side so he lay facing her.

"Holy hell," he said after a minute.

A giggle bubbled up. She buried her head against his chest to keep it down, but it refused to be contained.

"Hey," he protested. "Are you laughing at me? After you bit me and everything?"

"No, I'm just . . ." *Happy*. And wasn't that a ridiculous thing, given the situation? For just a few minutes, she'd forgotten everything but the sheer pleasure of being with Jake. The giggles disappeared, but the strange contentment did not. Jake stroked her hair without speaking, and her eyelids grew heavier and heavier. Eventually, she fell asleep, still locked in his arms.

A TAPPING SOUND BROUGHT Jake out of the half sleep he'd fallen into. Easing Tara's warm body away from his own, he slipped from the bed and opened the bathroom door to reveal Kevin.

"Walk?" the man mouthed, jerking his head outside. Jake held up his fingers, signifying that he would wait ten minutes after Kevin left to take off himself in case anyone was watching.

When he got outside, Kevin was shadowboxing in the cool night air.

"'Sup," Jake asked for the listeners. "Heard you leave. Didn't figure you for a nightwalker."

"Bea is becoming difficult. Disobedient."

"Really? She hardly seems the type."

"A dog can't serve two masters." Jesus. The guy was pushing his abuser role hard. "I told her to stay home and sleep tonight, but she insisted that the Leader would not want her skipping dinner. If she's gonna be mine, she's gonna be *mine*."

"Well, I hear that, but you knew when you signed on that everyone in here does what the Leader tells them to."

"Well maybe I'm sick of it. Maybe it's time to for me to take her and leave."

Jake began to walk, a meandering path that took them away from likely spots for listening devices. "Do what you've go to, I guess. Hey, you want to pick up the pace for a bit? Sweat off some energy?"

"Sure." They set off at a jog, out in the open, in the dark, shadowed spaces between the lamp poles, spaces where it would be difficult to install any kind of device. Jake filled in Kevin on what he and Tara had discovered. "So when you get out," he said, "don't do the exit ceremony. Pitch a fit and leave. And get Elizabeth to medical help ASAP."

"You should come, too. Once they hear my debrief, the feds will be all over Owen Stephenson like white on rice. This place is coming down."

"I can't. If we all go at once, they'll close up shop. You have to figure they have some kind of exit strategy, and we can't trigger it or we won't have any chance of getting the antidote. And we need it. We also need to know what kind of distribution network they're setting up. No one goes to all this trouble to keep the women in their little kingdom compliant. They have bigger plans, which means plenty of outside assistance. If the dealers have access to a running supply, we'll have to shut it down. So we need a few days to hack their computers, find the formulas. I'll start with Jonas. We know from Elizabeth's story that he's connected to the outside world."

"I'll stall them as long as I can. Everyone's gonna want a piece anyway—FBI, DEA, ATF—and alphabet soup always takes a while to make. The only issue might be if they mobilize a Joint Terrorism Task Force already in existence. That'd be quicker. But either way, I doubt I'll be able to hold them off longer than, say, Friday. In fact, I'd guess Friday after close of business. When the news day is over."

"That works. I don't want Tara ingesting that poison any longer than absolutely necessary anyway. When you get out, call Ethan Donovan. He and his fiancée are camped outside of town waiting for word. He can get messages to me. It's slow, but if there's something I need to know, tell him." He gave Kevin Ethan's cell number and the other man recited it back.

"So —" But before Jake could continue the conversation, a movement in the darkness signaled that they were no longer alone. Moments later, Samuel materialized.

"Out late this evening," he observed. "Any particular reason?"

"Nope," said Kevin, deliberately hostile. "What about you? Going to tell us to go back to bed like good little children?"

Samuel's eyes narrowed. "Is there a problem, Caleb?"

"And what if there is?"

"Then we will talk it out." But Samuel's hands tightened. He was more accustomed to using fists than words. Even Jake could see that much.

"Yeah, I'll think about that."

"The Leader wishes all the Chosen to be at peace. You should know that by now. You can bring any issue to him at any time." Samuel turned to Jake. "And you, Jacob? I would have thought you'd be at home this evening."

"Yeah, well, we went to bed early. Now I'm awake again, but she's asleep."

"You should return. Morning will be here soon enough. Caleb, I will make arrangements for you to speak with the Leader after breakfast."

Kevin grunted, and he and Jake began to walk back toward their shared cabin.

"Jacob," Samuel called. "A moment." Jake stopped and watched Kevin disappear into the night. When he was gone, Samuel spoke. "Did he confide his concerns to you?"

As if you don't know. Samuel hadn't approached until they were out of range of listening devices.

Jake had no doubt he'd heard every work of their early

conversation. He shrugged. "Not like we're best buds. He's having problems with Bea. He'll get over it or he won't."

"That's what he said? Problems in his relationship?"

"I don't recall his exact words. Something like that. I don't really feel right about talking about it behind his back, y'know? He and the Leader will work it out in the morning." Loyalty, reluctance, just enough information so they wouldn't believe he was shutting them out altogether.

Samuel nodded. "Just so. Thank you for your insight. Now, I am sure Serena would not wish to wake and find you gone."

"Oh, she's used to my midnight walkabouts," Jake said, "but I take your point." With a jerk of his head, he jogged off toward the cabin.

When he slipped inside he found that Tara had, indeed, wakened in his absence. Much to his disappointment, she'd also pulled on a T-shirt and wrapped herself in the quilt. She sat on the bed, knees drawn up beneath her chin and, despite all he knew of her strength of both body and mind, in that moment she appeared incredibly frail to him. He kicked off his shoes and crawled up the bed on all fours to plant a smacking kiss on her lips. Then he drew her over on top of him as he lay down and settled her head into the hollow of his shoulder.

"I thought you'd still be asleep. I never meant for you to wake up alone."

"I'm fine. You went exploring?"

Of course she would understand why he'd left. Why, then, did her question feel almost like a rejection? He stroked her hair, smoothing the wild mess he'd made of it earlier as he answered.

"Kevin has a plan to get him and Elizabeth out tomorrow morning." He explained the idea. "But it means we're going to have to speed up our timetable. We only have until Friday. John was smart enough not to keep anything on the box I am using to update their site, but I've identified at least three other terminals on the network. I'm trying to get into them, but they're protected. I have a pretty good idea which box belongs to who, and I just need the time and freedom from oversight to install the cracker program I have sitting on the server Ethan and I use."

"It will give you access to the other computers?"

"More than that, it will copy their drives onto our server. The only problem would be if they're keeping the important stuff on a completely dumb box with no connection to the network at all. But even though that's the smartest way to operate, almost no one does it."

"How long will the transfer take once you've installed the software?"

"Depends on how much data there is. But they're running a pretty fast network. And while some security-conscious companies shut down their networks at night, I doubt Owen would. I can't see his boys denying themselves hot and cold running porn, among the other advantages of the Internet."

Tara shivered, and he pulled her tighter into his body and brushed a kiss across her forehead. She was remembering Elizabeth's story. He wanted to swear such a thing could never happen to her, but he couldn't. He'd seen too much. Too many good, strong, happy people, people who lived carefully and did all the right things had their lives decimated—if not stolen—because they randomly crossed the path of crazy. And Tara had willfully entered a compound filled with it.

He bent his head and pressed a kiss to her lips, letting his hands wander the curves of her body. He might not be able to promise her safety, but he could show her he'd be beside her no matter what came.

She stroked his chest beneath his shirt. Her fingertips trailed down across his belly, and his dick jumped to attention, begging for her touch. She unbuttoned his fly and curled her hand around him and all tender, melancholy thoughts were subsumed beneath a surge of seething desire. He tried to push her over onto her back, but she was having none of it. She knelt astride him, leaning on her hands, which pinned his biceps to the bed.

"My turn," she whispered, and the shimmer of her breath over his ear dried his throat and raised his heart rate. Her hands moved to the hem of his shirt, and she let him up just enough to ease it off. In a single, fluid move, she lifted and twisted so she knelt beside rather than atop him, and in short order she worked his jeans over his hips and down his legs until he lay before her completely nude.

She still wore her T-shirt and panties, and he wanted to strip her of them, but the look in her eyes mesmerized him. She stared at his body as if he were a seven-course meal and she could not decide where to begin. But more than lust shone in those blue pools. Fear, hope, longing and something he couldn't—didn't dare—put a name to lurked in their depths.

She ran her fingers lightly over the skin of his belly and he shuddered. Her nails had always been short, practical, but well maintained. Now they were broken, ragged. They scratched as she explored him, the sensation not entirely unpleasant. But when she leaned over and pressed her hot mouth against his, the spell broke and he grabbed her shirt and dragged it over her head, exposing her gorgeous breasts and soft, smooth, skin. He sat up and captured one rosy nipple in his mouth, reveling as much in her gasp of surprised pleasure as in the taste of her against his tongue.

For a moment, Tara held his head in place, arching into him, but then she shoved him back. "I said it's *my* turn." She pressed hot, openmouthed kisses to his neck, then down across his chest. Her tongue flicked out to taste each of his nipples in turn and they tightened beneath her mouth and shot fire straight to his groin. His breath stuck in his lungs as she moved slowly down his body, her long hair cloaking her face and tickling his skin.

Gently she bit down on one of his protruding hip bones, then soothed it with her tongue. He clenched his teeth together and forced himself not to beg. And when she shifted to the other side, the slow slide of her silken hair across his skin was so precisely like his fantasies that he almost came on the spot.

Her hands, cool skin overlaying a pulse of hot blood, held down his thighs as she licked a line from his balls all the way up his throbbing cock. He fisted his hands in the sheets to prevent himself from grabbing her head and pushing it down on him.

She swirled her tongue over and around the head of his cock, and his hips jerked. He felt her smile against his skin.

"Like that, do you?"

"Jesus, woman, are you trying to kill me?"

Her fingers squeezed, massaged. "Now, what fun would that be?" she whispered, the brush of air sliding across his damp skin driving him even higher.

He reached down to pull her up, but she slid her mouth over his cock, sucking him deep, and he was lost. She made a tiny, satisfied hum in the back of her throat, and he felt it vibrate along his cock and, impossibly, straight through his heart. She began to move, advancing and retreating, squeezing his balls in time with the movements of her mouth, and he knew he wouldn't last.

"Sweetheart, please," he said, burying his hands in her hair and urging her up his body, "I don't want—I need to be inside you." At first he thought she might ignore him, but then she raised her head, shimmied out of her panties, and swung her leg over to kneel astride him. Holding him in position, she lowered her body slowly onto his. She was soaking wet, turned on just from giving him pleasure. He loved touching her, pleasing her, but hadn't believed she could feel the same kind of thrill. Her head fell back, and he wished he could raise himself up and suckle her, mark her the way she'd marked his shoulder with her teeth, but there was no time: with her first gyration atop him, his balls tightened.

He reached for her, determined not to leave her behind, but even before his fingers found their mark, he felt her spasms begin to milk him, sending him rocketing out into the stars.

And when he came back to earth, his only coherent thought was that nothing would ever be the same again.

CHAPTER EIGHT

THE MORNING HORNS woke Tara from a lovely dream, and
she burrowed deep where she lay with her head in the hollow
of Jake's shoulder to hang on to it for a last, precious second.
In that soft, sweet netherworld of dreams, Jake had told her
he loved her and though he held her now just as he had then,
cruel reality revealed all the world's hard edges disguised by
her dream state, and she recognized the fantasy for what it was.

Next door, she heard Kevin and Elizabeth stirring. Today
the fight to bring down the Chosen would begin in earnest.
She shivered, and Jake tucked her tighter against the heat of
his body.

"Ready, sweetheart?"

"As I'll ever be." The rusty, husky quality of her own voice
surprised her.

Jake tipped her head back and bent over to kiss her. "Then
I guess it's time to face the crowd." He released her and rolled
from the bed, and Tara had to squelch the urge to hang on to
him. A dream hangover, nothing more. She washed up and
dressed, and she and Jake headed for the dining hall. Kevin
and Elizabeth were nowhere to be seen.

At the door, Jake left her with a brush of his lips over her
forehead, and she found a seat next to an older woman, Leah,
with whom she'd been working on the linens. Still, Kevin
and Elizabeth did not appear. Had they been found out?
Disciplined? Owen usually liked to make such things public,
but what if he'd figured out that Kevin was DEA?

Leah passed her the pot of tea, and Tara's stomach rose into her throat. She fought back the urge to puke. *You have to drink it.* Not only would passing alert any watchers, but she could not afford to go through withdrawal, not when it had proven fatal in every case they knew of.

Up at the disciples' table, both Samuel and Aaron suddenly jerked to attention. *Pagers. Or cell phones set to vibrate.* Kevin must be making his move. Both men pushed back their chairs and headed for the door, causing a stir among the Chosen, who found anything outside their routine alarming. Many left their seats to investigate the disturbance.

Tara saw Joy among those peering out the windows and went to join her.

"What's going on?"

"I'm not sure." Worry lurked in the woman's fathomless brown eyes.

Kevin and Elizabeth came into view, flanked by Aaron and Samuel, and Owen walked out from the main house to meet them in the yard.

"What's the problem?" Kevin asked, loud and belligerent. "I thought you had an open-door policy. We want to leave, so we're leaving."

"Of course you can leave. We would never force you to stay. But come and talk to me—let's sit down together and so I can hear and address your concerns."

"I don't have any concerns. It's just time for me to be moving on."

"And what about Bea? And her baby? You think you speak for them, too?"

"Tell them you want to come with me, Bea."

She looked up at him, then at Owen.

"Tell them."

"I want to leave." Tara saw her lips form the words, but if she spoke them, she did so very quietly.

Jonas stepped out of the dining hall and approached the group. He gestured to Elizabeth and she stepped slightly behind Kevin. Tara could not hear his words, but she had a damn good idea what he was saying. She clenched her fists against the urge to storm out and beat the living hell out of him.

Owen apparently decided that arguing with the members of his congregation in public was counterproductive, so he backed away. "Go with our blessings, then," he said. "May the Powers always watch over you. Feel free to return if the Outside becomes too difficult, too depressing and grim." He glanced over at the dining hall, where almost everyone had gathered to watch the show. "Our day has been interrupted long enough." He strode back toward the hall, and the Chosen began to filter back to their seats.

Joy put a hand on Tara's arm. "Did you know they planned to leave?"

Tara shook her head. "Bea wasn't feeling well yesterday. Maybe Caleb just doesn't trust that she can get good enough medical care here."

"Deborah is an excellent healer." Joy's eyes narrowed as she watched Kevin and Elizabeth move in the direction of the front gate. "I doubt he is taking her away out of concern for her health."

It was the closest Tara had ever heard Joy come to criticizing, but then, she probably felt betrayed. She was a true believer.

"Maybe they'll come back. After all, they couldn't have been very happy on the Outside or they wouldn't have joined in the first place," Tara offered, and Joy nodded slowly.

The sermon that morning lasted even longer than usual, and Tara felt herself nodding off. She hadn't wanted to sleep at all the night before. Sex with Jake was like nothing she'd ever experienced, and it might never happen again. Sure, they were living together for the next few days, but between Jake's midnight explorations and the fact that she'd practically had to attack him to get him into bed, she had no idea whether he'd let his guard down again.

And once they were out of the compound, once life got back to normal, he'd be gone. Men like Jacob Nolan didn't fall for women like her in real life, despite what happened in fairy tales and romance novels. Men like Jake ended up with women like her friend Lucy—beautiful, smart, competent—women who didn't screw up their friends' lives as well as their own.

At long last, the sermon ended and food was passed down the table. Having missed dinner the night before, Tara piled eggs, potatoes, and toast on her plate. A few seats down on the other side, Aurora grinned at her, and Tara felt herself blush. She glanced over at Jake, and he had the balls to wink, which only increased the heat in her face.

Joy, seated opposite Aurora, watched the whole interaction. "I am glad things are working out for you and Jacob," she said. "Life among the Chosen is not for everyone, and when he first arrived, he seemed as if he might not be happy here."

No joke. Tara was honestly shocked that anyone bought Jake's cover. Sure, he had the experience and intelligence to back up the geek persona, but everything about the way he carried himself screamed "predator." How could they all miss it?

"Now that he has the website to manage, he's happier," she said. "I really hope he can learn to relax here, though. Outside, he was really into games and stuff, and I am a bit worried he'll eventually miss the excitement of all that."

"He's a thrill seeker?" Joy examined Jake. "Hard to imagine."

Hard to imagine? The woman had clearly been living in the compound too long.

"Well, at least online he is. And then there was the booze. And a few minor run-ins with the law. Nothing serious. But still. Being away from all that will be good for him if he can only accept it." She did her best to sound like both an eager convert and a woman blinded by love.

⌒

JAKE LOVED TO watch Tara blush. To be fair, he loved to watch her, period. But when she glanced his way and her face went hot, a ridiculous bubble of happiness rose in his chest.

"So I guess you had a good night," said the man to his left. He was a weaselly little punk named Jeremiah who also worked the sheds in the morning, and Jake would happily have smacked the leer right off his face, but he didn't have time to be stuck back in the hole for another three days. He chewed and swallowed the last of the toast he'd taken, counting backward from twenty.

"You should get a woman of your own," he said at last. "I highly recommend it."

Jeremiah made a dismissive sound. "Why settle for one? Twice as many women as men here. I get different ones pretty much every week."

How desperate—or drugged—did these women have to be? Of course, he couldn't ask Jeremiah that. But there was one thing he could ask about.

"You take them back to your bunk? Isn't that kind of lacking in privacy?"

"Nah, there are places you can find. Mostly, the women are pretty much up for anything, which you might not expect given the whole mother-earth vibe. Grab a couple of blankets and hike out to the orchard, or use one of the workrooms that's unoccupied."

Were the women "up for anything" because the drugs increased their desire? Was that why Tara had invited him into her bed? Was any of it real for her? When she got off the damned drugs, would she feel he'd violated her?

His stomach heaved, and he took a gulp of coffee to force his breakfast back down.

"Buyer's remorse?" asked Jeremiah, misinterpreting Jake's expression. "Don't worry about it. You get tired of her, you can trade her in. Happens all the time around here."

Like used cars. But the horn sounded, signaling the time to clear their plates, so Jake didn't have to answer aloud.

He dropped his dishes in the tray and stepped outside without looking for Tara. How was he supposed to face her? What the hell had he done?

He drew in a deep breath and for the first time noticed the thunderheads gathering. The sky had been completely clear when they'd left their cabin, but during his sermon Owen had gone on about the displeasure of the Powers and how it would show in the world, so he figured the guy had a weather radio somewhere. What would he have said caused the storm if Kevin hadn't chosen this morning to leave?

In the drying shed, the normally dim light was decreased even further by the thickening cloud cover outside.

"Gets much darker," he observed to his partner at the beam

after a few minutes of work, "I'm liable to cut off something I shouldn't."

"Yeah," the guy said. "We get a few like this every year. Once the rain really starts, work's over.

People generally hang out in the dining hall because there's electricity, so there's light. Of course, once in a while, a bad one will take out the electricity, too." As if to underscore his words, thunder rolled across the sky, shaking the shed.

And wouldn't a blackout just do wonders for the investigation? Jake needed both power and an Internet connection, because while darkness might improve his ability to sneak around unnoticed, he wasn't naïve enough to believe they wouldn't have backup power on the security systems.

A crashing boom rolled into a second and then a third. The pervasive and distinctive odor of ozone filled the air. An ululating wail sounded across the compound, and the men dropped what they were doing and rushed to the door.

"What's up?" Jake asked, following along.

"Fire," said one of the men at the very moment Jake smelled smoke.

One of the women's dormitories was alight, flames licking at the wood and shooting into the sky.

Jake stood back and let the others do their thing. In emergency situations, extra hands were apt to get in the way rather than assist. The ground trembled beneath him, lightning split the sky, and rain came down in thick, heavy drops. The storm had arrived in earnest.

A fire truck arrived from the direction of the main house, Samuel in the driver's seat. He and Aaron set up a system by which the truck drew in water from a small pond at the edge of the property, while three other men unwrapped and unrolled hoses they fitted to the truck and to each other until multiple lines of water were coming out.

One of the men grabbed Jake to back him up on a line, and he plunged forward, the hose a live, muscular serpent in his hands. Smoke billowed out from the building, making breathing difficult. None of the men wore masks, nor had they changed into any kind of protective gear. Samuel and Aaron stayed back, manning the pump itself, and none of the men went inside the building. But even so, the damned fire was hot on Jake's skin. He could only imagine how much worse it was for the man in front of him holding the nozzle.

The wind had picked up and water flew everywhere—from the hoses, from the sky—along with smoke and ash and sparks and cinders. Still, by the time the fire was out, the dormitory was gone. Most of the energy had gone into saving the buildings on either side. The storm still raged—how long had they been out there?—but despite the cool rain, a thick shroud of smoke hung in the air.

Everyone was soaked through, but even when the hoses had been rolled up and carried off and the engine put away in the garage behind the main house, men still hung around in small groups, talking. A number of them looked anxious, as if they'd like a cigarette, a joint, a shot of tequila.

Too much adrenaline. Too much testosterone. The women had remained inside during the blaze, but surely they'd stopped their work to watch the fire devour their home. Where would the dozen women sleep now? In the main house? Such a thing could be good or bad. Good, because upsets in routine always left openings, but bad because, with extra people in the space, security would be tightened.

The horn blew loud and long. Time for lunch.

"Better get cleaned up," the man beside him said. "Even after a fire, the leader expects respect."

I'll just bet he does. But he took the advice and jogged back to the cabin for a change of clothes.

Catching a glimpse of himself in the bathroom mirror, Jake decided more than a new shirt was in order. His face was black and streaked and pocked with red marks where bits of burning ash had landed, and he could smell his own sweat under the odor of the smoke on his clothes. He hopped into the shower and scrubbed away the grime in record time, then pulled on clean clothes and headed for the dining hall, hoping the power hadn't gone out.

At the sight of the cold, fluorescent lights glowing from the dining hall, Jake relaxed a fraction. But despite the stability of the power grid, the Chosen were restless, the noise level in the hall higher than he'd heard it even when Kevin had bucked the system by leaving without a private conference.

He searched for Tara and finally saw her in a corner with her pregnant friend Aurora. Her eyes beckoned, and he made his way toward her, catching snatches of conversations as he passed.

"The Powers are angry."

"The Leader says we need to . . ."

"Maybe I should leave, too."

"Did anyone get hurt?"

Tara greeted him with a chaste kiss on the cheek that nonetheless made her blush and filled him with entirely inappropriate desire.

"You two are so cute," said Aurora. "It's obvious how much in love you are."

Was it? Were they? Jake had never been in love. Until recently, he would have scoffed at the idea that the emotion—at least as portrayed in pop culture—even existed. But then his friend Lucy, the most relentlessly practical person he'd ever met, had fallen for a man almost as jaded as Jake himself. And Ethan seemed equally besotted.

Whatever lay between him and Tara, he wasn't prepared to label it. A healthy dose of lust, to be certain, but she also incited a long-dormant protective instinct, And something else, some ineffable tug, like an elastic around his chest that only relaxed entirely near her. When she'd lain with him in the infirmary, it was as if the bits and pieces of a puzzle he'd struggled with for years had slid into place.

Was that love? He'd loved his sister, but it had brought him nothing but pain. He loved his parents, but found no peace in their presence. No sooner did he sit down to dinner with them than his brain began working to figure out how long he had to stay.

His musings went no further as Owen Stephenson entered the room and the Chosen scrambled to find seats. When they'd settled, Owen raised his hands and spoke.

"We have seen evidence of the Powers' displeasure. But we know we are loved. None of the Chosen suffered injuries today, and in my communion meditation, I came to understand that Their anger is spent. The wind and rain shall pass, and we will rebuild."

In other words, this is Texas and the storm will blow out as quickly as it blew in. But Owen wasn't finished.

"This afternoon, we will remain in the dining hall. My apostles and I will circulate among you. If any of you are troubled, have concerns about today's events, feel free to discuss them with us."

A little time with their shepherd. How nice. But Jake's agenda didn't include an afternoon hanging around the hall.

He needed to get back to the computer, to tell Ethan what they'd discovered in case Kevin didn't get in touch with him.

While the Chosen assigned to the kitchen cleared the tubs of dirty dishes and silverware, several others went to the counter along one wall and opened the cabinets beneath. Board games, cards, and art supplies filled the space. The Chosen played as they seemed to do everything: earnestly and with devotion. He'd never seen so much attention paid to Monopoly. Even Chutes and Ladders became utterly engrossing when presented as a rare treat.

He saw Owen talking to Aurora and made his way through the crowd to his side. Tara noticed his direction and abandoned her group to join him and slide her arm around his waist.

"Plan?" she whispered, her mouth so close to his ear she might be kissing him.

In response, he wrapped an arm around her shoulders. "I need to talk to the Leader," he said. "You can go back to your group." But he didn't let go, and she understood the precedence of the nonverbal cues over his words.

"No, no. I'll come too, if it's okay."

"Of course." He pressed his lips to her temple, trying not to be distracted by the scent of her, by how right she felt glued to his side.

Aurora grinned at them as they approached. "Hey, you guys."

"Hey," Jake said, acid burning through his gut. What the hell had a nice kid like Aurora ever done to be drugged, possibly to death? Tara's arm tightened around him, and he realized he'd gone tense. "Do you mind if we speak to the Leader for a minute?"

"Sure." With a little nod, Aurora hurried away.

Owen blinked slowly, his pupils dilated despite the institutional brightness of the room. Did he indulge in his own recreational pharmaceuticals? "What can I do for you, Jacob? Serena?"

"I know you have the Chosen gathered with you and the apostles to calm us, but this many people, this small a space, it doesn't work for me. Might I be allowed to go about my usual afternoon task of working on the website?"

"I suppose that would be fine." Owen studied Tara, and Jake held perfectly still. Their embrace could work for him or against him. "And on such a troubling day, there is no need to separate the two of you. Take Serena with you."

Jake had a pretty good idea what Owen and the rest of his Peeping Tom buddies hoped would happen in front of the office security cams. And he'd indulge them, within limits. It would allow him to position Tara so she blocked the camera pointed at the computer.

"Oh, thank you, Leader," said Tara, all but batting her eyelashes at the man. "I can't wait to see what Jacob is doing for the Chosen. I know he'll be able to spread your message further, to all the people who need to receive it."

"It is important work," said Owen. "The digitalization of the world has isolated so many. It is only fitting the same tools should be used to spread the truth of the Powers and their desires for human community."

⌒

IN THE OFFICE, Jake tugged Tara into his arms and covered her lips with his own. *Cameras,* she reminded herself. *It's just an act.* But her treacherous heart beat faster, and she wound her fingers through his hair. She wrapped one leg around his lean hips, and he groaned. Hands at her waist, he lifted her to sit on the edge of the desk, pushing the computer out of the way. His tongue delved deep into her mouth for long minutes, stroking, sliding, tempting. At last, he pulled away.

"You sit right there," he said, his voice raspy. "I have work to do. The Leader didn't send us in here to fool around."

"I know. But could you at least explain what you're doing? I always felt left out before when you got involved with your computer stuff."

"Why didn't you say anything?"

"I did. But when you're in the ones and zeros, you don't hear me." She allowed a tiny bit of whine to creep into her voice, and Jake's lips twitched.

"Sorry, sweetheart." He booted up the computer and opened some windows. "So this is a server. It's where all the files that run the Chosen's website live. I can edit them directly on the server, but it's safer to download them, make changes, and re-upload."

"What kind of changes do you want to make?"

Jake began a mind-numbing description of work he was pretending to do as his fingers flew over the keys, opening the secret site he and Ethan had developed. He installed the software he'd told her about and, even watching, she wouldn't have realized it but for the fact that, beneath her gaze, he crossed his fingers.

"You know, the Leader should consider a Facebook page. I mean, I just stumbled onto the community because of my friendship with Pearl. And that only happened because I wound up here in town after . . . well, *after*. So many people could benefit from the Leader's wisdom."

Jake shrugged. "One thing at a time. This site is a mess, so let's get it as optimized as possible first."

"What does that mean?"

And he was off again. This time, beneath the coding for the homepage of the Chosen, which Tara vaguely understood, he opened a document showing nothing but a string of senseless numbers and letters.

A message from Ethan and Lucy. And a long one.

"Fuck," Jake said after a few minutes of silence.

"Jacob!"

"Sorry, sweetheart. I think there's a loophole here that might mean our customers' credit card information hasn't been transmitted securely. It would be bad if the Chosen got a rep for not caring for their customers' data." He checked the computer's clock, keyed in the date and time, and then began composing a coded reply.

He was deep in it when a floorboard outside the door squeaked. He shut the window and concentrated on an equally incomprehensible—at least to her—document.

"How's it going?" asked Samuel as he entered.

"Eh," Jake replied. "There's a bunch of stray code in here that looks like a loophole. I'm trying to figure out if I can safely close it."

"Show me," Samuel said, shoving Tara off the desk to lean over Jake's shoulder.

"It's right here." Jake pointed at the screen, and Tara held her breath. Did Samuel understand the data on the monitor? Was there an actual problem to be recognized?

Apparently he did, because he leaned in even closer. "What is that doing there? Do you know where it's storing or sending the data?"

"Not yet. I'm going to have to run through all the server scripts. I'd like to say your old computer guy just didn't know what he was doing, but this is deliberate and well hidden."

Samuel's eyes narrowed. "You're saying John was stealing from us."

"No. I'm saying he made it possible for someone, possibly him, possibly a friend of his, to steal from your customers. Maybe it was a fail-safe, a back door he installed and never used."

"Well, find out. I'm going to speak to the Leader." Samuel grabbed Tara's arm. "You, come on. Your boyfriend has work to do."

⌒

ALL AFTERNOON, TARA waited for Jake to appear from the office, but he remained inside even while the Chosen tidied the dining hall and prepared for dinner. Both Samuel and Aaron went in more than once and came out increasingly grim.

What had Jake told them? Would they trust him more for having uncovered the loophole, or would they believe he'd created it?

As plates were passed down along the long tables, Joy settled in next to Tara. "The apostles seem disturbed."

The apostles weren't the only ones. Tara had classified Joy as virtually emotionless, her default position after so long among the Chosen a calm acceptance bordering on catatonia. But in a single day she'd shown her disapproval of Kevin, and now curiosity and nerves.

Perhaps it wasn't surprising. The Chosen, after all, were pack animals. Humanity in general, despite its evolutionary sophistication, remained prone to herd behavior. The Chosen took their cues from Owen and, in his absence, Samuel,

Aaron, Jonas, and Francis. Samuel and Aaron glowered as they moved through the crowd. If they were supposed to provide a calming influence, they were failing.

Odd that neither Jonas nor Francis had been invited into the office conclaves. The greenhouse team had not even gone out that morning due to the weather. Did Samuel and Aaron not trust Francis or Jonas?

"I'm sure the weather has everyone on edge," she said to Joy. "It must be difficult to feel responsible for so many people, to worry about their happiness and satisfaction." God, the longer she stayed in the compound, the easier it became to sound as if she were drinking the Kool-Aid. How long before she actually believed the crap she spouted? Even without the drugs, repetition served as reinforcement.

"You are right, of course," said Joy. She poured herself a cup of tea and handed the pot to Tara. "It is not for us to concern ourselves with the doings of the apostles."

"Exactly." Gritting her teeth, Tara poured a cup of tea and passed the pot to the woman on her other side.

Jake slipped into the hall only moments before Owen ascended the steps to the stage. Head down, he didn't even glance Tara's way as he took his seat. What had happened? It couldn't be too bad, or they wouldn't have let him rejoin the group. Tara's hands shook, and she shoved them under the table and locked them together.

No hint of tension inflected Owen's pre-meal sermon and prayer. Had Samuel not informed him about the computer problem, or was he really *that* good an actor? Or maybe he found theft from Outsiders acceptable. She couldn't read him at all. How much of his own hype did he believe?

JAKE ATE QUICKLY. Not that it would do him any good, since the Chosen were excused from the table when Owen decided, not when they finished eating, but nervous energy pushed at him. He needed to talk to Tara. The media fostered an image of FBI agents, particularly profilers, as loners, but in truth they worked in teams. As a programmer, Jake considered himself damned good at making logical connections and seeing patterns. But personalities, the very illogical nature of humanity, confounded him. It was why he'd failed Lisa. Over and over he'd tried to explain that the heroin was stealing her life drop by drop. Over and over, she'd gazed up at him with those faded blue eyes big in her pale face and told him he didn't understand.

And, dammit, he didn't. Lisa hadn't been the first to accuse him of being as much a machine as the computers he programmed. But the others hadn't been family. And they hadn't died. Sure, one woman had thrown a shoe at his head as she left his apartment, but she—like all women he dated— had known what she was getting with him. Good food, good company, good sex, and nothing more. Despite her tirade— what was her name?—he hadn't suffered an ounce of guilt even after ducking the shoe. He hadn't failed her.

But he'd failed Lisa, and if he couldn't get a handle on what was happening among Owen's lieutenants, he'd fail Tara. And that might just be the end of him.

Beside him, two men discussed the fire. Both longtime Chosen members, they'd seen other fires and lived through other rebuilds.

"They'll pull most of us off normal duties tomorrow," one explained to Jake. "We'll clear the remnants, even if it's still raining, and Aaron and Jonas will pick up supplies. Won't take but a week to frame a new place. Another week and they can move back in."

Jake didn't have to ask what the women would do in the meantime. The pregnant ones from every bunk had been shifted into the infirmary and nursery, the others parceled out to spare beds. Joy and Mary were to share the bed in the second room in his cabin. Too much to hope that he and Tara would be left alone, but still disappointment and suspicion nagged at him. He could feel the eyes and ears, tickling his nerves, raising the hairs on the back of his neck and along his arms.

Every nerve screamed, *Run!* He fought back the sensation, took a deep breath, and let it out slowly. *Relax the toes, feet, ankles, calves . . .* He'd performed the exercise since his teens, when a doctor had prescribed it for hyperactivity, and it still worked. By the time he'd loosened his shoulders, Owen was releasing them from their seats, and he could walk casually across the room to join Tara. Mary and Joy came over, too, and he matched his pace to theirs as they sauntered through the gathering dusk to their cabin.

The moment they arrived, the urge to snatch Tara up and take off returned.

"Joy, Mary, you ladies go ahead and shower first. Serena and I can wait."

The instant they were alone, he dragged Tara into his arms. A brief, surprised hesitation, and then she melted against him. Her arms slid around his neck, and she buried her face in his neck. The most intimate embrace he'd ever experienced, it rocked him in a way no sexual act ever had. He let himself savor the sensation before whispering the word he knew would end it.

"Serena."

Tara tensed in his arms and her breath hitched against the skin of his neck.

"How did it go this afternoon?" she asked. "Did you figure out how to solve the computer problem for the Leader?"

"Not yet. And Samuel told me not to speak of my work." Christ, now he was parroting the self-consciously formal language of the Chosen. "I can say I've been taken off my work rotation in the sheds to spend more time bringing the computer up to speed."

She leaned back, looking into his face for cues, and immediately he missed the warm weight of her. "I have faith in you. You'll fix it."

"But you know how antsy I get chewing on a programming problem."

"It's stopped raining. Maybe we should go for a run. Like we used to. And then we can come back and burn off the rest of that excess energy."

"Oh, hell yes." Unable to resist, he buried his fingers in her hair, tugged her head back, and covered her lips with his own. She opened to him, hot and sweet and greedy, and he lost himself in the kiss.

Tara recovered first. She reached up and cupped his cheek in one small, delicate hand. "Run first, then fun. You can't concentrate on me properly until you get all that nervous energy out of your system."

In the basement security room, Samuel and Francis listened to the mics they'd planted that afternoon while delivering supplies for Joy and Mary.

"What do you think?" Samuel asked when they heard the door close.

"I wish we had eyes in there. Body language is a whole lot easier to read."

"No way. He's too paranoid."

"So you said." Francis massaged his temples. "And he did

find Jonas's extracurricular business, which is helpful. You'll deal with that?"

"I told Owen ages ago Jonas had to go."

"Don't bother Owen. Just do it."

Samuel's brows shot up. "And when he asks where his apostle is?"

"Tell him you confronted Jonas about filming porn inside the compound and he ran off. Or leave him in his room dead of an OD and let Owen figure out how to spin it." Francis watched as two figures jogged across a screen and then out of sight. "I don't care how useful this Jason Norman has been, I don't trust him."

"What about her?"

"She's broken. You could see it the minute she showed up here with Andrea. If it weren't for her reaction to him, for the fact that at least the relationship part of their story is obviously real, I'd have insisted Owen kick him the fuck out the second he arrived. We can't afford this when we're so close."

"How much longer?"

"The addiction curve is set. The only thing left is the euphoria phase. If it's strong enough to make them want more, they lose functionality and the ability to keep earning a paycheck." Francis grimaced. "Sometimes, it kills them outright."

"Shit, I thought we were past that."

"Look, the formula's not perfect. But with a few more weeks of experimentation, it can be. We've been at this a long time. One man is not going to fuck it up. Even if Owen does believe the 'Powers' sent him in our time of need."

Samuel snorted. "Yeah." He glanced at the monitors. "I wish he didn't keep going out of range."

"Yeah." Francis tapped his lips with his forefinger. "Take care of Jonas. Then run a deep check on Jason Norman. I

want to know when he took his first steps, his favorite restaurant, the name of every woman he's ever screwed."

"And her?"

"She doesn't matter. After all, all we have to do is kick her
out and cut off her supply, and she'll take care of herself."

Samuel grinned. "There is that."

OUT BEYOND THE reaches of surveillance equipment,
Jake slowed to a halt and Tara followed suit. But when she
expected him to speak, he dropped to the hard, wet earth,
pulling her down so she sat between his knees, her back resting against his chest. Did he worry about being overheard
even out here?

His arms came around her, locking her into position,
almost as if he expected her to run. A prison of pure muscle
surrounded her—his thighs and calves along hers, his chest,
his arms. But beneath all that solid strength, his heart beat
too fast. And not from that brief jog. He could probably
run a marathon at that pace without breathing hard.

"What happened after I left?" she asked.

"That loophole, it's how Jonas runs his porn business. I
saw it the first day I scanned the code, because I was looking
for anything out of place. I thought it might be a test, so I
had to 'find' it before too long, but I wanted to trace exactly
what it was first. The good news is that while Aaron and
Samuel were asking questions, they let slip which portal
belongs to who on the system. Aaron has very little tech
savvy, but Samuel's conversant enough to track down the
links himself once I showed him the oddities."

"He seemed shocked. Though he came into the room immediately after you mentioned it—like he had an office mic feed piped to an earwig while he was hanging out in the dining hall comforting the flock. He had to have heard what we were talking about before."

"Yeah." Against her stomach, his hand clenched into a fist. "I wish I were better at reading people."

"You're a *profiler*."

"But profiling's about data, not about people. At least, the part I do. There's a guy on my team, give him twenty minutes with a suspect and he can tell you every aspect of life that makes the guy uncomfortable, every time he thinks he's failed, every resentment he holds. That's not me. If you show me a data set—blonde women in their twenties, drowned, with their lips and eyes sewn shut—I can extrapolate from that what kind of monster we're hunting. And usually, more data is better. But the pieces don't fit together here, and I can only assume it's because we're hunting multiple monsters all operating in the same small area. And I can't separate them out because I can't figure out which results, which data, belong to which set."

"The porn versus the drugs."

"Like that, but even more. Who's really in charge? I'd bet serious money that Owen's passed from pathology into psychosis, too screwed up to run this complex an op himself."

It fit her own observations. "But he has to *know* about the drugs, even if he's not in charge. He told you I could never leave."

"Right. But why would a guy convinced he's the voice of God—or the Powers—drug his followers?"

Tara turned the question over in her mind, trying to examine it dispassionately, to separate it from Elizabeth's rape and Andrea's murder. "He has to believe the drug benefits people."

"I agree."

"But Samuel's no true believer," she said. "He has to have another motivation. Sure, he gets to leave the compound on occasion, and his quarters are probably luxurious compared to ours, but he wouldn't live out here in the middle of nowhere without a damned good reason."

"No."

"Aaron—" Tara considered her experiences with the man. "He's a follower. The kind whose loyalty you buy. Samuel brought him into the room with you, I saw that, but did he stay while you explained everything?"

"Yeah. You have an idea why?"

"It was a test. To gauge Aaron's reaction, see whether he and Jonas were in the porn business together."

"How can you tell?" Frustration bled through the words. Poor Jake, he really didn't like relying on other people. Or was it just that he didn't trust her instincts?

She took a deep breath. Exhaled. "Look, I know I screwed up Lucy's case."

"No—"

"Shush. Listen. I got . . . confused. There are good reasons not to let cops work cases involving friends or family. Being that close messes you up. It's too hard to untangle the past from the present, what you see from what you feel. This is different. When I look at Aaron, there's no residual information. It's all fresh."

She paused, sorting through her observations in her mind before laying them out. "He must be part of the drug business, because they send him out to the desert with the ones who come back and need to be cleaned up. So they trust him.

But they trusted Jonas, too—you could see that on Samuel's face when he came in."

"He was pissed."

"Yes. But also shaken. And he had to be wondering why, if you found the hole, John never did. Which brings up the possibility that John was helping Jonas. And if John, why not Aaron? All three of them—John, Jonas, Aaron—probably fall under Samuel's supervision."

"What about Francis?"

"You've spent more time with him than I have. He's rarely around during the day, and I've never been assigned to the greenhouse team."

"Our drive out to the greenhouses was a dance of distrust. Neither of us said a damned thing. The only information I gleaned was that he's smart and immensely suspicious. Not a lot to plug into the matrix."

She thought about Francis. Aloof, always busy with the greenhouses. "I don't have much to add. On one hand, he's been here since he was a kid, so he was already here when Owen brought Samuel back from med school. On the other, I don't believe they could run a large-scale drug operation without his knowledge."

"What does your gut say?"

That was easier than her brain. "I don't trust him. He may not be working toward the same end as Samuel, but he's using the Chosen—and Owen—just the same. Notice how Samuel didn't invite him into the office? He didn't need to test him." She waited for another question. When none came she posed her own.

"What did Ethan say?"

Jake sighed, his chest expanding and contracting behind her. "The cops he spoke to have noticed a higher than average number of ODs among the junkie population along with an increase in suicides. They put the ODs down to an unusually pure batch. That's the standard cause. Junkies know to the drop what they can take, and they'll shoot whatever they can handle. If they're used to stuff that's been stepped on four times, and what they get has only been cut twice, they pay with their lives."

He spoke clinically, but the words had to hurt, had to remind him of his sister. Tara tilted her head back and pressed her lips to his stubbled cheek. His arms tightened around her. He shifted slightly and suddenly she was sideways in his lap, the press of his body hard and hot against her own. His lips devoured hers, the simple kiss of comfort gone complex and hungry in an instant.

His hands slipped over her body, sliding beneath her T-shirt. She allowed herself the same liberty, running her fingers over smooth skin and bunched muscle. A quick lift and twist and she sat astride him, the hot throb of his erection against the juncture of her thighs.

He made a strangled sound. "Tara, sweetheart . . ."

Those two words, the sound of her own name in that husky, passion-rough voice almost sent her over the edge. She gripped the bottom of her own T-shirt and drew it off over her head.

"Oh, Christ," he said. "Baby, the ground is wet, it's cold. We should take this back to the cabin." But his eyes begged her to disagree. Not as if she had any choice. Her knees were jelly. If he wanted to go back, he'd have to carry her.

"I promise I'll keep you warm," she teased.

"You burn me alive," he said, and a shiver went through her at the intensity of the words. His fingers slid over her breasts, then found the clasp of her bra and freed them. "So fucking beautiful," he murmured before bending his head to suckle first one, then the other. The cold night air pricked at the damp, tender spots he left and sent lightning shooting through her from nipple to womb. She ground her body against his.

"Slow down, baby."

"I can't. I don't want slow." She slid her fingers between their bodies to cup him. They'd both changed into sweatpants for their run, and beneath the soft, worn cotton he was heavy and hot and pulsing in her hand. "Now, Jake."

"Jesus. Lift up." She did, and he stripped her sweats and panties. But he kept his own, settling her once more on his legs. He bent his knees and pushed her back so she lay against them, and his rough, calloused fingers found her center.

She was beyond words, beyond shame, beyond anything but the fire threatening to consume her. She arched back, offering herself to him, and he slid two fingers deep inside, letting his thumb caress her clit. She could feel the pressure building, and she wanted to protest, to insist on him being inside her when she came, but she'd lost her voice, and all that came out was a series of pleading sobs as he took her higher and higher until she exploded into a million fragments.

When she came back down, she reached for him, but he stopped her. "Not here. I want to be where we can really take our time, get comfortable. I want to lay you out in front of me where I can watch you . . ."

The words caused muscles impossibly relaxed to clench with desire, and she dressed as quickly as fumbling fingers and trembling legs allowed.

JAKE SAT ON the edge of the bed watching Tara sleep. He should have been sleeping himself. God knows, she'd worn him out. Sex, a shower, more sex . . . Every muscle was exhausted, but his mind wouldn't let him rest. He had four more days to get her out. And then what? He'd told her they'd find the antidote. But what if they couldn't?

Ethan's note had scared the shit out of him. Suicide after suicide after overdose after overdose. Jake didn't know much about people, but his sister had made him something of an expert on junkies and depression. Not all depression, even untreated, led to suicide. If it did, the population on the streets would be a lot smaller. No, suicidal ideation was something else entirely, more intransigent and harder to treat. What did the drug do to people that it sent them off that cliff, and so quickly?

And the overdoses. When junkies died from heart failure or the like, their deaths were rarely examined closely. Too expensive to screen the blood of every known user who dies with a needle in her arm. Had Samuel been testing an injectable form of the tea, cutting it into heroin for sale on the streets?

Tara shifted, then blinked up at him. "Hey."

"Hey." He bent to kiss her, and she wrapped her arms around his neck, getting to her knees so she could remain with him even when he sat up.

"You okay?"

"Yeah."

"Jacob." Even half-asleep, she remembered the microphones, used his Chosen name. He couldn't have asked for a better partner.

"Mmm?"

She stroked his cheek. "It's going to be okay. I know you're worried about failing the Leader, but you'll figure it out." She looked away for a minute. "I have faith in you. I love you."

His couldn't breathe. *I love you.* What would he give to hear her say those words for real? Had it only been a few hours ago he'd wondered whether he loved her? How could he have questioned it?

He kissed her again, just a brush of his lips against hers. "I love *you.* Always and only you."

For a heartbeat, she froze. Did she understand him? Her arms tightened and her breath hitched slightly. Confusion? Comprehension?

"Jacob . . ."

He laid a finger over her mouth, watching her blue eyes widen in the predawn light. Exerting a little pressure, he pushed her back down on the bed. She'd put on a T-shirt and panties before falling asleep, and he knelt between her knees and pressed his mouth to the spot where the two items of clothing met. Her belly contracted at the swipe of his tongue against her skin, and he grinned. So responsive. So sweet. So much better than anything in his life had ever been.

He kept his movements slow and deliberate as he kissed his way up her body, pushing the cotton out of the way inch by inch. When he reached her breasts, he lifted her slightly to strip the shirt off entirely so he could pay them proper attention.

His dick ached, but he felt no need to hurry. Which was crazy. Not that he'd ever rushed a woman—he always made sure they were satisfied—but sex hadn't been about savoring, either. With Tara, he just wanted to explore. To taste every part of her, to slide his fingers over the textures of her body and memorize the dips and curves, the soft fullness of her breasts, the oddly giving circles of her areolae, the stiff buds

of her nipples. The sweet, musky scent of her satisfied something deep inside him.

And though she squirmed beneath his ministrations,
Tara didn't push for speed, either. She stole his shirt, ran her
hands over his shoulders, slid her fingers through his hair.
Her breath came in quick little huffs, and he loved the sound
of it, the feel of it against his lips when he made his way up
her body to kiss her.

When at last he slid inside her, he felt complete, whole. It
occurred to him that what he'd found with Tara was more
than a relationship. It was home—and he'd kill, or die, to
defend it.

CHAPTER NINE

Between Caleb and Bea's departure and the fire, Jake expected the Chosen to be riled up at breakfast, but they were surprisingly calm. Extra-strong tea? Or were they just that complacent, that secure that their Leader would protect them from anything that might go wrong in their lives? How did people let themselves become so dependent on others to tell them what to do and how to think?

As for him, despite — or because of? — the night he and Tara had enjoyed, his nerves were wound tighter than usual. When they'd separated at the entrance to the dining hall, he hadn't wanted to let her go, and throughout the meal he'd had to stop his leg from bouncing with impatience.

He noticed the new camera the minute he entered the computer room. They hadn't even bothered to hide it. Large, round, white — with a bright blue light that shouted, *You're being watched!* — it hung at the juncture of the ceiling and wall, facing the computer monitor. No question how Jason Norman would react to such a thing — Jake stood on the desk chair and twisted the camera up to face the ceiling, then turned on the computer and waited for the reaction.

It didn't take long. Samuel stormed in before the computer even finished booting up.

"What do you think you're doing?"

"What you asked me to do. But I don't appreciate the evil eye hanging over my shoulder. If you want to see my work, you can. I've got nothing to hide. I showed it to you yesterday.

But that's not my gig. I told you that about any kind of surveillance in my cabin. It's not happening."

"And if we insist that we need to be able to see work that takes place on the computer? It is highly sensitive. Far more so than any of the work others of the Chosen do."

"Then you can do it yourself. That damned camera isn't even hardwired into a security system. It's just a wireless cam—anyone could tap into the stream if they wanted to, and that's not how I roll. You want to keep an eye on the computer when I'm not here, that's cool. I'll put it back in position when I leave for the evening. But if you insist on spying on me, we're done. I'll just take my girlfriend and go." Samuel's eyes narrowed and his fists clenched briefly, but then he smiled and, without another word, left.

Jake figured he didn't have long before the man came back, so he opened all the disguising documents, copied out the loophole code onto paper, and then, with the screen busy with cover work, ported into the server he shared with Ethan.

Reading didn't improve his mood.

Picked up good chunk of data from yesterday's dump. Haven't had a chance to go through it all, but if we're lucky we got what we needed. Problem, however: HS involved. JTTF. FBI has lead and they want in now. You don't have long. Doubt they will wait for weekend. HS JTTF claiming drug could be bioweapon. Lucy and I have no contacts, no in. We can't push them to wait. Work fast.

Well, hell. Any time Homeland Security or a Joint Terrorism Task Force got involved, things went to shit quick for those with boots on the ground. They were great ideas, and when they functioned properly, they saved a lot of lives. But all too often the whole thing turned into a clusterfuck. With a little luck the Trojan horse he'd inserted into the system would download the formula for the drug and for the antidote while it was grabbing all the rest of the Chosen's data. But he wasn't leaving without samples a lab could experiment on, too, just in case the antidote wasn't there, wasn't downloaded, or wasn't effective.

Hands moving quickly over the keys, always aware of the *other* cameras—the ones he wasn't supposed to know about—Jake fed Ethan the information he and Tara had come up with the previous night and asked for further research into all the apostles, then shut down the server connection and went back to working on the Chosen site.

Samuel returned and stepped right behind Jake's shoulder to see what he was doing.

"I haven't touched the loophole yet," Jake said. "You didn't tell me whether you wanted it shut." He handed Samuel the piece of paper with the code written out. "I think this is the whole thing, though. I don't see any harm to the site in pulling it out."

"Did you trace it?"

"Far as I could. Basically, it looks as if someone at this IP address"—he pointed to a line he'd written on the paper—"is using your credit card authorization portal. I can't see what happens beyond that because I'm damn sure not hacking a credit card acceptance company. If I had to guess, though, he's embezzling funds from you, too. Diverting them from your account to his own."

"And you think you can stop it."

"Sure. If I pull out that piece and reload the page, it should stop working for him, but your customers shouldn't see any changes. Is that what you want me to do?"

"Not yet. Can you set it up to flag any time that back door gets used?"

"Sure. You want it to send you an e-mail?"

"That will work." Samuel gave him an e-mail address and Jake wrote it down.

"This will probably take me a couple hours if I don't want him to realize what's going on. I'll have to bury it, in case he's looking at the code."

"That's fine. But it can wait till after lunch. Right now, you need to come along to the office to see the Leader."

"Ooookay." Jake made a show of getting up and tidying the desk before following Samuel out and across the main floor of the house to Owen's study. Once again, the man sat behind his big desk, fulfilling his role as father figure and commander in chief.

"Jacob," he said, gesturing to a chair placed in front of the desk. Hesitating just long enough so as not to seem cowed, Jake sat. As he had before, Samuel went to stand behind Owen. This time, Jake wondered whether the position was an intentional reflection of the man's actual status—was Samuel the power behind the throne?

"Samuel tells me you are considering leaving the Chosen."

"Did he tell you why?"

"He says you are uncomfortable with the restrictions on your life among us."

"That's not it. I don't like being spied on. Either you trust me or you don't. I won't be watched all the time."

"We could say the same. You don't appear to trust us. Samuel tells me you accused him of planting video cameras in your bedroom."

"Not him in particular. But look at what's going on in your

server. Someone here is up to no good. How can you expect me to overlook that?"

"I suppose that's fair. But we do trust you. And to prove that, I'm going to explain why you don't actually want to leave."

Jake leaned forward, resting his forearms on the desk. "Tell me."

But instead of an explanation, Owen began with a question. "Why did you come here?"

"We've been over this. I came for Tara. Serena."

"And she is happy here."

He shrugged.

"Think about it, Jacob. Remember what she was like at home, remember what you were like together, and tell me she's not better here."

"I guess. She's less volatile. More accepting."

"Exactly." A wide, creepy smile spread across Owen's features. "Now imagine if the whole world could be like that. More accepting. Calmer in spirit. Less dependent on outward displays of 'success' or materialism for their happiness. Wouldn't that be a wonderful thing?"

"Well, sure. But what's that got to do with me staying here?"

"That is what the Chosen work toward every day. In implicit ways, yes, but in explicit ways also.

The Powers want us to be happy, but they do not *make* us happy. That is for us to figure out. And we *are* figuring it out. Women need protection, food, and shelter to be secure, and work to make them feel worthwhile. Men need sex, food, shelter, and work. We provide those things. But we are also developing an herbal happiness supplement, a compound that allows you to see the world in its true glory and all the benefits you have to be grateful for."

"You mean a drug?"

Samuel took up the conversation. "You might call it a drug. We don't. It's more like a vitamin. Taking it makes you healthier, but in spirit not in body. People notice it right away, and when they stop taking it, the effects can be devastating. Suddenly, the world is not as bright, their work not as worthwhile, their relationships not as fulfilling.

"Your girlfriend has been taking it for a month."

"She has not! She would have told me."

"We serve it to the women here in their tea."

Jake wanted to howl and scream, to put his fist through Owen's smiling face, but he tamped the desire down. Jason Norman wasn't a warrior. He was a thinker. He'd be pissed, but wouldn't react physically. "You're drugging the women without them knowing it?"

Owen laughed. "You make it sound so sordid. I promise you, it's not. They are *happy*. You said so yourself. They're much better off here with us than they were in the Outside."

"In that case, what about the ones who 'go on a mission.' Why would any member of the Chosen kill herself if she was taking a happy drug?"

Owen sighed deeply and shook his head. "Unfortunately, we can't save everyone. Some are too damaged when they arrive. Serena's friend was one of those. We tried, but she took her life even before she'd been here long enough to fully assimilate."

"And you're working toward making this 'vitamin' universal?"

"Absolutely. Imagine a world without the dullness of the daily grind, where 'keeping up with the Joneses' is a thing of the past, where people only take what they need and leave enough for others."

Jake let his eyes slide from the fervor of Owen's to the

flatness of Samuel's. Let a little gleam of greed show through. "I want in."

"Suddenly you don't care that your girlfriend is taking drugs without knowing it?"

Jake shrugged. "It won't hurt her, right?"

"Not unless she tries to leave," Samuel said.

Jake frowned. "What do you mean?"

Owen leaned across the desk and covered Jake's hand with one of his own. "Seeing the true beauty of the world is like being wrapped in a cocoon of brilliant color. If she stops taking the tea, all that will go away. It can have devastating effects on people."

"Like how devastating?"

"Let's just say you don't want to find out. And you won't have to. She can keep taking it as long as you two are here, and your relationship will keep getting better. We've heard from several of the Chosen, both men and women, how much less inhibited they feel freed from the shackles of other peoples' opinions. And that's always a nice side benefit."

Bile rose in the back of his throat, and he swallowed hard.

"You can't think the whole world is just going take up drinking your particular type of tea."

Owen waved dismissively. "Samuel and Aaron are working on that right now."

Jake rubbed a finger between his eyebrows. "Look, this isn't my first rodeo. I've been around. You can call it a vitamin or an herbal supplement or anything you like. But it's a drug. I've got nothing against drugs, per se, but don't you worry about what will happen when people start taking too much?"

"We haven't seen any negative side effects yet, even at

quite concentrated doses, and we are well into the second generation. Kids now two years old who were born while their mothers were taking the supplements."

"Yeah, but if it makes them happy and they want to be happier?"

"Fuck, man, you ever hear of anyone OD-ing on antidepressants?" Samuel asked.

"No, I suppose not." Jake allowed himself to be convinced. "Still, I don't imagine you'd want anyone knowing what you're doing here."

Owen and Samuel exchanged looks. "It would be a shame if we had to stop before we could make the world all it could be," said Samuel. "We were hoping you'd see it that way, too. There are benefits to being among those who are helping free the world from the shackles of despair."

"Oh, really? Do tell."

"For starters, you'd need to be closer. You've already discovered a problem with the computer system in sales. There's a chance we might have another. So we'd move you and your girlfriend into John's old suite."

"Private bedroom and bathroom?"

"Absolutely."

"That *would* be nice."

"Naturally, you and she have to keep working. That's part of the life the Powers have laid out for us here on earth," Owen said, "but in the evenings you will be alone. If things work out over the next few weeks and we can clear up any security breaches, you'll even be given your own laptop."

Of course, he'd be long gone before that happened, but Jake made appropriately excited noises.

Owen nodded, satisfied that they were done. "Samuel, why don't you show Jacob to his new quarters. He and Serena can move in after dinner tonight. Then we can put a pair of women who are doubled up from the fire into their space."

"Very well," said Samuel, and ushered Jake out.

Following Samuel up the stairs up to the second floor, Jake examined everything as thoroughly as he could without being obvious. The stairs led to a balcony with heavy wooden doors all along it, and all the doors were shut.

"John's old room is down here." Samuel led him to the very far end of the balcony. The room was cool and dark and empty. Heavy shades kept out both light and heat, and someone had stripped the bed and thoroughly cleaned the space.

"Give it to me straight," Jake said to Samuel. "You're not really planning to make the world a better place, are you? I mean, I get that the Leader is, but you seem a lot more practical to me."

Cool gray eyes assessed him. "I believe in making the world a better place. But I don't see why I shouldn't get something out of it myself at the same time."

Jake nodded slowly, then turned his attention to the large bedroom. He remembered Tara's words about Samuel questioning John's loyalty. "You know I am gonna search this one for audio and video, too. Especially after finding that loophole in a program John ran every day. For all I know, he put it there himself and put cameras all over this place that are exporting out through the network."

"I expected nothing less," Samuel said. "I've already spoken to Deborah. One of the house girls will bring up fresh sheets and towels. She'll make up the bed. In the house, that is no longer your responsibility. But don't mistake the fact that you're in this bedroom for a decree of complete freedom. None of us has that but for the Leader. When you go to bed at night, you will stay in bed. There will be no wandering around the house as you do outside."

Keep your enemies closer. At least he understood why they were letting him into the inner sanctum.

"Deborah as in the one who runs the infirmary?"

"Yes. Deborah is in charge of the house. The infirmary, the kitchens; all the women who work inside during their pregnancies report to her. Her bedroom is at the opposite end of the hall from this one."

"I see." So they trusted at least one woman. Jake wondered what she'd had to do to earn that position. Even Joy, who had been at the compound since before Owen's arrival, still lived in a bunk with a shared bathroom. And he'd seen a couple older women, in their sixties or so, who ought to have been inside, away from the brutal heat of the summers. But none of that seemed to enter into the equation.

A young girl—no more than sixteen and at least seven months pregnant—entered with a pile of linens, and Samuel smiled. "Go over to your cabin and collect your own things. We will send Serena to get hers later this afternoon. See you at lunch." He slipped out, and Jake took the sheets out of the child's arms.

"Oh, you don't have to do that," she said. "I'm perfectly able."

"And so am I. My mama would have had my hide if I let a beautiful young woman like you wait on me."

The girl blushed, and Jake desperately wanted to ask her who'd knocked her up and under what circumstances. But he couldn't afford to let his concerns show. Samuel had been very confident that he wouldn't find any bugs in the room, but Jake refused to let his guard slip. A few more days—at most—and then the innocents like this little girl would get the help they needed. And he would descend like the wrath of God on Samuel and his ilk.

⟅

ONCE AGAIN, TARA hadn't seen Jake all day but for a passing glance at lunch when he'd winked at her across the room. When Samuel entered the room in the middle of her afternoon sewing and waved her over to follow him, her stomach clutched. What kind of trouble were they in now?

She made her excuses to the other ladies at the table and approached Samuel with lagging steps.

"The Leader would like to speak with you."

"Of course." She followed him back to Owen Stephenson's office. How odd to think that, for the man's father, this was a working ranch office, a place where he tracked stock and worked out crop and personnel issues. What did Owen do here? Track drug shipments?

"Serena," Owen said in his deep, hypnotic voice.

"Yes, Leader?"

"You are aware that Jacob found a problem with our computer system yesterday."

"Yes, Leader. He is very smart. I am sure he will be able to fix it for you if you give him a little time."

"His unique talents make him quite valuable to the Chosen. As such, we are moving the two of you into the main house. None of the others who live so close have bonded. This means other women in the compound will look to you for direction. Do you believe you are capable of advising them?"

"I'm not certain, Leader. I haven't much experience in being an advisor. Usually I am the one asking for aid."

"It is likely that none will ask outright questions, my dear. What you need to understand is how to behave in your new role. You have recovered well from your purification, but others remember your lies to the Chosen. You must be above reproach. Humble and obedient."

God, her mother would die laughing if she hadn't been in the ground for years already. Obedience and humility did not constitute Tara's strengths.

"Yes, Leader."

"You must obey not only Jacob, but any of the apostles who speak to you, without question. If you wish to ask questions, you must do so later, in private. When given the command, you must set an example by following it without hesitation."

And there wasn't really any possible answer other than: "Yes, Leader."

"Very well. At dinner, you will sit with the women as usual. We will introduce Jacob to the community and explain his new role. People may ask you afterward what you think. You will not have an opinion. Is that understood? To be prideful, especially when you yourself have done nothing worthy of note, is sinful in the eyes of the Powers."

And fuck you very much.

"Yes, Leader. Of course."

"For now, Samuel will take you back to your cabin, and you can bring your belongings to the main house."

Tara nodded, and Owen flicked his fingers at them to dismiss them. She followed Samuel out and across the yard to the cabin she and Jake shared. Gathering her things didn't take long. She had a half dozen pairs of jeans, three pairs of shorts, a couple of pairs of sweatpants, then tees and underwear. Piling up her bras and underwear under Samuel's watchful eyes—he didn't offer to help in any way—might have embarrassed her, but her brain was too caught on what she might be able to do with freedom of the house.

"The Leader did not say so, but you will be continuing with your duties. Nothing has changed in that respect."

"Of course. We must all do the work required of us." She tied the laces of her extra pair of running shoes together and hung them about her neck.

"Exactly. Are you ready?"

"Let me just get my toothbrush and brush and comb."

Jake's things were already gone. Had he picked them up himself, or had some oh-so-helpful disciple taken the opportunity to go through them in the guise of shifting them to the main house?

Awkward load in her arms, she followed Samuel back to the main house and up a wide, curved stair in the entry to a balcony lined with doors. He took her to one at the end of the hall and let her in.

The room was lovely. Heavy curtains had been opened, letting in the sun, and a fan hummed in the corner. Ah, electricity. She'd almost forgotten what that was like. A chest stood guard in a corner, and she carried her clothes over and began to lay them in the drawers.

"You may stay here until dinner," Samuel said. He looked at his watch. "There are only another twenty minutes until the horn sounds anyway."

"Okay." Tara nodded, choking back the *Yes, master* that wanted to pop out. He spun on his heel and left, giving her the distinct impression that she'd been checked off a mental list. *Girlfriend of new apostle resituated; back to the important stuff.*

Putting her things away took less than five minutes. Samuel hadn't told her she had to stay in the room, but she doubted they wanted her exploring. And security cameras almost certainly covered every inch of the second floor.

Still, it couldn't hurt. She wouldn't open any of the doors without knocking first and being invited in. If they took her to task, she could always say she was trying to familiarize herself with the place.

Four doors remained closed as she went down the line. She didn't dare, with the creepy, crawly feeling of being watched all the time, to try their handles and see if they were locked. Behind the fifth door, a woman's voice called, "Come in." She went in to find Deborah, who'd taken care of her in the infirmary, at a small writing desk. One wall of the woman's bedroom was taken up by a giant medical refrigerator with glass doors and a locked medicine cabinet. Well, that answered one question. Did Deborah also participate in the drug scheme, or were her medications on the up and up?

"Hi," Tara said. "I just . . . The Leader has moved me and Jacob into a bedroom down the hall. I am trying to figure out where everything is."

The woman watched her in cool silence.

"I didn't realize you lived here," Tara hurried on. "But I guess it makes sense so you'll be close by if anyone is really sick in the infirmary and needs you." She glanced at all the medicines. "Are you a doctor? I wish I were smart enough to do something like that. But I've never been much good at school. I took care of my granny when she was sick, but that was mostly just sitting next to her and holding her hand and reading to her. Occasionally helping her with, you know, personal stuff because she couldn't get out of bed."

"Would you like to assist me with the medical care?"

"Wow. Sure. But I really don't know anything about it. If you think I could learn, that would be awesome."

"Of course you can learn. You simply haven't had the necessary opportunities. I will speak to the Leader about taking you on in the afternoons."

"Oh, thank you. I would love that."

The woman nodded, dismissing her, and Tara continued on her way. No further knocks resulted in invitations, however, and the horn for dinner sounded as she was returning to her own room. She washed up—they had nicer soap and towels in the main house—and went downstairs and then out the front door to walk around to the dining hall.

As Owen had predicted, the women at her table at dinner asked plenty of questions when he spoke about Jake's special skills and how, having proven himself unusually useful to the Powers, he was moving into the main house. And, as directed, Tara professed herself ignorant of what any changes might mean.

"I remember John from when I first visited here," she said to Joy at one point. "I guess they need a replacement since he . . . went on a mission." She hadn't given John much thought. She'd been intent on proving that Andrea wouldn't have killed herself. And then, when the drug issue had arisen, it seemed as if maybe a precipitous depression might have been related to that, so Tara had let it go. But John wouldn't have been drinking the tea. He would have known better.

Which meant that whatever had happened to Andrea, John had been murdered.

Joy poured more tea into Tara's cup.

"It must be exciting for you. To move into the main house."

"I'm a little in shock, I think. I don't know how much will change. I'll still do morning duties in the laundry, but Deborah has invited me to learn about healing with her in the afternoons."

Joy's eyes narrowed. "You are going to assist Deborah?"

"Shouldn't I?"

"No, no, by all means, whatever path the Powers set before you is the one you should travel. But

Deborah has never taken an assistant before. She holds herself apart from the others in many ways."

"How long has she been here?"

"Oh, since she was a child. Like the Leader, she went away for a while to learn medicine and then returned to help the community. The Leader is caught up with the spiritual health of the Chosen; he needed help to provide aid to those in physical need."

"So she's a medical doctor?"

"I believe in the outside world she has the degrees, yes, though we don't value such things here. Here she is a healer and would be with or without the approval of the Outside establishment."

Lost women came in all shapes and sizes. Tara had seen it numerous times as a beat cop. Women who seemed to have it all together but were found beaten and bloody on a street corner or even in their own homes, women who should have been willing and able to get out of abusive relationships but stayed for reasons Tara would never understand. But Deborah was a *doctor*. You don't get that far in your life without having a certain level of self-confidence and ambition. Why had she returned to the fold?

The most likely motive was greed. If whatever drug they were developing resulted in something beyond a method of controlling the flock, it could be worth millions, or even billions. Deborah would be sitting pretty. But that would mean she had to have known about the experiments before she came back to the compound.

"How long has she been your healer?"

"Almost four years."

Wow. Talk about the long con. But if the rewards were great enough, it might be worthwhile.

"You're lucky to have access. In the town where I grew up, the nearest doctor was miles and miles away."

"The Powers provide," Joy said. "Just as they provided Jacob when we needed to replace John."

"Indeed."

The Leader released them from dinner, and Tara cleaned up her place and went to join Jake.

"Hey, babe," he said, dropping a kiss on her forehead and pulling her close as if it were the most normal thing in the world. " We can't go out at night here without sacrificing the Leader's security, so I want to take a quick run before bed. I'll meet you upstairs, okay?"

"Of course." Tara was beginning to feel as if she said nothing but "yes" and "of course." But it was only for a few more days. Then she could take off Serena's personality and slip back into her own.

She climbed the steps to her new bedroom and went inside. Would Jake have checked for cameras? Probably. But still, she looked to the best of her ability herself before stripping down for her shower. If they were watching, they could assume she'd caught his paranoia.

The bathroom was infinitely nicer than the ones shared

in the bunkhouses and cabins. To start with, it had electricity. Lights and an exhaust fan for the steam. Fluffier towels. A fresh bar of soap. Shampoo, even, when she was used to washing her hair with the hand soap in the cabin. A razor rested on the vanity, and a search of the drawers revealed fresh blades. So she turned the water on in the shower, noting its glorious pressure, and stepped in.

If she took longer than strictly necessary, well, she hoped the Powers would forgive her. But when she stepped out, she'd shaved, shampooed, and scrubbed until she felt almost herself. The luxuries of the bathroom did not extend to a hair dryer, so she walked out to the bedroom and sat on the bed in front of the fan. She tipped her body forward and let the air flow through her hair from underneath while combing it with her fingers.

She'd gotten most of the wetness out when she heard steps coming down the hall, and then Jake popped in.

"Hi honey, I'm home," he teased.

She grinned at him.

"I see you're enjoying the new accommodations."

"I am. I even checked for any video because I knew you'd want me to."

"I checked myself. But you did right. You can't be too careful," he said. "Let me take a shower. I feel pretty grungy from that run. Then we can test out the bed. Hell, it's a private bathroom. We could even test out the shower if you like."

Her whole body clenched in answer. *Yes, please.* But no way could she let down her guard like that in here. "I just got my hair dry. But I'll come in and chat with you while you shower."

"I'll seduce you into that shower yet," he said, and held out a hand.

Once inside, he turned on the shower and waited a couple of seconds before speaking.

"I checked pretty thoroughly, and I'm sure there's no video, but audio can be done through the walls and windows if they're determined, and I don't for a second believe putting us up here is a sign of trust."

"No."

"So for the moment, voices low, with running water. Or buried under the pillows on the bed. That should muffle any distance equipment."

He shucked his clothes in a quick, matter-of-fact motion that shouldn't have left her feeling as if she'd just watched a first-rate male strip show, but it did. Her breath stuttered and her palms went sweaty, and she plunked down on the toilet, thankful the lid was down.

When she had her breath back, she raised her voice above the shower's noise and told him about the job with Deborah.

"Hey, that's really cool," he said, also loud enough for any eager listeners. "You're a born helper, baby. You will be great at that. Deborah's lucky to have you."

"Life is going to be good, isn't it Jacob?" She let anxiety bleed into her tone. "We've found a good place, right?"

"We have." The water went off in the shower, and Tara squeaked and excused herself before being confronted with a wet, naked Jake.

In the bedroom, she slipped beneath the fluffy duvet that covered the bed—no scratchy blankets or low-thread-count sheets in the main house—and waited for Jake. Scraping and scrubbing noises indicated that he was shaving and brushing his teeth. Any hope she had that he might have dressed while out of sight was squashed when he opened the door.

Dear, sweet God, the man was gorgeous. Just when she

thought she was getting used to his physical impact, the sheer mass of sinew and muscle, the elegant grace and restrained power overwhelmed her again. He lifted the comforter and slid in beside her. His arm slid behind her neck, and she rolled closer until she was lying against him, her belly at his hip, her head in the hollow of his shoulder.

She breathed him in. He should smell like her. They'd used the same soap, the same shampoo. But he didn't. He smelled musky and dark, and she wanted desperately to lick him and see how that tantalizing scent tasted against her tongue.

But even after all the intimacies they'd shared, she couldn't.

Jake, however, had no such hesitation. He rolled to face her, tilted her head back, and kissed her. His mouth was hot, and he tasted of mint and musk.

"You're wearing too many clothes," he murmured, slipping a finger beneath the elastic of her panties.

"Yeah?"

"Definitely." He sat up, tossing the comforter to the foot of the bed, and knelt so that his calves trapped hers. Hooking fingers in either side of her panties, he pulled them slowly, oh so slowly, down her legs, then reached behind his own back to pull them off. Her mouth went dry and her core went wet. When he'd tossed away her undies, Jake brought his legs closer together, forcing hers shut. The sensation of her own skin pressing tightly against her flesh sent a shiver through her.

Jake grinned.

He leaned forward, and she felt his cock move over her mound. She tried to arch upward, but his position kept her down as he applied his considerable skill to kissing her. His fingers tangled in her still-damp hair, holding her head in place. His mouth hovered, nibbled, licked, teased until she pushed up and forced him to meet her full on. He stretched out his legs, letting her bear his full weight.

She wiggled her legs out from under his so that he lay between her thighs, his erection pressing hard against her center. He reared back just enough to get his hands beneath her shirt and yank it over her head, then came back down on top of her.

"Mine," he whispered against her neck. His mouth moved from her neck to her shoulder, down across her collarbone, pausing for a taste from where her pulse beat far too quickly, and on. His lips found her nipple and surrounded it with wet heat that dragged a sob from her lungs. Against her skin, she felt his grin.

His teeth took hold of her left nipple, gently teasing and scraping, while his fingers pinched her right.

She twisted beneath him, arms circling the breadth of his shoulders, then sliding down his back. She clenched her fingers into the muscles of his butt. He jerked in response, the blunt head of his cock sliding inside her a fraction. But he wasn't ready for that. He pulled back, sliding off the foot of the bed, and grabbed her ankles to haul her back with him. He positioned her on her forearms and knees, open to where he stood behind her.

Instinctively, she tensed, unaccustomed to giving up so much control. And what he must have been seeing—her mother's voice whispered horror in her head: *My God, Tara Jean, the size of your butt*—but then Jake was nudging his way inside her, and all thought vanished on a wave of scorching heat. He planted a hand flat in the center of her back, forcing her upper body down onto the bed, and pleasure screamed through her. She wiggled, trying to take even more of him, and heard him grunt, felt him begin to thrust.

Each thrust shoved her forward, rocked the bed, rubbed her sensitized nipples over the covers until she was sobbing, begging for him to finish her. And when he did, when he sent her flying over the edge and into a million tiny pieces, she felt him go as well, heard him call her name. Her real name. Tara.

That ridiculous, southern froufrou name she'd hated from the age of twelve had never sounded so good.

⌐

HOLY HELL. HE hadn't meant for that to happen. Sure, he'd checked for cameras and so had Tara, but he'd never meant to let his guard down while inside the compound. He'd set his goal to protect Tara and then had promptly lost his mind and taken her like a fucking caveman. He'd even called her by her real name. Not that that should surprise anyone who might have heard it—Jason Norman and Tara Jean Black had been lovers, so her pre-Chosen name would be likely to come to his lips.

He crawled up the bed and drew her along with him, anchoring her to his body. Nerves fired under his skin. He had to get her *out*, had to keep her safe. He pulled a pillow over their heads to muffle their voices.

"Tara—"

"They probably keep the drugs in Owen's room, right?"

He gritted his teeth. He wanted to talk about *them*, not the op. But she kept talking. "Or maybe Deborah's. She has to have access to them to add them to the tea. No way he does that himself."

He swallowed, forcing his mind back to the job at hand. "Those are the best bets. Owen's room will present the biggest challenge. But I can't see him taking personal responsibility for the drug program. He would want to be consulted at every step, but not be hands-on, so it makes sense that Samuel and Deborah control distribution and experimentation. If the drugs are in his room, they have access."

"I think he's too crazy for that," Tara said. "He really believes forces of evil conspire against the Chosen and against him as their leader. He's not going to want people — even his acolytes — tromping through his room."

A foreign sound intruded. A wail, like the fire alarm, but closer and higher pitched.

"What the hell?"

Tara stared at him, still holding the pillow over them. "It couldn't be. Not yet. Could it?"

"Fuck." If the raid had started, they were in serious trouble. Doors slammed and footsteps clattered in the hallway and down the stairs.

"I'll take Deborah's room, you take Owen's," Tara said, sitting up.

"No. We stick together. Deborah first."

Deborah's door was locked, and they didn't have time to pick it. Jake kicked it and it slammed inward. If the alarm turned out to be a misfire, they'd have to run. No hiding their true purpose now. But he couldn't risk Deborah or Samuel returning to destroy the evidence, leaving nothing for them to analyze. He'd set the Trojan horse program to download anything on the network, but depending on how paranoid or security conscious those involved were, the formula might not have been stored on a device with network connectivity.

"There was a laptop here," Tara said, standing next to a desk at the far wall. "She didn't even bother to unplug it — the cable's still here — she just grabbed it and took off."

Jake studied the various vials and jars and bottles in the refrigerator and in the glass-fronted cabinets. Some were labeled. Most were not. The labeled drugs — antibiotics, painkillers, and sedatives — came from both sides of the border.

An explosion shook the house and knocked several of the vials over. A second later, the odor of smoke drifted up.

"Fuck. They're burning it down."

Tara tore the comforter off the bed. "Here. We should get as many of the meds out with us as we can." She spread it on the floor and he dumped containers in by the armload. As he worked, Tara rolled, so that within seconds they had a secure, log-shaped package.

"Owen's room?" Tara asked as he hoisted the roll in his arms.

"Yeah." But when they stepped into the hallway, the smoke was too thick. He grabbed Tara's hand and ran for the stairs.

"The office," she said, coughing. "We should check—"

"Go!" That direction was clearer anyway. Smoke and fire engulfed the front of the house, but the back, where Owen's office lay, was merely hazy.

THEY HIT THE office at a good clip, and when Jake stopped dead in the doorway, Tara ran smack into his back. Her eyes were watering, but as she peered around him she could make out what had halted him. The office, while untouched by fire, had been completely dismantled. The massive cherry desk had been pushed closer to the door, and papers lay strewn everywhere. A piece fluttered by, caught by a breeze from the open window, and she reached out to catch it as Jake stepped over to the spot where the desk had once sat.

"Dammit," he said, bending down. Tara heard a creak. "Trap door."

She was stepping around the desk to see what he'd found when a loud *crack*, the unmistakable sound of a gunshot, ripped through the room. Jake stumbled backward two steps and went down.

"Jake!" She dove over to him. "Oh God, no. Don't you do this to me. Don't." Blood covered his face, and when she grabbed him beneath the armpits and began dragging him toward the window — the only likely exit — it quickly soaked into her shirt. He was losing too much, too fast. "Don't be dead," she ordered. "Don't you dare."

She shoved the window all the way open until it jammed at the top, and she did her best to lift Jake's unresponsive weight up and rest his midsection against the frame. Leaning out, she screamed for help. *Where were the damned govern-ment agents who'd started this whole mess?* She'd have to drop him, but at least she could arrange it so he hit the ground feet first.

She was lowering him as gently as possible when she caught movement out of the corner of her eye. She let go of Jake and tried to duck away from Samuel, but she was caught in the corner with no way to move, and he slammed a baton into her skull and the room went dark in a blast of pain.

CONSCIOUSNESS RETURNED IN fragments. A pounding head. The swell of nausea in her stomach and the back of her throat. A thrumming sound. The odor of oil. The occasional splash.

A boat.

Her hands and feet were trussed, and a blindfold had been tied over her eyes. A tight itch across her mouth extended out to her cheeks. *Duct tape.*

What the hell had happened? She shoved aside the ache in her head and tried to remember. The raid. The fire. *Jake.* Goddamn them, they'd shot him. For that, she'd kill them. She had no idea how, but that didn't matter. Before, she'd been content to wait for the good guys to round up the black hats, to throw them all in jail. But no more.

Where the hell were they taking her? And why? Why hadn't Samuel murdered her outright in the office?

There weren't that many places to go by boat from the compound. They had to be headed for Mexico. The boat bumped, then rocked as someone stepped off.

"Get her on her feet," Samuel said. "She's awake."

Rough hands grabbed her arms and pulled her to her feet. If she struggled, she'd fall overboard and drown, so she let them move her. She felt herself dragged up to a solid surface.

"Get the trucks," said Francis. "We'll wait here."

A few minutes passed in complete silence. Were they hiding from police? Should she make noise? But right now, at least, she was safe. Right now, they weren't interested in killing her, which was more than might be said for whoever might find them. If they were, indeed, in Mexico, the police weren't the only men out patrolling.

The rumble of several motors brought her to attention. She felt the air move across her face as one of the trucks pulled up in front of her. Hands pushed her forward and others lifted her into the back of what she assumed was a pickup. They forced her to the floor, and rough cloth covered her.

"Stay still, or I'll put a bullet through your fucking skull, just like I did your boyfriend's," Samuel said. Behind the blindfold, tears burned, but she squeezed them back, grateful that the duct tape wouldn't let them see her lips tremble. Weights were piled atop her body. They felt like bags of produce. Potatoes? Oranges? A booted foot kicked her hard in the side, and the truck jolted into motion.

They were stopped twice, and both times a foot rested casually on the side of Tara's face while the truck driver answered questions she couldn't quite hear. Both incidents ended in laughter. The apostles had cultivated friendships with whoever controlled these roads. She and Jake had hypothesized about the Chosen being in bed with the cartels. Evidently, they'd been correct.

"Did the Leader say what to do with her?" asked a voice she didn't recognize when the truck slowed for a third time.

Christ. Owen had escaped, too? Had the damned raid caught none of them? What had the feds been doing?

"Put her in one of the basement rooms. Chain her. If she gets out, you'll pay in blood." Francis. So far, she recognized him and Samuel. But there had been several others on that boat with them. Did they have a full compound in Mexico, similar to the one they had in Texas, with workers blind to the reality of the operation? And how did they plan to explain her presence if Owen had the faithful as his housekeepers on the other side of the border as well?

She was hustled out of the truck and half carried into a house. There, the bindings around her ankles were cut off and the blindfold removed. A swarthy man stood to her right with an M4 pointed at her head. He smiled.

CHAPTER TEN

JAKE WAS TWELVE. He'd been playing catcher—and doing a damned fine job of it despite his parents' objections to his fascination with sports—until one of the kids on the opposing team let go of his bat at the end of a swing and it clocked Jake in the noggin. They were going to be so pissed. He'd have to miss school.

"Jake?"

That wasn't his mother. That was . . . *Lucy.*

He wrenched his eyes open despite the pain in his head. He winced at light's reflection off the white and stainless surfaces surrounding him. Machines beeped and hummed. Tubes ran to his arm and under the light hospital blanket that covered him.

"Tara . . ."

"We're looking for her. Are you okay?"

"What do you mean?" He struggled to sit up, setting the machines into overdrive. A nurse hustled in.

"Agent Nolan, you're awake!" She leaned over his bed, peering into his eyes. "And you're looking much better. But you need to stay calm."

"Like hell."

"Jake, please." Lucy took his hand. "We're working on finding her. Until we do, you need to get your strength back."

"How long have I been out?" Frustration ate at him. Where was Tara? What were they doing to her?

"Almost twenty-two hours. We found you outside the

main building, which burned to the ground. You'd been shot in the head. They airlifted you here for surgery."

"Fuck. Twenty *hours?* There was a trap door . . ."

"Yeah. The task force guys found it. Led to a tunnel. A big one. Looks like they had vehicles in it. First tunnel led out to the greenhouses, and from there out under the walls. They found evidence of several boats. Far as we can tell, they've gone to ground in Mexico."

Jake reached for the IV to pull it out of his arm.

"Stop that!" Lucy and the nurse spoke in concert.

"Mexico's a big country. I called in a favor. Got a friend figuring out where she might have been taken. Until we know, we can't move. So relax and get better."

"I can't do that. For Christ's sake, Luce. She's on that damned drug, too. Did you get anything from the computer?"

"We did. Both the formula and the antidote. They rounded up the women and they're dosing them at about a half dozen different hospitals. Too many to fit in just one."

"The pregnant ones?"

"We found nine women in different stages of pregnancy. No one has any idea what detoxing will do, so they're being monitored extra closely."

"Aurora?"

"Who?"

"Never mind. She was one of the girls. Nice kid. I was hoping you'd found her."

"I don't know all their names. But your DEA friend Kevin has worked with us nonstop to identify them all."

"And Elizabeth? His girlfriend?"

"She's here. With a couple of the other pregnant women. She's been a tremendous help keeping them as calm as possible under the circumstances."

"Who escaped?"

"We don't know. Owen died in the fire. That's certain. He was facedown when they got him out, so he could be identified by sight. Some weren't so lucky. Aaron was shot trying to run away. He's still in critical condition. Most of the guards gave up without a fight once they knew they were dealing with the JTTF. They were just hired guns, not willing to go to jail on a terrorism charge. A few of the Chosen were injured but only three seriously enough to require hospitalization. The ones we could get to agree were bussed here to El Paso where there are counselors and LEOs helping them figure out what to do next."

The door opened and Ethan stuck his head in. "They're here."

"Thank God." She squeezed Jake's hand. "I am going to step outside. Ask nicely, and maybe this lovely lady will take out the cannula and catheter."

"Well, you ready?" the nurse asked as the door shut behind Lucy.

Nausea boiled in his stomach and everything he looked at too long wore a white halo, but he nodded. The sooner he was free of tubes, the sooner he could go after Tara.

"The doc says you can try standing up," the nurse said after she freed him. "Just hold on to this IV stand, and ease your way over to the side of the bed."

He did. The world spun a little faster but eventually settled. Weight on the IV stand, he pushed to his feet.

"You can take a little walk. Your friends are just outside, past the nurses' station in the waiting area. You can sit with them if you like."

Hell yes, he liked. The nurse helped him put on scrubs underneath his gown, and he shuffled out, feet sticking to the floor in the nonslip green socks she had given him to go with the scrubs.

In the waiting area, Lucy and Ethan sat huddled with a man whose dark hair was liberally streaked with silver. A light-haired man with a crew cut dressed in black cargo pants and a black T-shirt stood at parade rest behind them. Although he listened to the conversation, his eyes never stopped moving. Who, exactly, had Lucy brought in?

Then the older man turned in his direction, the light catching on a silver guitar pick earring, and Jake knew. The older man stood and held out a hand.

"You must be Jake. I'm Nash Harper."

Jake took Harper's hand. Everyone in the law enforcement community knew—or at least knew of—Dwight "Nashville" Harper. He ran one of the biggest, best-funded private security organizations in the country. And he had contacts everywhere. Although his public background information said he'd served in the Army, scuttlebutt claimed he'd really been CIA.

"I didn't realize you and Lucy were friends."

"A book she wrote helped my cousin immensely. I owed her a favor. She called to collect. I'm a bit disturbed she didn't call sooner—I understand she had trouble of her own over the past few months."

Ethan slung an arm over Lucy's shoulders. "We handled it."

The corner of Nash's mouth quirked up. "So I see. But this requires, shall we say, a different skill set?"

Jake would gladly smack that half grin off the bastard's face. Harp Security Enterprises might be entirely legit, but rumors flew about the kinds of activities they engaged in. He'd heard blackmail, theft, hacking . . . all kinds of accusations, though nobody had ever proven any of them.

Blondie leaned forward, feeling the vibe Jake wasn't trying to hide, but Harper shook his head. The smile disappeared.

"This woman is important to you. Asset protection and recovery is our area of expertise. We will find her, and we will bring her back."

"Not without me."

Harper cocked his head. "Let me be blunt. I've investigated you thoroughly. That's my business. What I see is that you're a very smart, very driven individual, just the kind I like to have on a team. But nothing in your background indicates skills in tracking, SERE, or combat. You'd be more use to us staying here."

"Not going to happen. If you leave me behind, I'll find my own way and probably fuck up whatever plan you put into action. I can hold my own."

Harper looked over his shoulder at Blondie, who nodded once.

"Fine, then. This is Trey Godwin. It's his op. If you want in, you understand that it's his show. His orders." The subtext was clear: Jake couldn't ask about the man's training; he either accepted the situation or he didn't.

He examined the man, who met his gaze without flinching. He'd never come up against any of HSE's operatives, but like most security companies, Harp tended to recruit former military. No question that's where this guy had come from. And despite his youth, there was a coldness to him that bespoke a deep immersion in violence.

"All right," he said at last. "It's your op."

"Good." Trey checked his watch. "I'll call Reno and see what he's got for us."

He stepped out of the waiting room with its multiple "no cell phone" signs.

"Trey's former Army. A Ranger," Harper said, apparently willing to volunteer information since Jake had not asked. "And he's a medic. I think you need to be prepared for your friend's situation to be fairly grim."

Not like he didn't know, but hearing it said so baldly brought the fact home hard. He lowered himself into one of the chairs.

"What do you have so far?"

"They're definitely in Mexico. Chihuahua. Somewhere outside Juárez. Reno—he's our communications and tech guy—he thinks he should have an exact location within forty-eight hours. But that land is heavily cartel-controlled. Between the Zetas and the *Hijos* . . . even the Juárez cartel is a possibility. They're down, but not out."

"I thought the *Hijos* were on the wane," Jake said.

"Who are the *Hijos*? And the Juárez?" Lucy asked.

"The Juárez were big in the nineties," Harper explained. "Their leader died in, oh, ninety-seven or ninety-eight, I think. They faded for a while, but they seem to be back on the upswing. And with Z-40 in custody, there's a good chance they'll try to take over a portion of the Zeta profits."

"And the *Hijos*?"

"*Los Hijos de la Madre Muerte*—Sons of Mother Death. Sort of a cross between a cartel and a cult. Like the Knights Templar. But there's plenty of evidence they're heavily into cocaine and heroin production and distribution. Their first leader came over from Colombia in the sixties. When he died, his son took over. But here's the problem: no one, and I mean no one, knows who their leader is these days. Juan Carlos Muñoz, who took over from his father, married an American girl from Idaho, if you can believe it. They stayed married for about fifteen years, near as we can tell, and then daddy died and she suddenly got a taste of what it meant to be married to a cartel boss. At which point she either ran, or he had her killed."

"No kids?" Jake asked.

"A ten-year-old son with his long-time mistress. But with Katherine, the Idaho wife . . . there are rumors. We're almost certain they had a daughter named Elina, and they might have had a son named after his father. But neither of those kids was ever confirmed. Never photographed, never even seen in public. If they existed at all, they disappeared with their mother. They'd be in their late thirties or early forties now if they lived, though, too old for any of Owen Stephenson's apostles."

"When did Juan Carlos die?"

"Seven years ago. The cartel took a hit, the way they always do, and the Zetas took over, but the *Hijos* only had about a two-year hiatus. Then they came back, more brutal than ever."

"That has to be when they got involved with Owen and Samuel. Maybe they were looking for a new distribution channel to fund their power struggle."

"Makes sense," Lucy agreed.

"Still, we don't know what home base is for them. Reno is looking at a couple of different big houses in the area. The problem with an area that's seen so much violence over the years is that anyone with bucks builds themselves a damned fortress, so we can't just point to one and go, 'That's it.' When he pinpoints the spot, we'll go."

"Forty-eight hours is too long. Tara could be dead in two days."

"She could be dead now. You wouldn't be ready if we left today anyway. You're barely able to stand. You were shot in the head. That the bullet bounced off your skull is a miracle of physics. If the shooter had been in front of you instead of below you, you'd be toast. Use the time to get better."

"Well I'm not getting better in here." He looked at Lucy. "Get me out. I need real food, and real clothes."

⸺

AT GUNPOINT, HANDS still bound, Tara was taken down to a basement room that reminded her of the isolation sheds in the Chosen's compound, with a few upgrades. In the corner squatted a stained and chipped sink and toilet—the industrial type, with no tank she might be able to disassemble for weapons. A metal table and chair dominated the rest of the small space, and chains hung from u-bolts in the cement walls. The man who brought her down snapped one end of a pair of cuffs to her left wrist, the other to a link about halfway down the chain. It left her enough room to sit without having to have her arm in the air, but she couldn't get near the door. Once she was safely snapped in, he pulled out a hefty knife and used the serrated back edge to cut through the duct tape around her wrists.

He left her alone, and she immediately began looking for anything she might use to open the cuffs. The chains were thick and heavy, each link probably two inches wide, with not a single spot of rust; no breaking those. A bobby pin would be ideal—her first instructor at the academy had taught them all how to create a cuff key from a bobby pin—but her hair fell loose around her shoulders. She hadn't even put a rubber band in it when they'd run from the bedroom during the raid. The floor had been swept clean of any objects, though a layer of sandy dust covered everything.

Obviously, they hadn't had "guests" for a while. Lucky her. A small window high on the wall had thick, chicken-wire fencing outside as well as bars on the inside. If she could convince them to let her off the chain, she could reach between the bars, break the glass, and pull free the fencing to unlock the cuffs. She'd still have to find a way out of the room, but it was a start.

Hearing voices in the corridor outside, she quickly dropped her head to her knees. It wouldn't do to let them see her studying the window.

"You have been a real pain in the ass, Tara Jean Black, or whatever your name really is," said Samuel as he entered. "And don't think I won't find out. Things will go a lot better for you if you just tell me right now."

Oh, right.

"Don't worry," said Deborah, propping a hip on the table and pulling out a small black case. "She'll tell you anything you want."

"Truth serum?" Tara asked. "Really? How pedestrian." And how seriously fucked she was if crazy Deborah had access to Sodium Pentothal. "Given all your fancy games, I would have thought you'd have a much more nifty experiment planned."

Deborah laughed. "We don't play games. And we don't bother with 'truth serums.' Everyone knows they're unreliable. No, we have much more effective means of getting information. But for now, I have to be sure you don't . . . expire . . . before it's convenient."

Hell. She'd managed to forget the suicidal side effect of withdrawal. How long had she been without the damned tea? Outside the tiny window, the light was already dimming. She'd lost most of a day.

Deborah pulled a vial and needle from the black case, along with a piece of rubber tubing, and Samuel reached for Tara. She ducked away from his arm, but the chain yanked her back and he slammed her into the wall, which left her left arm outstretched. "Perfect," Deborah crowed, tying the rubber tightly around Tara's arm. "We've never tried the antidote in injectable form before, but it should work fine. We don't have time to have you drink it." She drew about a quarter of the vial into the syringe. "Now, let's check out your veins."

And damned if she wasn't cursed with excellent veins. With an O negative blood type, she made sure to donate regularly, and the hospital lab techs always told her how good her veins were.

Apparently, Deborah agreed, because she jabbed the needle smack into the hollow of Tara's elbow and depressed the plunger. "Does it burn?" she asked, tilting her head to watch Tara's reaction.

And yeah, it burned. But that was the least of Tara's concerns. "Doesn't this crap occasionally kill one of your subjects? The guys who go out into the desert with Aaron and never come back?"

Deborah shrugged. "You know what they say. Only the strong survive." She collected her works, and Samuel let go of Tara. "See you in the morning."

"Wait!"

"What?" Samuel asked.

"I need to go to the bathroom." Which she'd originally said out of desperation, but once the words were out, her bladder woke up and started screaming.

"You really think we're gonna fall for that?"

"Just hook her farther down the chain so she can reach

the toilet," Deborah said impatiently. "She won't be in any shape to cause a problem."

"You're awfully fucking relaxed," Samuel muttered, but he did as she ordered, unlocking Tara's handcuff and reattaching it at the end of the chain so that she could reach the toilet, if not the door.

And she could reach the window, which she did the moment she'd taken care of the rest of her business. Unfortunately, as she watched, booted feet passed by. She waited a few minutes, and more feet passed. Guards. They would undoubtedly hear the glass breaking if she tried to reach the wire.

And then the shaking started, and she collapsed onto the dirty cement floor. The chain rattled with each wave of tremors, and the rattles echoed in her head. Her stomach heaved, and she crawled over to the filthy toilet. Waves of nausea and cold sweat rolled over her. When the cramps started, she seriously thought she might have been better off dead.

～

THE NIGHT WENT on forever. At some point, sleep snuck in and carried Tara off, and when she woke she lay on the floor beneath the window, the sun already high in the sky. At least she hadn't passed out in the toilet. The trembling had subsided into the occasional quiver in her hands. Exhaustion begged her to remain on the floor, but she forced herself to stand. She splashed a couple of handfuls of tepid water across her face and wiped her gritty eyes on the shoulder of her T-shirt.

On tiptoe, she peered out the window, looking for guards.

None she could see. Time to get to work on the cuffs. She shucked her tee and wrapped it around her hand, then tapped lightly on the glass. If she could break out a small corner, it would be less noticeable when Samuel came back. No luck. She hit it a bit harder. But the glass refused to break, taunting her. Her third try shattered the glass into hundreds of pieces. Damn. That would be extremely noticeable.

In fact, the very sound had attracted attention. Footsteps pounded down the hallway. She grabbed the biggest piece of glass she could find and stuffed it quickly into the center of the cardboard of the toilet paper roll that sat on the edge of the sink and yanked her shirt back on.

Two strange men rushed into the room, guns drawn. A moment later, Samuel arrived, followed by Deborah.

"Really? The *window?* What did you think, you could call for help?" Deborah shook her head. "You don't get it, do you? There's no one here who will help you. You're on your own." She surveyed the broken glass and gestured to one of the men. "Clean that up. And make sure she didn't keep any of the pieces.

"Now, let's have a little chat. Before you waste your time lying to me, we already know your name is Tara Jean Dobbs and you are — or were; that part you can clarify for us — a cop."

Tara kept her mouth shut.

"And then there's your boyfriend. He's been a little harder to track, but we found him about two this morning. FBI. So we have a few very simple questions for you: Exactly what did you tell your friends on the outside, when, and how?"

Tara crossed her arms, clanking the chain, and stared Deborah in the eye.

Samuel walked over and leaned close to her face. "Answer her."

When Tara refused to speak, he clocked her in the temple with a massive fist. She stumbled to the side, catching herself against the wall.

"I said, answer her."

No fucking way. The minute they got the information they wanted, she was dead. Her only way out of this mess was to delay until they left her alone again so she could free herself from the cuffs.

"You're only making this harder on yourself," Deborah said. She jerked her head at Samuel, who left the room, a smirk on his face. Bozo One cleaned up the glass and then left, too. "When Samuel comes back, things are going to get very bad for you, Tara Jean. Very bad. So I advise you to give it up now."

Tara continued to stare until Deborah sighed elaborately and shook her head. She leaned up against a wall behind the table with a faint sneer on her face and glanced at her watch.

Samuel entered the room carrying a hefty, battered toolbox.

Not good, TJ. Her mouth went dry, but she kept her expression neutral.

The toolbox screeched out a nails-on-a-chalkboard warning as Samuel dragged it across the metal table toward the end where the chair was positioned. Tara refused to look at the various items he was laying out with great care. She let her gaze drift to the ceiling and counted the spider webs clinging there, but she could still see his movements out of the corner of her eye.

"Bring her here," he said at last.

Bozo Two grabbed Tara's left arm, and she reacted without thought, slamming the base of her right palm up into his nose. He dropped her arm and howled, backing away. "What the fuck?!"

"What did you *think* she was going to do, you moron?" Samuel asked, though Tara saw him jump a little and move two steps back. She didn't blame him. She'd kind of surprised herself. But now that she couldn't avoid looking at the damned table, there was no way on earth she was going to let them tie her into that chair without a fight. "Get Juan and Curt down here."

Bozo Two left, cursing steadily, and Tara moved to the farthest corner from the table and the pliers, hammer, knives, and mallet laid out there. If they used any of that shit on her, no way was she going to be able to keep from telling them whatever they wanted. She knew her limits.

"Do you know that there are certain places on the human body where nerves cluster very close to one another, very close to the surface?" Samuel asked, picking up the pliers from the table and tossing them from hand to hand. "One of those very sensitive spots is the tip of your finger." He studied his forefinger as if he were looking for his own nerves. "Have you ever lost a nail? Closed your finger in a car door, maybe? Or hit it with a hammer? Hurts like hell. But your nail doesn't come off for a few days. It turns black and blue underneath, swells up, your nail separates from the skin naturally, and the new one starts to grow in. Eventually, the one you damaged just falls off.

"But when you rip a nail off, now, that's a different matter entirely. Your nails are quite firmly attached, you see. The body doesn't like to give them up. There's a remarkable amount of blood. And quite a bit of pain, I understand. I've never experienced that part myself."

Two men entered the room, one dark, one fair. Tara pressed herself even farther into the corner.

Even in peak condition, Tara doubted she'd be able to take on the two thickly muscled men, and she was far from her peak. Still, they approached carefully. Probably they'd had a good look at Bozo Two's face. The thought gave her a little thrill of triumph despite the circumstances.

The men glanced at each other, then rushed her. One reached for her arm, but she ducked under and grabbed the roll of toilet paper with the shard of glass in it and struck out, using the roll as a handle. She felt it connect, drag, and pull as it sliced through skin, and one of the men shouted. Then a forearm slammed across her throat and pinned her to the wall. She tried to knee her attacker in the balls, but he just leaned harder against her, cutting off her air supply until black spots swam in front of her face.

"Don't kill her," said Samuel.

"Not a problem," replied the blond. "But I'm not planning on letting her fuck up my face. I saw Tom's upstairs, and now she got Juan, too."

"Bitch!" The dark-haired man hissed. "She fucking cut me."

"I see that. Just strap her in the damned chair and go clean yourself up."

The two men dragged her across the room and shoved her into the chair, tying her down with leather straps, one across her chest and under her arms, another over her thighs, and the third and fourth binding her legs to the legs of the chair.

She was still gasping for air when they left, and Samuel leaned on the table and got up into her space. Not so close she could head butt him in the nose, but close enough that she could feel his breath on her face. "Now, let me tell you how this is going to go. I'm going to hurt you. You're going to scream. You can't answer questions while you're screaming, so I won't bother asking. When we're done, Deborah will ask. You'll answer. If you don't, you and I will spend some more quality time together."

Tara straightened her shoulders. "You do know that studies show torture doesn't work, right? You hurt me, I'll tell you whatever I think you want me to say, whether it's true or not."

"That's the beautiful thing about our questions," Deborah said. "You'll either be able to answer — in which case you most certainly will — or you won't."

"For example?"

"She's stalling," Samuel said.

"So what if I am? You claim you're going to get your answers one way or another. So try me. What is it you want to know?"

"Let's start small," said Deborah. "You obviously know about the tea. Tell me what it does."

"Creates addicts," Tara spat.

"Very good. Now, who else knows?"

"I have no idea. Getting the word out was Jake's responsibility. He had access to the computers."

Samuel and Deborah exchanged a glance. They'd circle back to this topic, Tara felt certain. "And what do you know about the distribution network?"

"Distribution?" *Fuck.* If she told them the truth — that she and Jake had never even considered distribution — they'd have no reason to keep her alive. She took a deep breath, let it out slowly . . . and changed the subject.

"This is pointless. Your whole precious scheme is going to go down because Jake found the antidote. When your drug doesn't send people spiraling into a fatal depression as soon as they stop taking it, it loses considerable value. If I were you, I'd pack in the whole operation now."

"Suicide was a side effect, not a desirable outcome," Samuel corrected her. "We didn't name our experiment American Dream for nothing. It won't just provide us with the American Dream, those who take it will believe they're living the dream, too. So, yeah, getting off is hard. And we were talking about distribution."

"How did you avoid getting addicted yourself?" Tara asked Deborah. "You drank the tea when you ate with the Chosen."

"Distribution," said Samuel, but Deborah shrugged.

"Addiction isn't bad as long as you have a steady supply of the drug. That was the whole point. It can cloud your thinking, though, so we made sure that the antidote could be taken prophylactically."

"That's enough of your damned questions." Samuel grabbed her left hand and slammed it down on the table. He leaned hard on her forearm, holding it in place with the side of his torso. She yanked on his hair with her right hand and, when that had no effect, tried to shove him away.

"Dis. Tri. Bu. Tion."

Tara gritted her teeth and slugged him from the awkward angle as hard as she could, then tried to wedge her right hand between the two of them to grab his throat, but Deborah seized her right hand and wrenched it up and back, behind her head.

Time rippled, slowing, speeding, as Samuel took the needle-nose pliers and pried up the edge of the nail on Tara's forefinger. The cold metal felt almost like a balm against the sudden sweat on her skin.

"Common wisdom dictates you pull off a Band-Aid as quickly as possible," he said, bending the nail back slightly, then sliding the pliers down to get a better grip. "But we're not common. Are we?"

He wrenched, and she screamed.

JAKE PACED THE floor of his room at the hotel where Lucy, Ethan, and Harper and his men were all staying. Lucy had stocked the room with plenty of food and drink, but she'd still insisted he order room service the minute she got him inside.

"You need your strength. I've sent Ethan to buy you some better clothes. Not that those scrubs aren't lovely, but the good people of El Paso are already looking askance at us."

Yeah. Not like he'd missed the side eyes he'd gotten checking in wearing the pale green pants and shirt they'd given him at the hospital and with both eyes black-and-blue. Or the subtle shifting people did to stay away from Trey and his buddy, Marco.

So he'd eaten, and he'd waited for Ethan to bring him fresh jeans. And then he'd showered and changed and rested as much as he could with Lucy calling every hour to be sure his concussion was okay, and now it was afternoon and he was damned well ready for action. But they still didn't know who'd taken Tara, or where. Harper had called a meeting, which would be held in Jake's room in another ten—no, eight—minutes.

He rolled his shoulders back and forth. A few kata would be good to get him back in shape, see how his reflexes were doing. Maybe after the meeting.

A knock at the door, and Lucy and Ethan came in, followed by Trey, Marco, and Harper. Trey set up an easel in the corner of the room, and they all took seats where they could see it. Harper handed him a map, and Trey shook it out and clipped it to the easel.

"Okay, here's what we know: Of the bigwigs among the Chosen, two escaped—Francis and Samuel. Kevin Reasoner says there was a woman who stayed in the main house, too— Deborah—and we haven't found her, either."

"She ran the medical side of the drug concern," Jake said.

"Like Owen Stephenson, she had a medical degree. She counts as a bigwig."

"Noted. So that's three. They went down a tunnel in the office, and we tracked them across the river into Mexico." He put an X on the map. "They're in a building here. It's a private home, but it's *big*. And it sits smack in the middle of almost seven acres of property outside of Ciudad Juárez. Unfortunately, the land around Juárez is inhospitable. Scrub, desert, rock, with too few trees for reliable cover and the occasional house with occupants we don't want to endanger. We can't go in heavy, and sneaking in will be problematic."

"Not to mention crossing the border carrying weapons," Ethan said.

"That's not an issue," Harper said. "We have contacts in Mexico who can provide whatever we need. Advantage to working in private sector."

"So we get to Mexico, then what?" Jake stared at the map, trying to remember the landscape of Mexico. The last time he'd been there, he'd been working a case with the Mexican police, a border-crossing killer who'd given him nightmares for weeks thereafter. He had left the police station only rarely. He'd certainly never ventured into the countryside.

"We're going to drive in because—despite the off-putting black eyes and bandages of Agent Nolan, here—we'll attract less attention telling them we're taking our buddy who's just been in an accident on a vacation than we will hitting customs any other way. We'll meet up with Miguel, our contact, in Juárez. He's found a rental apartment about ten miles from the mansion. We can run the op from there, but too many civilians live there for us to go back once we've extracted the asset."

"Tara. Her name is Tara."

Trey didn't even glance at him. He inked a spot on the map. "This is the apartment building. There's virtually nothing on satellite as far as cover between it and the mansion. But if we go in this direction"—he indicated with the pen—"there are more trees and fewer houses. Still far from ideal. Most of what I am calling trees are actually bushes.

"But we have no idea how many people are at the mansion. Miguel did a drive-by and said he saw at least a dozen, but couldn't identify innocents versus targets. If we needed to eliminate everyone, that would be no problem. But we can't. And we can't afford to wake the entire area by choppering in to grab her, because there might be far more soldiers involved than we know. So we're going to have to sneak in, extract, then call the chopper and fly out."

"You're just going to casually cross the border in a helicopter?" No wonder LEOs hated Harper if he pulled that kind of shit on a regular basis. "You don't think that will be a problem?"

"Nope. The mansion is a hundred miles from the border. I have no intention of crossing in the chopper. But sat photos show a host of vehicles around that house, and we can't possibly outrun them all without air support. So—and I think you'll appreciate the irony here—we'll fly out, take the river by speedboat, and land right in the middle of the cleanup operation on the Stephenson property."

Well, yeah, he could appreciate that. Every branch of law enforcement would have representatives combing the compound. Tara would be completely safe, no matter which of the Chosen remained on the loose.

"When do we leave?" he asked.

"Tomorrow morning," Harper answered.

"Why not tonight?"

"Because arranging the types of things we need is not

precisely easy. Even for me. Besides which, three guys heading to Mexico for fun are a lot less suspicious in the morning. And you won't be able to approach the house until after dark tomorrow, so there's no rush."

"Fuck. I don't have my passport." He hadn't even thought about it.

"I do," Lucy said. "I brought it down to Twin Oaks as soon as you asked me and Ethan to come."

He sucked in a deep breath, let his muscles ease as she dug through her purse and handed him the slick booklet. "Thanks."

A few more odds and ends and the conference was over. Harper and his men left, but Lucy and Ethan lagged behind.

"Are you certain you're okay to go?" Lucy asked. "You look like hell."

"I have a mirror. But I'll be fine." He looked into her blue eyes. "I fucked up, Luce. Big time. I can't—I can't do this again."

"Don't count her out, Jake. Tara Jean Dobbs is one of the strongest women I've ever known. Even when she was just a kid, she was that way."

He held on to that assurance the whole time he lay in bed, waiting for dawn, waiting for the call that would tell him it was time to go. He held on and hoped that, this time, he would be enough.

⌒

TARA REGAINED CONSCIOUSNESS when cold water slapped her across the face. She had—*thank God*—passed out still tied to the chair before Samuel and his pliers had even finished removing her nail. Fainting hadn't done much for her ego, but at least she hadn't had to live with sharpest of the agony any longer. Her whole hand throbbed, and she wanted to vomit from the unceasing streaks of fire that shot up her arm from where it dangled limply at her side. They hadn't bothered to bandage the finger, so blood dripped steadily down into a pool on the floor. *Splat. Splat. Splat.*

Heat swelled up over her body, followed by ice.

Samuel stood over her, holding a bucket, Deborah beside him.

"That was fun," he said. "Now that you understand the situation, perhaps we can have a more productive conversation."

She shook her head.

"Now, now." He reached for her hand.

"Can't talk. Gonna puke."

Quickly, he stepped back.

"Go get her a bottle of water," said Deborah. Samuel hesitated, then turned on his heel and left the room.

The moment he was gone, Deborah leaned on the table with both hands. "Samuel likes pain, you know. He likes the particular smell of it coming out of your pores. And he'll get tired of your fingernails eventually. He always does. If you think you feel sick now, wait until he's broken a few of your bones and refused to set them. There's no point in holding back."

"Fuck you," Tara managed.

"Now, me," Deborah continued, "I prefer more humane methods. I can make you feel good. I can make you forget all about what he does to you. All you have to do is tell me how much you found out. Every detail you know."

Tara pressed her lips together.

Deborah shook her head. "Stubborn. You're the only one who will suffer, you know. It's not as if your silence hurts us."

Samuel returned with several bottles of water. He uncapped one and handed it to Tara. She didn't want it. What if they'd tainted it, the way they had the bottles in isolation? But she needed to stay hydrated at the very least. The body could last only three days without water, and she had no idea how she would get sustenance once she escaped.

She took a few small sips. Despite the ache in her hand and the shocks that traveled up her arm, her stomach settled a bit.

"Time to talk," Samuel said. "How much did you tell your Fed buddies about product distribution?"

"I told you, I don't know what Jake managed to communicate. You didn't give us a lot of free time. And you were watching him on the computer." She shivered, waited out a wave of nausea and sweat. She needed to keep them talking. Maybe, just maybe, even if she couldn't escape, the FBI could shut down the entire operation by using the information Jake had sent to Ethan. If they could trace the distribution, they might even make their way back here, though that would require cooperation from the Mexican government.

Stall.

"But why do you care what he knew? Surely the government will know it soon enough when they analyze the data on your computers from the compound. Or are you counting on the fire having destroyed them all? That's a big risk, isn't it?"

"The fire did its job," Samuel said.

"Shush," Deborah hissed. She narrowed her eyes at Tara. "It doesn't matter why we want the information. We do. So let's assume he sent out everything you knew before your friends invaded our private property. What would they know about our network?"

"Nothing." It was the safest answer. If Samuel and Deborah

believed they could continue as they had been, they had a far better chance of being caught. If they holed up and stopped talking to any of their people on the outside, the police might never find them.

"Bullshit. What brought you to the ranch in the first place?"

"Andrea."

"That was your *cover*. Who tipped you to what we were doing before you moved to Twin Oaks?"

"No one. I moved to Twin Oaks. I became friends with Andrea. She joined you. Or do you think she was undercover, too?"

"No." Deborah made the word last a full second. "But you could easily have befriended her because you knew about John."

"I didn't. I came to the Chosen looking for her. Ask Owen. I didn't know she was dead until after I got there."

"Owen."

"What, do you call him 'capo' or whatever the Mexican equivalent is now that you've moved to Mexico and shown your true colors?"

"The Leader. Yes. No, we don't call him 'capo.'" Deborah's fumble confirmed Tara's belief that Owen wasn't the real power behind the drug sales, despite his title. "But you know his name. So you didn't just come to the Chosen to find Andrea."

"I did. But as you pointed out, I used to be a cop. And if you'd done your research well enough you'd know it was 'used to be.' So I tend to look before I leap. I researched the Chosen and found out the current Leader was Owen Stephenson. Mildly sociopathic, pathologically narcissistic, God complex. But, fuck, I've dealt with men like that in all walks of life. This guy was just living his delusion a little louder."

"She's fucking lying." Samuel rapped his pliers on the edge of the table.

"Why would I lie? It's too easy to check! I found the cemetery. That's the only reason I even started investigating. If you'd let Andrea live, none of this would have happened."

"No way. Not with your FBI friend showing up a few weeks behind you."

"For fuck's sake," Tara snapped, "do you think we would have done that intentionally? If we'd been *together*, we would have come up with a far better cover. Andrea disappeared, so I came looking for her. I disappeared and he came looking for me. As you say, we were *friends*." The thought came with physical pain almost as intense as the one in her hand. Poor Jake.

"No way." Samuel reached for her left hand, and she waved it around trying to stay out of range, still trapped in the chair. Fire raced down her finger as the air swished by, and it was pointless anyway. There was nowhere to go.

CHAPTER ELEVEN

Again, Tara woke to water in the face.

"This passing out shit won't save you forever," Samuel informed her.

A bubble of hysteria formed in her throat. "Sorry," she choked out. He'd taken her center fingernail this time, and if the thought of raising her hand wasn't so painful, she'd have flashed it at him.

"Leave her to me," Deborah said. "I'll get it out of her. And if my way doesn't work, we can always go back to yours."

Samuel gritted his teeth, then shrugged. "What the hell? The Leader wants that information."

Deborah left the room, and Samuel leaned against the table. "Who'd have believed a fucking cop would have such a weak constitution? I thought for sure you'd be more fun to play with."

So glad to disappoint you. But Tara didn't dare speak the words. She had no desire to trigger Samuel's temper.

"We read a lot about you and your boyfriend when we finally got your last names," he said. "It makes what's about to happen so much more entertaining. It's a damned shame he's not still alive."

Don't ask. Don't ask. Don't ask. "What do you mean?"

"Well, with his sister and all, having a junkie for a girlfriend would have been absolute poetry."

Fuck. This was *not* how she wanted to go down. She tried to remember what she'd learned about heroin use as a patrol cop. Generally, unlike meth heads, junkies wouldn't fight you.

They'd be too relaxed to do much of anything. But a junkie in withdrawal was like a wounded animal: approach with caution. Would she be able to get out of the cuffs if Deborah injected her? Would she lose all desire to?

"I've told you guys everything."

"Too bad you're a cop. If you were Jane Doe who hadn't spent the last two months lying to us, even after your stint in isolation, you could maybe convince me of that. But now? No way."

Deborah reentered the room with her little black leather case.

"I hear heroin makes you throw up," Tara said. "You could at least untie me so I can get to the toilet."

"How long's this going to take?" Samuel asked.

"We should be able to question her in ten minutes." Deborah studied her. "But she's right. With our luck, she's going to puke. So get ready to untie her the minute it hits her system. We'll leave her for a bit, go get some dinner, come back. She'll be good and wasted for at least four hours."

Four hours. That wasn't so bad. If she sobered up after four hours, it would be the middle of the night and she could work the wires in the window loose. They wouldn't bother checking on her then.

Samuel grabbed her arm and slammed it down onto the table, causing her bloody fingers to slap into the metal. Despite herself, she screamed as the shock of pain traveled up her arm.

He grinned. "Aw, did that hurt? It's your own fault. Liars don't fare well around here."

Deborah pulled out her vial and syringe. "You're about, what . . . a hundred-twenty pounds, give or take?"

Tara weighed more like one thirty, but the lower estimation might encourage Deborah to lighten the dosage.

"That's what I weighed before you dragged me out of the Chosen and starved me and made me puke."

Deborah shrugged. "Good enough." Squeezing in next to where Samuel held Tara's forearm tight to the table, she tied the rubber tubing around her biceps. That done, she lifted a vial with a vaguely dirty-looking liquid in it and sucked about a third of the liquid into the syringe.

"Enjoy the ride," she said as she jammed the needle into Tara's arm and depressed the plunger.

The injection stung a bit, though not as badly as the antidote to the drug they'd been feeding the Chosen. Immediately after Deborah pulled the needle from Tara's arm, Samuel began cutting the leather straps that tied her to the chair.

Tara was prepared to fight, to punch and kick and do as much damage as possible the minute she was free despite the pitch and roll of her stomach, but before Samuel had even gotten to the strap around her first foot, her whole body went soft, weak, and warm. Every muscle relaxed at once, and even the ache in her fingers disappeared.

"Nice, isn't it?" Deborah asked.

Tara wanted to say no, but she couldn't. In truth, despite the fact that she was forming words in her head, she was pretty sure she wasn't saying them aloud. Samuel and Deborah left, but she had a hard time caring. She did her best to keep her injuries and her desperate situation in the forefront of her mind, but they kept slipping away.

Her body was so loose and relaxed that at one point she slumped down and fell off the chair. Which struck her as hilarious. She should just lie down on the floor and rest. That would be nice. But her mouth was very dry, and there was water on the table. Although it seemed like an enormous effort, she climbed to her feet and reached for the bottle. It took two tries to get the cap off because, despite the warm, comfortable fuzziness surrounding her, her injured left hand refused to do any work.

And then, when she'd sucked down the water, nausea struck again in crippling waves. She crawled over to the toilet and vomited up all the liquid she'd consumed. Christ, she was tired. She put her head down on the floor and dozed off. She woke because her skin itched, and her first attempt to scratch her right arm when she forgot about the condition of her fingers send a brutal shock of pain up her left that chased off the cloudy comfort. Her limbs still felt heavy, her muscles unwilling to work, but her brain came partway back to life.

How long had she been in dreamland? How long until Samuel and Deborah came back to question her again? She forced her feet under her and went to the window. Dusk covered the sky. She felt as if she'd been imprisoned for weeks, but it had only been a day. She needed out. Now. She reached between

the bars on the window and grabbed the chicken wire, wiggling it back and forth to loosen it. Before she could entirely free it, however, she heard the key in the door behind her. She scuttled backward into the space between the toilet and the wall, the only place that offered any cover.

This time, Deborah had the blond goon—Curt—with her. She also carried the little black case.

"Ah, Sleeping Beauty is awake," she said. "Perfect. I imagine you're feeling pretty good."

And Tara was. Her hand hardly hurt at all. After the initial jolt, when she'd scraped her nail-less fingers over her skin, the pain had subsided again to a dull throb. But damned if she'd tell Deborah that.

"I can make sure the pain doesn't come back," Deborah

said. "All you have to do is tell me how much you and your electronics-obsessed boyfriend discovered about our operation. In detail."

"I don't want your drugs," Tara said. "I may be feeling the effects, but I'm not stupid."

"Ah. I thought that might be your answer. It's one of the problems with being high. You forget what pain feels like. Curt?"

The man didn't even bother coming to get Tara. He just grabbed hold of the chain and yanked. She tried to remain in her corner, but her muscles wouldn't cooperate and she felt herself being dragged forward. At first, she stayed on the ground, where she had better leverage, but it was in vain, and she didn't want to be on the floor at his feet, so she stood to face him. He grinned.

Tara was having a hard time breathing. Her lungs didn't seem to want to expand. She watched the glitter in Curt's eyes and her lizard brain screamed for action, but her body simply refused to fight back. Deborah produced a pair of handcuffs and—though Tara twisted and wriggled and ducked—snapped her wrists together behind her back. From his pocket, Curt pulled a heavy-duty folding KA-BAR knife. Tara's father had used the same one as a hunting knife. It didn't inspire either pleasant memories or confidence.

With Deborah standing behind Tara and holding her in place, he sliced through the cotton of her T-shirt, the knife's tip leaving a paper-thin line of blood from her collarbone to her waist. She didn't feel it at first, and then it began to burn. Curt put the tip of the knife against the top of her right breast and with a quick twist of his wrist cut a divot out of her flesh as if he were coring a tomato.

Tara's breath left her in a rush and a scream. Instinctively, she tried to bring her hands up to press down on the wound, but they were still cuffed behind her, so instead she sank to the floor and pressed her chest into her knees.

"That was just a little reminder," Deborah said. "Anything you want to tell us?"

"I don't know what you want."

Deborah sighed. "We'll be back." She unsnapped the cuffs. "There's a guard outside. If you change your mind, you can call him to get me."

Tara's whole body hurt. Impossibly, given the circumstances, she'd fallen asleep again. But then, she'd seen junkies sleep under the most extreme conditions. Through the window, she could see the moon high in the sky. She pulled at the wire, wiggling and yanking until the whole rectangle came free of the window. Cement, dry and crumbly, coated the corners.

Her left hand was useless, so she stood on the mesh with her left foot to stabilize it and worked one wire loose. When she had about two inches unwrapped, she carried it over to the table and used the edge of the table to work it up and down until it broke free of the rest. Then she rolled up the larger piece of chicken wire and stored it next to the toilet, where it was less visible.

She turned her attention to the handcuff holding her to the chain, ignoring the sight of her bloody and swollen fingers. She inserted the wire partway into the cuff's lock and bent it, then bent it again, creating a small, S-shaped hook.

And now for the hard part. She'd spent hours practicing to beat her classmates in lock-picking skills, but that had been years ago, and her skills had no doubt gone rusty. She inserted the hooked end of the wire under the lip of the cuff lock and felt for the catch. No joy. A deep breath and she tried again.

And again.

On her fifth try, she felt the pin in the lock lift, and the cuff slipped open.

Now what?

The only object in the room she could use as a weapon was the chair. They wouldn't be expecting her to wait for them next to the door. Not only wasn't the chain long enough, but she'd so far held herself far away from her tormenters. Next time they came, she'd take out whoever walked in first, try to grab a weapon, and hope for the best. It wasn't much of a plan, but she didn't have many options.

But of course, now that she was ready for them, neither Samuel nor Deborah returned. Hours passed, and the aftermath of the injection threatened to suck her under again. She forced herself to stand and stretch out each of her limbs in turn. She would do some Tai Chi forms. That would keep her awake.

She was well into the third form when footsteps echoed in the corridor. She snatched the chair from its spot on the floor and took up position next to the door just as a key turned in the lock. The door opened, and she brought the chair crashing down on Samuel's head. He went down like a sack of potatoes.

Deborah shouted and guards came running. Tara reached for the gun holstered at Samuel's hip—he hadn't worn it the other times they'd come for her, and she couldn't stop to analyze its meaning—but before she could free it, one of the guards landed on top of her.

"Don't kill her!" she heard Deborah yell, and then the guard bashed her head into the hard cement floor.

Dazed, she felt herself dragged back into the room. The guards held her down while Deborah prepared a syringe and injected her again.

"If it were up to me," she said coldly. "I'd give you to Samuel to play with. I wouldn't count on him being kind next time."

Kind? Tara almost laughed, but the nausea slammed into her and all she could do was retch. And then, hard as she fought it, the deep, soothing warmth flooded her veins and relaxed her muscles, sending her to that place where nothing hurt and no one yelled and she was beautiful and graceful and loved.

⌒

TREY COULDN'T HIDE his military background, not with that haircut, but when he met Jake in the lobby the next morning, he had changed into a T-shirt that said, "Bad Girls Do" and a pair of ratty jeans. For his part, Marco wore a plain white T-shirt with the sleeves cut off. The color emphasized his dark skin and shaggy dark hair. He could easily have passed for a Mexican native, which was, perhaps the point. Each man carried a single piece of carry-on luggage, the same cheap brand Ethan had brought Jake's new clothes in. Nothing for an inquisitive ICE agent to worry about.

Despite Jake's twin black eyes and the prominent bandage that circled his skull, the border guard barely glanced at them before stamping their passports and wishing them a good day.

Have a nice time in Juárez, folks. Try not to get dead, Jake thought as the man waved them through. Not for nothing had Juárez frequently been called the murder capital of the world. Sinaloa, Juárez, *Los Hijos*, the Zetas . . . every major Mexican cartel had a presence in the city. But when Marco had told the border agent he was taking his buddies to taste his second cousin's cooking so they could see what real Mexican food was, the man hadn't even blinked.

In the peculiar way of cities like Detroit that those with means to do so frequently fled, Juárez seemed only half-alive. Well-maintained buildings backed to crumbling disasters. They parked in front of a small walk-up and went inside. After fifteen minutes in the empty lobby, they exited out the back. Trey led them down a garbage-strewn alley then out into a larger street, where a van idled at the curb. Marco slid the panel door open and they hopped inside.

"Any trouble?" the driver asked. He was dark complected, with almost blue-black hair, but he wore it short and curly where Marco's was long and straight. He was also, Jake noted, built like a tank. Not made for running, but his hands handled the van with absolute assurance on the rough roads.

"No trouble. You heard anything?"

"Not a word. Who's the new guy?"

"Jake Nolan." Jake reached forward from the back seat, and the guy stuck his hand over the seat and shook.

"Miguel Perez. I'll be your pilot."

"Ah. So you work for HSE as well?"

"Miguel's an independent contractor. He helps us out from time to time."

The man laughed. "You make me sound charitable. Nash Harper pays me well for my assistance."

"That's between you and him. Jake here's FBI. The asset is a friend of his."

Miguel glanced back at Jake. "You going to be okay going in?"

"Damned straight." Or so he hoped.

"Did you get everything?" Marco asked.

"Yes. Though I must say, it was not easy to get the rifles. A four-sixteen and a four-seventeen, along with the handguns. They cost a pretty penny."

"As long as they work."

"They work. I field-tested each of them. But you'll need to see for yourself. Make adjustments. We'll do that now."

Weapons. Harper hadn't been bragging when he claimed his contacts could get them what they needed. The Heckler & Koch 417 was popular among snipers, being basically a larger, heavier version of the 416, their standard assault rifle. But neither the HK416 or HK417 would be as easy to get in Mexico as a standard M4 used by most of the American military. Which meant that either Marco or Trey was a trained sniper, because snipers were notoriously unwilling to use unfamiliar weapons. He'd bet on Marco. The man hardly ever spoke and carried himself—when he wasn't playing laid-back half-Mexican dude on vacation—with a particular stillness.

"Scopes and suppressors, too?" Marco asked, confirming his suspicion. "Of course. Do I not always find what you require?"

"That you do," Trey said.

After more than an hour's drive on the highway, they turned off into a sparsely populated area. Another forty minutes passed before they pulled up in front of a low, white stucco building. Miguel jumped from the van and opened the door. Inside, Saltillo tiles covered the floor, and large ceiling fans circulated cool air. It could be any private home in Texas.

"Don't let the decor fool you," Trey said. "This is Miguel's place. All the cinderblock under the stucco is steel-reinforced, just like the door. And he turned off the booby traps remotely on our way up. No one comes here without him knowing.

But if it looks like too much on the outside, it attracts attention he doesn't want."

"Gotcha."

"Come through here. Can I get you something to drink while we get the targets set up? Limeade, perhaps? I would offer a beer, but I have become accustomed to Mr. Harper's men preferring not to indulge."

"Limeade sounds good," Jake said. The others agreed.

"And the distance?" Miguel asked as he led them through to a spotless and well-appointed kitchen.

"Five yards, ten, one-fifty, two-fifty, four hundred, and five hundred." Trey said.

Miguel issued orders into a walkie-talkie, then served them their drinks. After they had refreshed themselves, he led them out the back to a bench facing into the desert.

"People who come sometimes ask me why I have this bench here. I say I like to sit here and watch the sun set over the desert. Which is true. But it is equally true that all the way out here, no one hears when my friends need to use the desert as a shooting range."

An SUV pulled up and two men climbed out. "Targets are set," said one. The other lifted the back hatch to reveal a virtual armory, all laid out nice and clean in separate compartments of a custom-designed liner with associated magazines.

Trey reached in and hefted the HK416. "I didn't ask for a rifle for you," he said. "Figured you were more of a pistol man. We got Glocks, Sigs, Berettas. Didn't know your preference."

"Sig," Jake replied. He reached for the familiar weapon, checked the magazine, and took aim at the closest target. Unfortunately, the black outline of a man was surrounded by bright, fuzzy glow, a remnant of his concussion. Goddammit. He hadn't noticed it driving around, but when he tried to concentrate, tried to focus on the paper waving slightly in the breeze, it reappeared.

"You okay?" Trey asked.

"I'm fine." He squeezed off a shot. Nicked the edge of the paper.

"Really?"

"I just re-qualified three months ago, okay? New gun, new situation."

"Three months ago you hadn't just taken a bullet to the skull. If you can't see, you're just going to slow us down."

"I can see just fine!" He sighted, adjusted, and fired again. This time he hit the chest of the silhouette.

"Better," grunted Trey. He, too, held a Sig Sauer. Aiming at the second target, the one thirty feet away, he fired off a series of shots. They left a nice, neat, triangular hole in the target's head.

"Show-off," Marco commented. He was still assembling and checking his rifle.

Jake ignored them both and continued to practice.

They stayed out on the makeshift range for two hours, putting each weapon through its paces. Then Miguel fed them lunch and drove them out to the apartment where they would stay until they made their move on the mansion.

"I have to gas up the helicopter and check it over," he said as he helped them carry duffle bags up to the small apartment. "I'll pick you up at oh six thirty."

The one-bedroom apartment was furnished in early modern Goodwill, but Jake had stayed in rattier.

"Get some sleep," Trey said. "We leave at ten thirty tonight. We'll drive within a couple miles of the property, then hike in. The plan is to be in by oh three hundred, out in less than an hour. We've got three miles to the LZ."

⌒

TIME BENT AND twisted, expanded and contracted. Deborah and Samuel came in and shouted questions at her. Samuel held a gun to her head and all Tara could think was that, if he fired, at least the peace would go on forever. *Would that be such a bad thing?*

Deborah injected her. Once more? Twice more? Three, four, five times? The period between the injections seemed to get longer, but that might just have been because every time she came down, her body screamed in increasing pain.

And always there were the questions, though they'd ceased to have any real meaning. Soon, they would realize she had nothing to tell them and they'd kill her.

⌒

JAKE, TREY, AND Marco approached the two-story stucco mansion in perfect silence. As well as weapons, Miguel had provided clothing and tactical gear. They all wore headsets, but at the moment stealth was their ally and words unnecessary. The weather cooperated, a heavy cloud cover hiding the three-quarter moon. Their night-vision goggles gave them a clear view, but the guards at the mansion were not likely to be so well equipped. They were about a hundred yards out from the fence marking the edge of the property when Trey called a halt.

"Two exterior guards," he whispered into his headset. "Marco?"

"Not a problem."

Marco set up. The shot from this distance wouldn't be much of a challenge for a sniper, and sure enough Jake heard two soft pops from the HK417—the suppressor at work—almost immediately.

"Clear."

"Pick it up. We don't have long before they're discovered."

They took off over the desert at full speed and for the first time Jake felt as if they were doing something. *We're coming, Tara. Just hang on.*

They hit the fence and paused briefly while Trey checked for electronic triggers or alarms. A keypad dissuaded them from going straight through the front, and they had to detour around to the side of the property and then go over the barbed wire at the top. Security seemed too light to Jake, which set his nerves jangling. They had Tara. Shouldn't they have been worried about law enforcement coming after her? They must have considered that they'd covered their tracks very damned well.

Still, he was grateful for any advantage they could gain.

The main floor windows at the back of the house had all been outfitted with iron bars. Trey handed Jake his rifle, then pulled a folding pole and a hook with a rolled-up, soft-sided ladder attached to it from his backpack. The pole folded out and attached to the hook, which he slipped onto the roof and tugged to secure. He pulled the pole clear, nodded at Marco, took the rifle back, slung it across his back, and began to climb. Jake put a foot on the bottom rung to follow him up, but Marco held him back. Trey disappeared into the second-story window. A minute later, he stuck his head out and beckoned them up.

Jake and Marco climbed while Trey covered them. Slipping his leg over the sill, Jake found himself in a bedroom.

At one point, it had belonged to a young girl. Miniature horses, posters of princesses . . . all the trappings suited a kid. But the room was musty and a fine layer of desert grit covered everything.

"Fucked up," Marco whispered, echoing his thoughts.

Trey shrugged. "At least she's not here to see what's going on now."

"True that."

Trey cracked the door and peered into the hall. "There's a room across the hall. Jake and I will clear it. Marco, you cover us from the hall. Then we move. You and Jake will take the next, and I'll cover.

Repeat."

Jake's heart slammed against his ribs and sweat slicked his hands. He wiped them on the MultiCam cargo pants Miguel had supplied for him and clutched his pistol more tightly. Harper had been right about his lack of experience in tactical maneuvers, but no way could he have allowed himself to be left behind. So he followed first Trey and then Marco as they checked rooms. The first held a bathroom, the second another bedroom. Gunfire erupted almost the minute Trey turned the handle on the third door, and all three of them jumped back, flattening themselves against the wall. Marco stepped quickly out and hit the door with a burst from the 417. Shouting exploded downstairs, but Marco paid it no attention, kicking in the destroyed door. In the bed opposite the door, Samuel sat, his back against the headboard, an AK-15 in hand, his eyes wide and blood pouring from a gaping wound in his chest.

A savage satisfaction filled Jake, but he couldn't take time to enjoy it. Movement to his left had him spinning, pistol in hand.

"Please, don't hurt me," said the woman huddled in the corner.

Trey hesitated, but Jake didn't. Obviously, she didn't recognize him in face paint. "Not on your fucking life, Deborah," he said. "You probably killed him yourself so he couldn't give you away."

Trapped, she raised her hands from her lap where she'd hidden them in pretend modesty. Jake saw the pistol and reacted instantly, putting three bullets into her before she got off a shot. He turned to the door and found that his teammates had already dispatched two men coming up the stairs and that those two had fallen backward, taking a third down with them. The man was struggling to his feet when Marco put a bullet in his brain. Jake ran to a door on the far side of the bedroom and shoved it open, hoping to find Tara, but he saw only another empty bathroom. Another door revealed a closet.

Two doors remained closed upstairs. Trey kicked one in and backed quickly out of the way while Marco cleared it and the bathroom and closet within. They reversed positions for the second, where they found Francis, his hands over his head. Jake identified him for the others and enjoyed a moment's savage satisfaction when Francis's eyes narrowed in recognition.

"Bring him with us," Trey said. "He may be useful."

Jake grabbed Francis's wrists and slammed them down behind his back, securing them with flex cuffs. "Move," he said, jabbing his Sig into the man's back. Out on the landing, they paused while Trey watched for movement below.

"Want to tell your friends to be careful where they shoot?" Jake asked Francis.

"Fuck off, asshole."

"Your life." Jake shrugged.

They moved carefully down the stairs, sidestepping the dead bodies of the three guards.

A bullet splintered the wood next to Jake's head, and he, Marco, and Trey fired in the shooter's direction simultaneously. Francis took the opportunity to try to duck free, but Jake caught him.

"Where's Tara?"

"Dead."

Jake's nerves flashed fire and ice, and he almost, almost let his trigger finger tense. But Trey saved him.

"I don't think so. You don't drag a woman across the border when you could shoot her on the spot unless you have other plans."

Slowly they cleared the main floor. Off the kitchen, they found another staircase, long and narrow, leading down.

"Ah, a little basement dungeon? How traditional of you," said Trey.

They descended the stairs, Trey in the lead firing forward, while shouting that they had Francis as a prisoner. Marco covered their six.

⌒

TARA FLOATED. IF she remained perfectly still, the whole word disappeared into a beautiful pinkish blue haze, like cumulous clouds tinted by dawn's earliest rays. When she moved or thought too hard, pain burned olive, rust, and black.

At the edge of her consciousness, beyond the fog, strange sounds intruded. Voices. Thuds. Bangs.

She buried herself more deeply in the haze of the pink

cloud. If she worked at it, she could almost imagine the comforting warmth was Jake's arms around her. But inevitably the truth burned through. Jake was dead. She'd killed him.

A sudden crash and the door to her cell was flung wide. Filling the jamb, an angry, blond-haired angel carved of granite with blue diamond eyes.

"Got her," the angel shouted over his shoulder, his voice echoing through the cavernous void in her head and heart.

And then, behind him, Jake appeared. Like the angel, he wore camouflage, and his face was streaked with strange, stone-like colors. Until this moment, she'd assumed angels smiled all the time, but the blond angel practically sneered as he stepped toward her, and Ghost Jake's mouth was set in a flat, grim line.

"She's high as a fucking kite." Even the angel's voice grated like rocks grinding against one another.

And he was right. She knew it. But Jake's appearance had pierced the pink cloud, and sadness crashed over her.

"I'm sorry," she said. "I'm so sorry. I never meant to kill you."

⌒

WHAT THE HELL? Jake yanked off his NVGs and squatted in front of Tara. "Sweetheart, you didn't do anything to me. I'm right here." She reached up to touch the bandage that covered his stitches, and he saw the raw, oozing tips of her fingers where the nails had been ripped away. Her shirt had been cut open, and he saw both cuts and burns on her chest and neck.

"I'm sorry," she said again, tears streaming down her face, every drop a bullet in his chest.

"You have nothing to be sorry for."

"We need to move out," Trey reminded him. "We don't know how many of them will have heard the gunfire."

"How do we take her?"

"Fireman's carry. You handle transport. We'll handle cover. I've got the prisoner."

"Jesus, that's going to hurt."

Trey's eyes narrowed. "My mission, my orders. Pick her up and let's get the fuck out of here."

Jake knelt before Tara, trying to focus on her eyes and shut out the sight of the marks the torture had left on her. "We've got to move you, sweetheart. It's going to hurt. Try to stay relaxed." He hoisted her up and draped her body around his neck, one arm between her legs, gripping her right wrist and forearm to hold her in place across his shoulders.

They headed up the stairs, Trey in the front, the pistol in his left hand jammed between Francis's shoulder blades, the assault rifle in his right. Jake followed, carrying Tara. She panted, her breathing shallow and uneven, and muttered off and on, though he couldn't make out her words.

Trey shoved Francis out the kitchen door, then slammed Jake to the side as Francis stumbled back in a storm of gunfire.

"Too bad, so sad," Marco said as the man tumbled down the stairs. On the other side of the door, a babble of confused and angry shouting ensued, along with the occasional bullet fired to keep them in place.

"No time like the present. You set?" Trey asked Marco, who'd used their trek up the stairs to mount a grenade launcher to his rifle.

"Good to go." Marco leaned around the corner and fired. A resounding crash, and dust and debris rained down on them in the stairwell.

"Go!" Trey shouted, leading the way through the decimated

kitchen, hopping over the bodies on the floor, and heading for the front door. Marco cleared the whole doorway by simply firing a round through it, and Trey checked for trouble.

"Fuck. We've got company. But there are vehicles around the left side. Jake, put her down. You and I are going to hold off the guards. Marco, go get us something and pick us up."

Marco disappeared into a room to their left, and Jake let Tara slide off his shoulders, propping her in the corner.

"Give me a gun," she said, her voice surprisingly clear.

"Tara—"

"I'm right-handed, and you need all the help you can get. Even if all I do is confuse them."

Trey darted back and grabbed one of the AK's off a dead guard. "Give her your pistol. You take this."

Although Jake hated Tara's pallor and the dazed look in her eyes, and he worried she'd further injure herself, he respected her too much to argue with the decision. She needed to take control. He handed her the pistol and hefted the rifle.

Trey leaned out the door and let off a burst. The guards responded. "You're low, I'm high on the next one," he said. "You aim nine to twelve. Short bursts. Let's see if we can't take a couple more of these fuckers out of the equation."

On Trey's count, they fired for several seconds, and then Jake heard Marco's voice over his headset.

"Coming in hot. Ready to roll in two. Just have to take out—" A resounding boom from the side made Jake wince.

"Ready? Three, two, one . . ."

A Humvee slammed to a halt in front of the door, raising an enormous cloud of dust. Immediately, it was peppered with bullets, but Marco fired back and Trey darted out. Crouching behind the hood of the vehicle, Trey laid down suppressing fire to keep the guards from coming forward while Jake helped Tara to her feet and rushed her into the backseat.

The Humvee jolted forward and spun into a turn. Tara slid across the seat, smacking into Jake with her left side. She cried out, then curled over as if she were going to vomit.

"Get her down. You cover the rear."

Jake helped Tara to the floorboards, where she would be safest, wishing he could make her more comfortable, then took position with his rifle out the glassless rear window. Two men were chasing them on foot. Jake put a bullet in one, and the other stopped. A third man joined him, and they ran around to the side of the house where Marco had found the Humvee.

"Gate closed," Marco said, handing the grenade-launcher-equipped rifle to Trey. "Loaded."

Jake laid down a spray of fire left to right behind them as Trey leaned far out the window, pointed the grenade at the gate, and fired. Marco didn't even slow down, merely driving on through the cloud the explosion generated, the wheels of the Humvee bumping and crunching over the wreckage of the fence.

"Don't head straight for the LZ. Miguel won't be there yet, and we can't secure it for any length of time if they've called for backup. We've got fifty minutes." He reached into his ammo pouch and reloaded the grenade launcher. Then he switched out the magazine from his own weapon for a fresh one.

Jake heard another vehicle behind them coming fast but saw no lights. Dragging on his NVGs, he searched the darkness until he found it. "Behind us," he called. "Looks like three men in a Jeep."

"Range?"

"Five hundred yards? Maybe a bit more."

"Swap," said Marco. A quick change and he was in the passenger seat and Trey was driving. Then he crawled into the backseat. He took Trey's rifle and rested it on the back of the window.

"Straight and smooth," he ordered.

"Yeah. Like that's going to fucking happen on this terrain," Trey replied, but Jake noticed he held his hands steady on the wheel.

A bullet whizzed by their right side. Marco took in a breath, let it out, and fired. Another breath, another shot. "Driver down," he announced. "Let's get out of here." They reached the landing zone without further interruption twelve minutes before Miguel was due.

Jake helped Tara out, and Trey slid from the driver's seat.

"Ditch the vehicle," he ordered. "At least two miles away. That should give us time." Marco nodded and headed out.

Tara sank to the ground and rested her back against the trunk of a small bent and withered tree. Her face was the color of the sandy ground, pale with a yellow undertone, and shivers wracked her body. Jake knelt in front of her. "How you holding up?"

"Fine." But her eyes darted from side to side and her leg bounced. Jake had seen both of those behaviors before.

"Isn't there anything you can do for her?" Jake asked Trey. "Aren't you a medic?"

"I'll treat her wounds on the chopper. The heroin she'll have to deal with on her own." He studied her. "How long have you been using?"

"She's not a fucking junkie, for Christ's sake. She's a *victim*."

Trey shrugged. "Not mutually exclusive."

Jake half rose, but Tara put out her hand and stopped him.

"I'm not even sure what day it is at the moment. They started shooting me up when I wouldn't give them what they wanted."

"Why didn't they kill you?" Trey asked.

"I'm sure they would have. Deborah hoped I'd give up in withdrawal and detail what we knew about their operation so they could change what was necessary and leave the rest of their distribution network alone."

"So she was in charge?" Jake asked.

"No, she said Owen wanted to keep me alive."

"Owen?"

"Well, she insisted on calling him the Leader. God knows why."

"Because it wasn't Owen. He was killed in the raid," Jake explained. "For whatever reason, she didn't want you to know who it was."

"Paranoid," Trey said. "On the off chance you escaped—as you did—this 'leader' didn't want you to be able to identify him."

"Could she have meant Francis?" Jake asked.

Tara shook her head slightly. "I don't think so. I always got the feeling that she and Francis were colleagues, for want of a better word. Not boss and employee."

In Jake's ear, he heard Marco's voice. "On my way back. But they're looking. I've seen two SUVs. Miguel's gonna have to be in and out damned fast. I should be to you in couple of minutes."

"He's ten minutes out. We'll be ready for whatever comes."

Marco jogged in, gun and pack on his back. "Set them a bit of a false trail," he said. "Though there's not a lot that can be done in this territory. If they spot us, we're toast."

They waited, searching the darkness, until the *whomp-whomp-whomp* of helicopter rotors alerted them to Miguel's impending arrival. Trey lit the landing area with a laser marker so that Miguel would know exactly where they were, and then Jake just crossed his fingers and prayed their enemies wouldn't find them first.

⸏

Miguel landed safely, but they were no sooner aboard than an SUV came racing toward them. Jake took aim, but held off when a man shouted "Stop! Police!" When the rotors kept moving, a bullet pinged off the front of the chopper. *"Alto! Policia!"*

"Can't buy a damned break," Jake said, peering out. The SUV was unmarked. Who even knew whether these guys were for real?

Miguel took off, and Marco aimed out the door.

"You can't shoot at police!" Tara reached for him, but Trey shoved her back into her seat.

"He's not shooting *at* them, he's shooting *near* them. Provided you don't fuck up his aim." Marco kept up steady fire until the chopper was well away. Then they all donned new headsets with heavy, noise-reducing cups over the ears. When Jake went to hand Tara hers, she was sitting with her head between her knees, shaking.

"I don't like it," Trey said. "If that's the cops, they'll be tracking us in no time flat."

"I can stay under radar," said Miguel, "but they have to know we'll be heading for the border. If they really are law enforcement, they'll have their own air support."

Trey shrugged, though Miguel couldn't see it. "Nothing for it now. The boat is still our best chance of getting her back to the States. Just keep your eyes and ears peeled."

Setting aside his rifle, he slid his pack off his back and unfolded the front to reveal a panel of medical supplies.

"Let me see your hand," he said to Tara.

"I can wait till we're over the border." She didn't uncurl, didn't raise her head, and Jake's stomach churned. He laid a hand gently on her back and felt her bones and muscles, all shifting, twitching beneath the filthy, sweat-soaked cotton. They hadn't even had a chance to let her change; she'd run with them in a T-shirt sliced from neck to navel.

"You need to let him treat you, sweetheart. If anything happens, we could be delayed getting to a hospital."

She shook her head.

"Baby, please. For me. Let Trey help you."

She began to rock, her whole body tilting back and forth, back and forth on the seat, ripping his heart out. He rubbed her back, then slid his hand down and took her right hand in his.

"Can't you give her something?"

"You want a painkiller?" Trey asked her.

Tara's head shot up. *Fuck.* Jake hadn't even considered her addiction, but desire for the drug shot tension into her muscles and flowed through her skin, entering his own where he touched her as despair. Five breaths. Each one dragged in and pushed out, never taking her eyes from Trey's.

"No."

"Good. Now, give me your hand."

She shifted her gaze to Jake.

"I'm right here, sweetheart. You need him to stop, you just say so and he will. I swear it. Right, Trey?"

The man's nod was infinitesimal, but Tara must have seen it. She pressed her eyes shut and her lips together and eased her hand out of the protection of her body. Throughout

Trey's exam, cleaning, and bandaging, her face lost more and more color until it seemed a vampire had snuck into the chopper and drained her. The hollows beneath her eyes lay like smudged charcoal on parchment.

When he finished with her hand, Trey soaked a cloth in water and pressed it against one of the spots where her T-shirt crusted to her skin, then began to peel the shirt from her skin. She flinched, and a small cry slipped from her throat.

"Enough," Jake said.

"We don't have any idea how bad those wounds are."

"We're almost to the boat," Jake countered. And then, to be sure Trey wouldn't force the issue, he gathered Tara into his lap, wrapping her tight in his arms.

TREY'S POKING HAD started the fiery streaks back up her arm, and her skin had shrunk to a thin, tight, itchy veneer atop a boiling mess of pain and fear. Still, she'd managed—though Jake's hand was probably broken from her clutching at it—right up until Trey had reached for her shirt. Her chest didn't even hurt as much as her fingers. Or she didn't think it did. She'd lost track of which injury caused what pain.

And then Jake pulled her into him, and she could smell his sweat, feel his strength, and it was oh so much better than the pink cloud. Not that the hunger was gone. It skulked in the shadowy corners of her mind and under her breastbone, but the vivid, aggressive tension that made it impossible to stay still seeped away.

Trey handed her a pill. "Broad spectrum antibiotic.

Won't do much, to be honest, because infection has already set in, but it's better than nothing. You'll do much better in a hospital. This is just in case."

She swallowed the pill with a long swig of water from the tube Trey offered that led to a pouch built into the side of his backpack. When she tried to hand it back, he shook his head. "You're dehydrated. I can tell just looking at you. Even if you can't manage food, you should drink. Slowly, but drink."

"Did they feed you at all?" Jake asked.

"No." God, her voice sounded so strange. All scratchy and harsh. She took another slug, letting the water soothe her throat on the way down. "But I don't think I can eat anything." The adrenaline hit from the fight had driven away the constantly lurking nausea, but in the relative safety of the chopper it returned. Puking in front of the men who'd come in to rescue her would cap her day off just perfectly.

"Coming in for landing," said her other rescuer. He and Trey pulled down the NVGs they'd shoved up on their heads and began to scan the surrounding area.

They put down softly, and Trey told her and Jake to stay while he and the other man—Marco—scouted. Moments later they returned with the all clear. Jake helped her to the ground while Trey conferred with the pilot. Then the chopper lifted off.

"Can you walk?" Trey asked.

"I—yes. Not fast." In fact, air felt like molasses, thick and heavy, and lifting her feet seemed to take forever. Even breathing was an effort. But she'd be damned if she admitted it.

"If you can walk," Trey said, "you can walk fast. Luckily, right now you don't have to. If the need arises, your adrenaline will do the rest."

"If the need arises, I'll help her," said Jake.

Marco chuckled. "He's being an asshole. He enjoys it. Push comes to shove, he'd be the first one to pick her up and toss her over his shoulder."

Trey shrugged. "In K and R, the asset always comes first. We come back without you, the client's not happy. And since, in this case, the client's our boss, I have a distinct desire to keep him happy."

"See?" said Marco. "Asshole."

Trey turned on his heel and led them through the trees that grew thicker, greener, and stronger than any she'd seen around her prison. Even the air smelled different. Moister, earthier, less dusty.

"Where are we?"

"Close to the Rio Grande. We're going to take a boat across. The place they held you was much further inland, in the desert."

She started to ask where they planned to land, but she tripped over a root. Jake hooked her around the waist before she could fall and drew her close to him. "I've got you." He helped her over the rough ground, never letting go.

"I hate this."

"Not top of my list, either."

And, hell, how could she have forgotten his sister? Seeing Tara in this condition must be doing a number on him. "I'm sorry."

"Now you're just pissing me off."

"What?"

"Quit apologizing."

"I didn't mean —"

"Stop. I can already tell you're about to apologize again. Don't. Okay?"

What else could she say? "Okay."

They trudged on until Trey held up a hand. He put a finger to his lips and gestured for Tara and Jake to stay put while he and Marco left the cover of the trees and headed for the river.

And now I should apologize. But he couldn't. Because he couldn't discuss drugs without pictures in his head of Lisa laughing and lively as a kid warring with those of her still and cold in the morgue—with the occasional screaming battle over drugs and booze thrown in for good measure. And those memories still had the power to rob him of breath, to leave him battered, shredded by his own guilt and surging anger.

How was he supposed to cope with Tara going down the same path? He'd told her he loved her. But they'd been undercover. Did she have any idea that he'd meant it?

The words were there, waiting. Given half a chance, he'd say them today, tomorrow, every day for the rest of his life. But maybe he needed to back off. The words had never comforted Lisa. In fact, she had accused him of using love to manipulate her.

You just say you love me to get your way, to guilt me into rehab. If you only love me when I'm straight, you don't love me at all. She'd stormed out that night, and he hadn't seen her again for five months, when she had called him to bail her out after being arrested in downtown DC. And then she'd blubbered all over him, telling him she loved him so much and she'd never meant to hurt him.

Would his love be a burden to Tara as well? Would she feel as if he was bludgeoning her with it, trying to remake her? And if she couldn't remake herself, if she couldn't get back to the person she'd been before she was taken, could he live with it?

Trey called softly for them, interrupting the never-ending spiral of his thoughts, and Jake helped Tara down to the bank, where Marco and Trey dragged a speedboat from the woods.

They made good time across the river, hitting the north bank as the sun peeked over the horizon and the water in the east went from black to pink. Before they could set foot on land, however, four armed men drove up in a battered olive drab Jeep. They all wore standard US Army combat gear, but Jake wasn't about to risk Tara's safety by believing the uniforms. He slipped his pistol into the patch pocket of his cargo pants, where he could easily access it, despite their orders to disarm and placed himself squarely in front of her in the boat.

"Look, guys, we're citizens," said Trey. "No need to get all uptight." With a glance at Marco that Jake interpreted to mean not to relax his guard, Trey laid his rifle on the floorboards and put his hands up. "I'm going to step out of the boat. Very slowly."

He did. The soldiers looked at Marco, who checked his watch and sat right where he was, though his weight tilted slightly. If the soldiers made a move to fire, Marco could capsize them instantly. It might not keep them safe for long, but every little bit helped.

Trey stood in front of the men, hands on his head. "If you look in my lower right pocket, you'll find my passport. And there's a piece of paper in there, too, with a phone number on it. You call that number, you'll find out that we're all okay to be right where we are. We can wait."

Two of the soldiers came forward and frisked Trey, pulling not only his passport, but all manner of spare weapons from his pockets. They slapped flex cuffs on him, and then one of them stepped back to the vehicle and used the radio to make a call.

Jake couldn't hear what was being said, but the guy's face turned boiled-lobster red, and his jaw set. He took a deep breath before returning to the river's edge.

"I'm to tell you that the word is 'percolate.'"

"And the response is 'ruined.'"

Still, the officer hesitated a long moment before pulling out a knife and cutting the flex cuffs from Trey's wrists. Trey signaled to Marco, who set down his gun and disembarked. Jake, too, stepped out, though since he had never shown the men his weapon, he felt no need to give it up. Trey and Marco might have believed their job was done. His was not.

When Tara stood, she shook so violently that the boat threatened to go over. She sat back down and turned pleading eyes on him. "I can't."

"Not a problem. I can." He waded down into the sandy mud at the edge of the water and helped her up. Then he reached over and slid one hand beneath her shoulders and the other beneath her knees.

"Oh! You don't have to —" But she wrapped her right arm around his neck and let him lift her out of the boat.

"I'm going to drop them off at HQ," the soldier who'd cut Trey's ties said to his men. "Then I'll be back. Call in if anything odd happens."

⌒

IF EVERY LIMB didn't feel it weighed fifty pounds, Tara might have objected to Jake's hold. Being carried to the waiting vehicle hardly projected the sensible, capable, intelligent cop image that had helped her survive in a predominantly male profession. But the drugs had sapped her of will, so despite the embarrassment, she allowed the indignity.

Jake settled into the back of the Jeep with her in his lap, and Marco joined them. Trey took the front with their guard. Despite the jolting, bouncing ride and the steep climb from the riverbank up to the ranch, Tara's eyes first glazed, then shut. The outside world drifted into the comfort of sleep.

She was not so far gone, however, that Jake's whispered "We're here" when they arrived at the compound failed to wake her. The front gates lay open, guarded against intruders by more men in military uniforms. Their driver spoke to one of them, who in turn spoke into his radio and waited for a response before passing them through. Just as they pulled up in front of the ranch house, the front door swung open, and Lucy and Ethan ran out, followed more slowly by a man Tara didn't recognize.

"Tara!" Lucy cried, rushing over to the Jeep before it even came to a halt. "Oh, my God, what happened?"

"It's kind of a long story." And she didn't have any desire to tell it more than once.

"She needs a hospital. One with a good trauma unit," Jake said. He shifted her off his lap, then climbed from the vehicle and reached in to help her get out. Even once she was out, she leaned heavily against him.

"Of course. We'll take her where we took you. That girl you asked about—Aurora—she's there, too."

"You found Aurora? How is she?" Guilt struck. She hadn't spared any of her fellow Chosen a second thought from the moment of her capture. Aurora and her baby, how were they surviving the withdrawal?

"She's fine. The pregnant women are still at the hospital. In fact, most of the women are still in the hospital, but they're coming up to the point when they can be released. From the studies we found on the computers, three days should allow the drug to get out of their systems. The psychological effects they can be treated for as outpatients, and they will be. Believe me when I say there is no shortage of doctors anxious to study the Chosen's membership."

The man who'd come out with Lucy and Ethan had spoken with both Trey and Marco and now tapped Lucy on the shoulder. "I'll call for a chopper to fly them to the hospital. We'll drive down and meet there, and we can use the medical center waiting room to talk. If the Feds want a more formal debrief, the field office isn't far."

"Thank you, Nash. That's more than kind. Tara, this is Nash Harper. The two men who came with Jake to get you, they work for him."

"Harper as in Harp Security?"

"That's me," said the man.

"Well, I am more than grateful. But I can make it in a car as long as I don't have to drive it. You don't need to supply another helicopter just for me."

"Haven't looked in a mirror lately, huh?" asked Lucy.

No, but she could imagine. She tried to smile, but Lucy's face blurred and melted, and the earth spun. She reached out to steady herself on something, anything, but her hand simply disappeared, and blackness swept over her.

Tara's body sagged against him. Her speech had slurred, so he'd had a tiny bit of warning, but still he almost let her fall. Instead, he held her against him and sank to the dirt himself so he could cushion her.

"Fuck."

"It's the smack," said Trey, holding her wrist lightly between her fingers to check her pulse. "Her heart's still pumping. If you can keep her breathing, she'll be fine."

Lucy knelt in front of him. "I am so sorry, Jake."

"I'll be fine, okay? Can we please worry about Tara?"

"Chopper's on the way," said Harper. "ETA twenty-five minutes."

"Twenty-five—isn't there anything closer?"

"Not that we can hijack. And even that far out, it will still get her to the hospital faster than we could driving."

Jake slipped his arms under her. "We'll take her inside, then." He carried her into the house and laid her on the couch, twisting so he could sit with her head in his lap.

"Get a cold, wet cloth," Trey said to Marco, "and a glass of water. And crackers, if you can find them."

"They dosed her?" Harper asked.

"Repeatedly."

"For what possible reason?"

While Trey worked over Tara, cooling her face and listening to her heart and checking her breathing, Jake caught the others up on what they'd learned.

"So you think Francis was in charge?" Ethan asked. "Nothing in the computer files—we turned them over, but kept copies—indicates who actually ran things. Authorities have already busted stash houses in San Antonio and Oklahoma City based on information your Trojan horse program pulled from their server, but everything's coded. They named their drug American Dream and referred to themselves by numbers. So it's all 'One says American Dream is key to getting what we deserve' and the like."

"Any idea who kept the notes?"

"Deborah, we think. And as far as we can tell, she was Three. So there were One and Two above her."

"Francis and Samuel?" Harper asked.

Jake's gut twisted. "I don't—nothing about Deborah's relationship with Samuel spoke to her having a subservient position. If anything, I'd have bet on her being the boss. I'm not the best judge, but that's my feeling."

"You think we've missed someone."

"I hope not. But when we have a chance to talk to Tara, when she's more clearheaded, maybe we can figure it out."

The sound of chopper blades beating the air signaled an end to their conversation. Jake carried Tara out to the court-yard, where the rescue helicopter was landing. He handed her off to a uniformed medic and then climbed aboard himself. As the aircraft rose once more, he saw the others running to the cars parked behind the ranch house.

THE CHOPPER LANDED on the roof of the medical center and doctors were waiting to rush Tara inside. The medic had asked Jake a steady stream of questions during the flight, transmitting the answers to the hospital so that by the time they arrived he'd passed along everything he knew about what had happened to her.

"Her pulse and heart are strong," the medic assured him.

"And this is a Level One trauma center. She couldn't be in better hands."

Still, as Jake paced the floors of the waiting area, memories of other hospitals assaulted him, promises from other doctors who'd told him his witnesses, his suspects, his sister would come out cured. Doctors were human. They did their best, but they couldn't save everyone.

He got coffee. Drank it. Got more. Drank that. And still, no word from the team that had taken Tara into surgery. What the hell could be taking so long?

Lucy and Ethan arrived, followed by Harper and his men. Lucy disappeared for a couple of minutes, and when she came back she was towing Aurora and Joy behind her.

"Jacob!" Aurora ran over and hugged him. "They told me you went to get—is her name Tara?"

"It is. And you can call me Jake. And you?"

"Jennifer. But I've decided to keep Aurora. I like it so much better. And I like me better as Aurora, too."

"I'm glad to see you're doing well," Jake said. "Tara was very worried about you. And Joy? What's your real name?"

"I've been Joy forever," the older woman said. "I was among the Chosen before the Leader, that is, before Owen Stephenson took over. I lived at the ranch with my mother."

"Since neither of us has any family, we're sticking together," Aurora said. "Joy said she's helped out with lots of babies at the ranch, so she can help with mine." She laid a hand on her belly. "The doctors did a test and told me he's a boy. Would it be—Would you think it's weird if I named him Jacob?"

Jake's knees went weak. He gestured for Aurora to sit on the couch so he could do the same without looking like an ass.

"I would be honored. But why?"

"Well, I don't know if Tara told you, but my boyfriend, he beat on me. My dad did the same thing to my mom. When I got in with the Chosen, I thought they were all really good, you know?"

Jake nodded.

"And then, it turns out that they're selling drugs to people like my ex. I mean, not all of them, but how am I supposed to know which ones? I thought about naming him for a character in a book or a movie, but I decided I wanted him to have the name of a real person I could tell him did good things for others."

"That's . . ." he cleared his throat. "That may be the nicest thing anyone's ever said to me."

"So then it's okay?"

"Definitely."

The door to the waiting room swung open and a doctor appeared. He looked around, then zeroed in on Jake. "You came in with Tara Dobbs?"

His heart stuttered. "Yes."

"Could you come with me, please? She's out of surgery, and we've got her in recovery, but she's causing a problem."

"A problem?" Jake followed the man down a hallway. But then they entered the recovery room and he understood. Though her left hand was bandaged, she was trying to use it to pull the IV from her right arm. Two nurses held her, but as he watched she broke free from one of them and took a swipe at the tubes.

"She's coming out of anesthesia," the doctor said. "I don't think she realizes where she is. Given her history, I don't want to put restraints on her, but I will if I have to."

"No. I'm on it." Jake displaced the nurse standing on Tara's right and sat on the edge of the bed. The nurse had been gripping Tara's arm, but he took her hand, instead.

Leaning over, he placed his lips near her ear and whispered. "It's okay, sweetheart. You're safe. I've got you."

She quieted, and a tight, hollow sensation between his shoulder blades relaxed. She recognized him. And even unconscious, she trusted him.

"Talk to her," said one of the nurses. "Once she wakes up, we can move her up to the postsurgical floor into a room where you can have a proper visit."

Recovery wasn't designed for visitors, so he continued to sit on the edge of the bed waiting for her to wake up as the nurses went about their business with other patients. He talked about Lucy and Ethan and teased her about being his date for their wedding. He was in the middle of relating Aurora's desire to name her child Jacob when Tara yawned deeply and blinked.

"Hey," he said.

"Hey." She looked around. "Oh, hell. What happened?"

"They haven't told me yet."

On cue, one of the nurses came over. "Nice to see you," she said. "How do you feel?"

"Umm . . . I don't feel much of anything."

"That's fine," the nurse said. "That's the anesthesia and the pain meds. You'll be wobbly for a bit, but now that you're awake, I'll call transport and have you taken up."

"Pain meds?" Tara tried to loosen Jake's hand and go after the IV. "I can't. I don't want to take anything!"

"I understand," the woman said, "and I'm sorry. But it's not just to keep the pain away. It's also so we can regulate your withdrawal. You've had a lot of stitches, a lot of surgery. Going through withdrawal all at once could be fatal."

Tears welled in Tara's eyes. "I don't want any more drugs."

"I know, sweetheart. But they'll wean you carefully."

"We will," the nurse said.

Tara gritted her teeth and gazed at the IV for a long moment before sucking in a deep breath and nodding.

"Excellent," said the nurse. She fixed a stern eye on Jake. "But now you have to go back to the waiting room. Or you can go up to the third floor and we'll let you know when she's in a room so you can visit."

"Okay." He pressed a kiss to Tara's forehead and patted her hand. She was sliding back into sleep even before he left the room.

∽

WHEN JAKE RETURNED to the waiting room, Ethan and Lucy were sitting alone. Joy and Aurora had gone back to Aurora's room, and Harper and his men had headed over to the FBI's field office, where the JTTF was headquartered. Relief slid through Jake. He appreciated everything Harper had done, but he was done with people. He wanted to be alone with Tara. He led Lucy and Ethan up to the postsurgical floor, and by the time they arrived, Tara had been assigned a room.

When they entered, a nurse was explaining to Tara what had been involved in the surgery. The mere description of the process they'd used to clean the infection from her fingers brought the coffee he'd drunk earlier boiling back up into his throat.

"Will they heal?" Tara asked. "Will I get the sensation back?"

"We can't ever say what will happen. But the doctor was

happy with how the surgery went. He can tell you more about the prognosis and what you'll have to do when he comes by later on."

"And the rest?"

"Well, let's see." The nurse looked at the chart. "All told, thirty-six stitches. All over the place, which won't be comfortable. It's easier to deal with if they're all in a row. The infections were the worst of it. But now we've got you hydrating and on a high dose of antibiotics, so you should be fine."

"Thank you," Tara said.

"You're apt to be nauseous for a little while longer and your records show you haven't eaten in several days, so I am sure the doctor will want to start you off slowly, perhaps with liquids." The woman smiled. "Y'all have a good visit. Stay as long as you like." The moment she was out the door, however, Tara asked to speak to Ethan alone.

Jake understood. Ethan had lived through his own brush with addiction, so she probably wanted to talk about it with him, but he couldn't help feeling as if she'd kicked him in the gut. He took her non-bandaged hand and brought it to his lips for a kiss before he and Lucy left her alone with Ethan.

In the waiting area, he collapsed into a chair.

"Give her time," Lucy said, touching his knee as she settled next to him. "She's confused. She needs to get back on her feet."

"I could help with that."

"But she can't let you. She has to do it herself. Or she thinks she does. With a little luck, Ethan can convince her otherwise."

"Like he did with you?"

"Oh, I never wanted to take on the world alone. I just didn't believe anyone would be on my side. There's a difference.

When we were kids, Tara thought she could do anything, best anyone. This past year has sucked all that away from her. She will get it back. And when she does, she'll want a partner."

"You're telling me she won't want a protector? That I should back down?"

"I'm telling you that before she can learn to lean on you without resenting it, she has to believe—deep down—that she can stand on her own again."

"You're talking about therapy. Possibly years of it."

"I am. And I have no doubt she and Ethan are discussing the very same fact. You have to consider all the things she's been through recently and understand that she's dealing with a form of PTSD. That kind of thing never *really* goes away. You have to decide whether you can cope with that."

And there it was again, the question that had faced him in the darkness of the Mexican night. Only hours earlier, and yet the answer now was so easy. "I'll have to learn."

"Good."

They sat together for several minutes after that until Jake spotted Ethan coming toward them down the hallway. He limped, giving away his exhaustion, but managed a smile for them all the same. "You're up," he told Jake.

TARA THOUGHT, AFTER talking to Ethan, that she was ready for Jake. She was wrong. When he pulled up a chair so he could sit next to the bed and took her hand in his, she could feel her throat tighten and tears press against the back of her eyes. Damn her emotions; they were all over the place.

"You okay?" he asked, tilting his head to catch her eye.

"Not really."

"Want to talk about it?"

"Not yet. Is that okay?"

"Of course. But there's something I have to tell you. I don't—I've been waiting because I don't want to hurt you or freak you out."

"Oh." She tried to pull her hand away, but he held on.

"Don't. Please. I need to touch you."

"You do?"

"I do. Listen. I need to apologize. In the woods, what I said . . ." He blew out a breath. "It's hard for me to talk about Lisa. But the thing is, you deserve to hear about her because I suspect you think you're alike. You think seeing the needle marks in your arm makes me remember her. And it does. No doubt about it. But you're not her. She made a choice, several choices, to take the easy path. Even with the full knowledge of the likely outcome, she still chose going back to her dealer rather than calling me or our parents and asking to come home or go back to rehab.

"She was my little sister. I was supposed to look out for her. That's what big brothers do. But there's only so far a person can go. I held out my hand, but she wouldn't take it. In my more sensible hours, I know that.

"But you're not her. I've known about your strength since before I met you. Lucy used to talk about you. You're one of the few good memories she had of her childhood. I was prepared for a tiger."

"What if I'm not a tiger anymore? What if I lost that?"

"You didn't. Because a tiger has more to do with heart than with claws." He reached across and touched her bandaged hand. "You saved Lucy's life when she was a kid. You went into a viper's nest because you thought your friend Andrea was in trouble.

When we pulled you out of the prison, even before we got to the hospital, you wanted to know about Aurora." He rested a hand on the slope of her left breast. "You have an amazing capacity for caring. I've never met anyone like you."

"Jake . . ." She shook her head, trying to prevent the tears from slipping out again, but they escaped nonetheless.

"Let me get this out. I love you. I'll help you any way I can. I just don't want to lose you."

Oh God. He'd said he loved her. "What if I screw up?" The words came out a whisper through the miniscule passage in her tight throat.

He shrugged. "Then you screw up. It's part of being human."

"You make it sound so easy. I don't want to disappoint you."

"You won't. Well, you might. If you don't at least tell me there's a chance you might be able to love me back." His tone was teasing, but his eyes had gone slate-gray and held no humor.

"I do. How could you even ask? Of course I love you. I had a soft spot for you the first time I read Lucy's book, but if you were prepared for a tiger, I was prepared for . . . anything but you."

"Yeah? Do tell." He wiggled his eyebrows.

Impossibly, she laughed. Of course, it made her stomach churn and her head throb, but the lightness of heart was worth any discomfort.

"Maybe later. Much, much later."

He sighed. "Well, okay."

There was a light tap on the door and Aurora poked her head inside. "Hi."

"Aurora! It's so good to see you."

Jake stood and pulled another chair over so the pregnant girl could sit down. A moment later, Joy, too, came in. Tara couldn't believe how well both women appeared to be recovering. Of course, Aurora was full of chatter about what had happened since the raid on the compound.

"What will you do after you have the baby?" Tara asked when Aurora began to wind down.

"Oh, the—"

An explosion rocked the room, the sound loud and close. Alarms rang out and people ran by the room shouting.

"Should we evacuate?" Joy asked, standing and putting a hand on Aurora's shoulder.

"Not yet," Jake said. "We might be safer staying put. You guys get ready to go while I check out what's happening."

No sooner had he stepped outside than Joy jumped to her feet and in a single, smooth motion grabbed Tara's portable IV pole and swung it around to club Aurora in the head. The IV tore from Tara's arm, and Aurora fell sideways over the arm of her chair to the floor. Tara scrambled for safety, but Joy was on her in an instant.

"Bitch," the woman hissed. Tara grappled with her and called for help, though she doubted she'd be heard over the ruckus in the hall. And then Joy reached into the waistband of her jeans, pulled out a gun, and jammed it into Tara's stomach.

"Get up," she said.

Fuck. "How did you get that into the hospital?"

"Don't be silly. You don't think they check on those of us who go in and out all the time, do you? I've been bringing things back for Aurora every day. Now get up. We're leaving."

Delay, delay, delay. Jake would return soon. "Joy, you're confused. I understand, you lived as a member of the Chosen for years. But all the things the Leader told you about the government, well, he was a little paranoid."

"I never believed a word that asshole said."

Okay, she hadn't expected that.

The door opened and Jake dashed in. "I don't—Shit."

"Shut the door or your girlfriend here dies."

He held up his hands and kicked the door shut. "What's going on, Joy?"

"Joy." She laughed, a bitter, desperate sound. "You killed every bit of *joy* I ever had. Get over next to your girlfriend." She stepped away from Tara out of range of his hands.

Jake moved toward Tara. In the instant his back was to Joy, he caught Tara's eyes with his own and then dropped his gaze to the right cargo pocket of his pants. *He still had his gun.*

"The Chosen wasn't what you think it was," he said, standing between Tara and Joy, his body a protective barrier.

"I know exactly what it was. It was mine. Just like Deborah and Francis. My heritage was stolen, and you stole my children, but you won't get away with it."

"You're Elina Muñoz."

Joy's eyes glittered. "I am."

"Who?" Tara asked.

"Elina Reina Muñoz," said Joy. "Daughter of Juan Carlos Muñoz and the lying, traitorous bitch he married. My father called me *princess*. He intended me to be a *queen*. And then she ripped me away from my home and took me to that godforsaken ranch. She wanted me to work in the *fields*."

Tara stepped out from behind Jake and edged in front of him, blocking Joy's line of sight to his right side. She could feel his irritation, his desire to protect her, but if he couldn't access the gun, they were both dead.

"That sounds terrible," she said. "How old were you?"

"Fifteen. I had just had my *quinceañera*. I was a woman, capable of making my own decisions. But she stole me away in the night."

"Didn't you have a brother, too?" Jake asked.

"He died the year before we left."

"That's terrible," Tara said, infusing as much sympathy as possible into her voice. "So much tragedy. How did he die?"

A smug smile twisted the woman's features. "He became ill. No cure could be found."

Jesus. Fourteen years old and she'd murdered her own brother. Tara swallowed, then stepped forward, trying to keep Joy's attention fixed on her, not Jake. A patch pocket wasn't exactly a quick-draw holster.

"Stay where you are!"

"What happened after your mother took you to the ranch?"

"Why should I tell you?"

"Because you feel guilty?"

"I have nothing to be guilty about!"

"Not even for hurting Aurora? She never would have done you harm. Or how about for the part you played in your children's deaths?"

Behind her, Jake stiffened. But antagonizing the woman was a calculated risk. She needed to have Joy's total focus.

"I never, ever hurt my children! From the moment they were born, I told them who they were, about their double heritage."

"Double?" She felt Jake shift—getting his gun?—and leaned forward. Although fear and adrenaline shook her, she was still fascinated by the woman's perverse logic.

"Every child has a double heritage. I made sure mine were well protected on both sides. Their father was Hal Stephenson. They owned that ranch. All they had to do was eliminate that fool Owen and then they could step forward as the other heirs. They owned the land. And they owned the drug trade. It was their birthright." Her eyes narrowed. "And you killed them. I was going to take you outside during the evacuation, use you to trap the others who went to Mexico with you, but they were hired mercenaries. They don't really matter."

"If you kill us, you'll never get out alive," Tara said.

Behind her, she felt Jake press three fingertips into her back and tap three times. She took a slight step forward, and Joy shouted at her to get back.

"Okay. Okay. Okay." She nodded three times, agreeing to Jake's count.

THANK GOD, SHE'D understood. Jake inched his right hand down into his pocket, pushing his hip up as high as he could without Joy noticing, and got a grip on the Sig. When he had it secure, he tapped Tara's back with one finger, waited a beat, then tapped her with two fingers, waited a beat . . .

And she threw herself down and forward, out of the line of fire, tackling Joy from the ground as he fired repeatedly. Joy went down on her back, her pistol firing. A bullet creased the outside of his arm and slammed into the wall. The next one crashed through a window. He dove on top of Joy while Tara struggled to grab the gun from her hand. Blood covered Joy from a wound at her shoulder and one in her side, but still she fought. Tara slammed her hand down into the floor, and she released her grip on the gun.

The door burst open and two uniformed officers shoved through, guns drawn. Lucy and Ethan crowded in behind them, and Jake had never been so glad to see anyone in his life. They'd neutralized Joy, but he needed to see to Tara, whose arm was bleeding from where the IV had been torn out, and who was sitting on top of Joy's arm, the pistol held tight in her hands.

He gently closed his fingers over Tara's and removed the gun from her grip, then helped her to her feet.

"It's over." He handed Joy off to Ethan and one of the cops with a quick explanation of who she was and passed both pistols over to the second officer, then wrapped his arms around Tara. Moments later, two more officers arrived along with medical personnel. Nurses went to care for Aurora where she lay curled around her belly on the floor. The cops cuffed Joy—screaming curses—in front and then lifted her from the floor as if to take her out on foot, but the nurses insisted on laying her on a gurney as they had with Aurora and starting an IV while the police officers held Joy down. Then they all left the room in a single, rushed cluster.

In the sudden silence, one of the officers who stayed behind cleared his throat. "I'm sorry, but we have to ask you to come with us for a bit, Agent Nolan. The two of you need to be questioned separately if we want your story to hold up in court."

"You can't be serious. Can't you—"

"No." Tara lifted her right hand and touched his lips, drawing his attention. A bit of color had returned to her face and her eyes had cleared. "You go. They'll have to move me anyway, and Lucy will stay with me." She glanced at her friend. "Right?"

"Of course. Jake, you go. The sooner you do, the sooner you'll be back. Tara won't be alone for a second, I swear it."

More medical personnel arrived, and a woman helped Tara into a wheelchair.

"Are you sure this is okay?" He knew procedure as well as anyone, but he'd fight it if Tara needed him.

"I'm sure. Get this over with."

The police did him the courtesy of questioning him in an empty room, but even so they made him tell his story over and over. The uniformed officers were replaced by two detectives, who were later joined by an agent from the El Paso FBI field office. Jake held it together for nearly an hour before he put his foot down.

"I'm done. I've explained everything. You've recorded it. Now I am going to see Tara. If you have a problem with that, arrest me and I'll call a lawyer."

"You killed at least two American citizens in Mexico along with God alone knows how many others. And you shot a woman right here in this hospital."

"And I'll answer for it. But every one of those shootings was justified. Righteous. And you know it, or I'd already be cuffed and stuffed. Since I'm not, I'm done." He strode to the door and pulled it open, shoulder blades twitching the whole time. But no one stopped him, so he jogged to the stairs and up to the post-op floor.

⤴

"I'M A MESS," Tara said once they'd settled her in her new room and the police officers and nurses had left her alone with Lucy.

"Oh, totally," her friend teased. "I mean, you look as if you just survived a near-death experience. Oh, wait: you *did*."

"I don't mean outside, though thanks for that. I mean . . . what if I don't get the feeling back in my hand? And what about the drugs?" She reached her bandaged left hand over and touched the IV the nurse had hooked into the back of her right hand. Her left elbow veins were shot from the rough injections she'd been given in Mexico, and her right was bandaged where Joy had torn out her original IV. "Right now I am fine, but what about when I leave and they stop pumping me full of morphine?"

Lucy grimaced. "I'd like to say none of that matters, but the truth isn't that easy."

Tara's throat went dry and her eyes burned. She lifted her water to her lips to hide her face.

"Tara, listen to me. As long as it's important to *you*, it matters. But only for that reason. Do I care whether your fingers work properly? Hell, no. You could have had them amputated and I wouldn't care. Neither would Jake. He *loves* you. All he wants in the world is for you to be well and safe."

She swallowed and asked the question eating at her. "How could he ever want to tie himself to an addict?"

"Well, for one thing, there's no guarantee that once they take you off the morphine you'll be what any of the rest of us think of as an addict. If *you* think of yourself that way, then you'll work at fixing the problem, but you're the only one who can tell how you feel inside, how bad the urges are."

"Does Ethan's addiction scare you?" At first, Tara thought Lucy might not answer, but after a moment she nodded. "Yeah, it does. I don't worry about him backsliding. He hates even remembering those days. And when the urges strike—and they do—we talk through them. But he isn't over the insecurity, the idea that he's a lesser man for having the dependence, and I don't know that he'll ever completely beat it. He worries about being a bad husband, about being a bad father, about not being strong enough to face up to the challenges. Those concerns are based on his addiction, not on reality.

"Jake understands what he's getting, and he wants you. You can, of course, decide that *you* don't want *him*, but it's not up to you whether he loves you or not. He does."

The tears she'd been holding back slipped down her cheeks. "Are you sure? What if he just feels responsible? What if I remind him of Lisa and he wants to rescue me since he couldn't help her?"

"I knew Jake when his sister died. Believe me when I tell you, the way he feels about you is anything but brotherly."

"But he's a white knight. What if I'm no more than another project?"

"You're not. I've known you all your life. You're a fighter, Tara Jean Dobbs, a white knight in your own right. And that's exactly what he needs: a woman who can take care of herself."

"I'm not doing such a great job of that. I don't even recognize myself."

"Oh, sweetie. I know. Even the most independent of us need help sometimes. Believe me. And I am the last person in the world who'd ever tell you to listen to what anyone else says about you, but in this one instance, you need to let go and trust the rest of us. We still recognize you. Jake doesn't see you as a project any more than he sees you as a sister."

Tara took a deep breath and let it out slowly. "You think so?"

"Absolutely."

Tara attempted a smile. "So how bad do I look?"

Lucy laughed. "Bad enough. Luckily, you have another six months before you have to be my maid of honor."

"I can't believe you're getting married."

Jake pushed the door open a few minutes later. "Hey," he said, walking over to the bed. He wore a fresh bandage over his arm, and the stitches on his head looked rather worse for wear, but he was smiling, and Tara's heart lifted at the sight.

"Look who's back," Lucy said. She stood, leaving her spot

on the edge of the bed open for Jake, who immediately sat. "They kept you quite a while."

"Yeah, well, I have an accounting to come still. They didn't give you too hard a time?"

"No. I had to tell them everything that happened here. They said someone else would be by to ask me about Mexico, but that it could wait."

"It can."

"I'll leave you two alone," Lucy said. On her way out, she gave Tara a quick wink and pulled the door shut.

The moment the latch clicked, Jake leaned over and gathered her up. She wrapped her arms around his waist, careful not to pull out the IV, and felt his whole body sigh.

"Tell me again," he said.

"Tell you what?"

He growled, surprising a giggle out of her. "Tell you that I love you?"

"Yeah, that."

Her heart thumped painfully against her ribs, beating all the humor out. "It doesn't solve anything, though."

"It doesn't have to. We'll deal with whatever comes." He leaned back slightly and looked down into her face. "Tell me something. If you could do anything at all, what would it be?"

"Get out of this hospital. Go home."

"Where's home? Surely not Dobbs Hollow."

She hadn't even considered that. Once her father had died, she'd put her childhood home on the market, and the lease on her apartment had expired after she left town. A storage locker in Dallas — her first stop when she left Dobbs Hollow — contained the few possessions she cared enough about to keep, and a safety deposit box held her weapons and papers.

"I guess I'm homeless. Lucy gave the police her address in

Houston when they asked where I could be reached, but I don't care for cities so I don't know how long I'll stay. Besides, she and Ethan will want to be alone." She shrugged.

"Have you ever thought about leaving Texas?"

"And going where?"

"Virginia? Plenty of small towns there."

She gaped at him, then snapped her jaw shut. *Virginia?* "You're going back to the FBI?"

"The FBI isn't the only employer in the state. But yeah, I have to go back and talk to them. I promised my superiors I would when I asked for their help and contacts when I realized I was going to join the Chosen. After our . . . adventures . . . they won't allow me the kind of latitude I've had for the past couple of years. I'll have to fish or cut bait.

"All I promised was a conversation, though. I could retire. There are beautiful small towns in upstate New York. Horses, farmland, the whole bit."

"New York?" Tara's mind spun. "Why New York?"

"A comment Nash Harper made. HSE is in New York City, and I could probably get a consulting gig with him. I wouldn't have to be in an office all the time, but I'd want to be close enough to go in when necessary."

He was planning his future. And he wanted to share it with her. "What would I do?"

"Whatever you wanted. I'm sure you could get a job with a police department—there must be a process for people who move across the country. Like I said: you're a tiger; you'll get any job you decide on."

Did she want to go back to law enforcement? She believed in the creed, deeply and completely, and always would. But maybe there were other ways to protect and serve that would better suit her. She'd started over in two separate departments and couldn't imagine doing it a third time.

"When I was a rookie in San Antonio, I enjoyed the whole community outreach thing. Going to schools, talking to kids and adults about personal security, stuff like that."

"So then set up a business. Teach self-defense and personal security and firearm safety. Go to schools or work at a shelter. People need you. *I* need you."

"I can't just move with you."

"Okay, then we'll stay in Texas."

"No, no, I'm not tied to the state. I'm just not ready to start a new life yet. I have so much to hash out with my old one. Can you deal with that?"

"I can. And I'll help you as much or as little as you want. Just promise that when you *are* ready, you'll give me a chance to be in your new life, whatever it looks like."

"I can't imagine going on at all without you, and that's terrifying in and of itself. I'm used to relying on *me*. Right now, if it weren't for the fact that you're here, I'd probably lock myself in a small, dark, windowless room and never come out. When I left Dobbs Hollow, the lawyer told me it would likely be months before my father's will could be properly executed, and my brother didn't even have one. I'll have to call him—the lawyer—and see how far he's gotten. I try to imagine things like selling my parents' house, facing the fallout from my brother's crimes, living with the—God, the *need*—for that stupid drug for the rest of my life. It makes me want to curl up in a ball and hide." Or cry. Which she was doing again. It seemed all she'd done since her return was weep. She forced the tears back.

"Talking to Ethan didn't help?"

"It did. But it scared me, too. He said I wouldn't ever be the same person I was."

"What the—"

"No. He was being honest. He said I had to think of it like I would any other major life change. Change is part of being human. Addiction makes your life a little harder but so does, say, having chronic pain. He asked me whether I'd ever had to kill on the job, and when I said no, he asked whether I'd ever drawn my weapon on duty. I have. Seven times. And every one of those times has altered the way I viewed myself and my work just a little. The first time . . . it was a seismic shift in perception. I don't have to tell you."

"No, I understand. And the first kill is worse."

"I'm not sure I want to find out what that's like. I could do it. I realized that in Mexico in a way I hadn't ever really considered, even through all the psych exams and questions and practices. Even after drawing down on a guy in a domestic assault who was going after his wife with a broken bottle while he pointed a revolver at me and my partner. At that point, I knew in my mind I could fire, could kill him if he didn't surrender. But in Mexico, I knew in my heart.

"As much as the drugs, that's something I have to work out before I can get on with my life."

"You know, there's a reason they make you go to the department shrink after every shooting."

"I have a feeling this is going to take more than a few sessions."

"Yeah, well, you've got a lot of ground to cover. But we've got all the time in the world. If nothing else, neither one of us is going to be able to move on until the various law enforcement entities get their pieces of the *Hijos*-Chosen pie. So we'll just take it one day at a time. Slow and steady. Sound about right?"

"It does. But Jake?"

"Yeah?"

"Not too slow, okay?" She leaned up and pressed her lips to his, tasting the smile that formed there.

ACKNOWLEDGMENTS

This book owes a great deal to various groups as well as individuals. For starters, my gratitude goes to MWA and Sisters in Crime for teaching me about weapons and taking me shooting, and to RWA for the conference at which I learned the ins and outs of a Joint Terrorism Task Force. The services these organizations provide is priceless.

But when the research is done, you still have to write the book. And for a hospitable spot and all their attention in the time it took to write this, I owe the staff at the Village Social my deepest gratitude. Always on hand with more caffeine and—when that's not enough—something deliciously chocolate to keep me going, without them there would be no book.

I also need to thank my editor, Leis Pederson, and my copy editors, Andy Ball and Lynda Ryba. Carrie Devine made the cover suit the story and Keith Snyder made the whole thing into a book. I cannot imagine a better team.

Last but not least, as always, thanks go to my husband. He knows why.

ABOUT THE AUTHOR

Laura K. Curtis gave up a life writing dry academic papers for writing decidedly less dry short crime stories and novel-length romantic suspense and contemporary romance. A member of RWA, MWA, ITW, and Sisters in Crime, she has trouble settling into one genre. She has published four romantic suspense novels (*Twisted*, 2013; *Lost*, 2014; *Echoes*, 2015; and *Mind Games*, 2015), two contemporary romance novels (*Toying With His Affections*, 2014; *Gaming the System*, 2015), and a host of short stories, many with a supernatural bent.

www.ingramcontent.com/pod-product-compliance
Lightning Source LLC
Chambersburg PA
CBHW062022190726
48284CB00014B/1847